Dan,

Thank you for having.
Group and for _ now."
I hope you enjoy it.

Edw...

Ghost Writer

Cover Design by Dakota Hobbs from a concept by Edwin Frownfelter. Images used by permission from Shutterstock.

Quotation in Chapter 14 from Muriel Rukeyser, "The Speed of Darkness," *The Collected Poems of Muriel Rukeyser*, copyright 2006 by Muriel Rukeyser, used by permission of ICM Partners.

ISBN-10: 1496188624

ISBN-13: 978-1496188625

To the Scribes, and to Deborah, for
the Rule of Threes and so much more.

Ghost Writer

A Novel

by
Edwin Frownfelter

Chapter 1

"Great to have you on the team again.
We're buddies. We're partners!" said Barry.

"I must be out of my mind," muttered
Doug.

"Of course you are. So am I. That's why
we're such a great team!"

-- David Shepherd, *Finger of Fate*

The door to the doctor's office opened and a
dark-haired man stepped out. "Mr. Trovato?"

Ben stood up. "That's me."

The doctor looked to be of Indian ancestry,
perhaps in his forties, with an easy smile and
relaxed manner. He reached for Ben's hand. "I'm
Dr. Menon. Come in, have a seat. Would you prefer
Mr. Trovato, or may I call you Ben?"

"Ben's fine. Uh, I haven't done this before. Do I
lie on a couch or something?"

The doctor laughed. "That's a stereotype. We
just sit and talk." He motioned through the door.
Ben entered and sat on one of two upholstered
armchairs. The doctor sat across from him, his pad
on an end table by his chair, a coffee table bearing a
box of tissues between them. The décor was
modest, with a few certificates and decorations, not
as plush as he expected a psychiatrist's office to be.

"So this is your first consultation, Ben?"

"Yeah, I never felt the need before. My mental health has always been pretty good. I'm a take care of yourself kind of guy."

"So what brings you here?"

"Well, I have this problem I don't know quite what to do about. I don't know if it's some sort of syndrome or something, but I thought I should have it checked out. I thought maybe some sort of therapy or medication or something might get rid of it."

"What sort of problem?"

"I've been, uh, I've been hearing this voice. That isn't really there."

Dr. Menon made a note on his tablet. "You're hearing voices?"

"Not voices, a voice. One particular voice."

"Oh? What does this voice sound like?"

"A man's voice, baritone range. Sonorous, like a guy used to speaking at length. Excellent vocabulary."

Dr. Menon leaned back in his chair. "A particular voice? Like, a particular person?"

"Oh, yes. I know exactly who he is. He's the guy who used to live in my apartment."

Dr. Menon's pen hovered over the pad. After a moment he said, "This is someone you know?"

"I didn't know him, really. I do now, but now he's, well, he's dead."

"You're hearing the voice of a dead man? A particular dead man?"

"Yes. Exactly."

"I see, I see. And is this voice ... what is it telling you?"

"He has something he wants me to do."

"I see." Dr. Menon leaned forward slightly. "And what is it he wants you to do?"

"Take dictation."

Dr. Menon sat up. "I beg your pardon?"

"He wants me to finish this novel he was writing when, you know ...'

"A novel?"

"Yes."

Dr. Menon sat silent for a moment, seeming lost in thought. Then he said, "So tell me, when did you first hear this voice?"

"About three weeks ago when I moved into my new apartment," said Ben. "Let me tell you how it all started."

Chapter 2

> Doug's stomach did a flop as the coroner's assistant pulled out the drawer. In thirty years as a sleuth, you see a lot of stiffs. But you never get used to it.
>
> -- David Shepherd, *Neck of the Woods*

The siren caught Ben Trovato's attention. Ben looked out his office window, but it faced east, away from the main boulevards of the business district of Kansas City, so he couldn't tell where the siren was coming from. He was surprised he could even hear it. Maybe from Hospital Hill, a mile to the south. His apartment building on Grand Boulevard was near the hospital, so he learned to tune the sirens out. But in the early evening long after close of business, it was the only sound in his office, except for the low whirr of his computer.

The siren probably got his attention because he was ready to be distracted from work on a Friday evening, after a work week now in its sixty-eighth hour, forty-nine of them billable. This was normal for Ben as a fourth-year associate attorney in the large Kansas City law firm of Block, Stahl, and Stonewahl.

Ben picked up the smartphone on his desk to check the time: 7:17. Now that it was November, his window looked out into darkness. He leaned into the window and looked at the office projecting from the corner of his floor to the south. The light was still on in the office of Mark Masters, his supervising partner. Mark's voice would be influential when the question of Ben's possible elevation to partnership came up in the meetings of the managing partners in June, so Ben made a practice of always staying longer in the office than Mark. Ben was ready to leave, but he would have to wait until Mark's light blinked out.

Ben sighed and looked back at the screen on his credenza. The electronic document on his computer screen demanded much of his client, a manufacturer of wire cables with an unfortunate tendency to separate into their constituent parts at the least opportune of moments. He stared glumly at the page:

> 57.   Please identify all individuals with knowledge of Quality Control Protocol 27, and provide addresses, telephone and fax numbers, email addresses, job title, job history for the past ten (10) years, educational and professional qualification, and supervisors, and provide all reports, memoranda, notes, correspondence, drafts, letters, faxes, email messages, and other written descriptions, accounts, reactions, records, and other documentation of any sort whatsoever regarding the application of Quality Control Protocol 27 and/or any other quality control protocols, procedures, examinations, reviews, and actions of any

nature whatsoever at any time thereafter, regarding to the incident of June 21.

RESPONSE:

Ben typed in the response space, "fypara/," which launched the text string his assistant Lesley made into a shortcut, after typing it more times than she could stand:

58.   The interrogatory is objected to as being vague, overbroad, as immaterial and irrelevant and unduly burdensome and not reasonably calculated to lead to the discovery of material evidence, as calling for information which is protected by attorney client privilege and calling for the thoughts, impressions, and work product of counsel in preparation for trial.

He knew he would have to devote some actual thought to answering the questions, but not at 7:17 on a Friday night.

This was what Ben did: discovery, the endless exchange of demands for information, parried to the extent possible by the recitation of canned defenses, and met, when defense failed, by the production of staggering quantities of documents. Ben spent the last four years of his life managing the flow of these rivers of argument and information into and out of Block Stahl's corporate clients. He slogged forward, enduring the often numbing boredom of sheer repetition, in the hope he could so achieve partnership, and with it earn the privilege of delegating the drudgery of this same work to other hungry young lawyers.

A moment later the plastic brick on the surface of his desk rattled. A pleasant trio of ascending beeps told him who was calling. He picked up the phone and read the screen anyway: LIS.

"Lis" was Melissa Sturgeon, with whom Ben enjoyed an unofficially but de facto monogamous relationship for the last eighteen months. He knew that about this time on a Friday, she would be hungry.

Ben thought the ringtone he chose for her reasonably sentimental, but Melissa was not impressed. Her ringtone for him was "You Take My Breath Away." For this reason Ben tried not to call her when he knew she would be around people. He was expecting her call.

He picked up the illuminated slab. "Hi, Lis."

Her voice came through the phone. "Let me guess. You're still at the office."

"Uh, yeah, just finishing up a few things."

"You do know, don't you, that it is 7:20? On Friday?"

"Is it? I sorta lost track of time."

"Well," she said cheerfully, "Since I'm on a winning streak, I get another guess. Mark is still there."

He glanced again across the bay. Mark's light was still on. "Uh, I didn't see him go. What does that matter?"

"I know, you don't leave until he does."

Ben felt a spark of annoyance. If they stayed together, this was for her sake, too. "You know he'll have a big say in the decision when I come up for partnership in June. I'm a fourth year associate. There aren't too many fifth year associates."

"And then if you do make partner, you still get to stay as long as he does? Doesn't he have a family?"

"Yeah, but sometimes I think he'd rather be here."

She sighed. "Are you going to be like that when ... when you have a family?"

Ben didn't need this. "Come on, Lis. The hours come with the life. You know how important the partnership is to me. "

"Of course I do. I'm sorry, babe, I know how hard you work. But when do you think you'll be done? I'm starving. I only had an apple and a cup of yogurt all day. Oh, and a bag of chips from the vending machine about 4:00."

He leaned over and looked down the hall. The light was still on. "Uh, would eight be okay?"

An interval of silence a second or so too long informed him that eight would not be okay. Finally she said, "Well, I'm so hungry, and kinda tired. I think I'll just heat up something from the freezer, read a couple of chapters, and go to bed." Alone, her tone of voice added.

"Okay," he said, trying not to project either disappointment or relief. "Call you tomorrow?"

"Will he call her tomorrow? Only he knows!" Melodrama queen.

"I'll call, I'll call."

"Okay. Good night. Don't stay too late. I love you."

"Yeah, me too. 'Night," he answered, and the phone clicked off. Oh, well, sometimes an evening alone was a relief after a long week. He looked back at the screen but couldn't stand to read another line. He closed the document, and clicked on a sports website to see who would be playing in the NFL on Sunday.

A few minutes later, he saw the light in Mark's window click off. He sent the page he was viewing to a printer Mark would pass on his way out. He leaped out of his chair and strode briskly to the printer. By the time Mark passed into the hall outside the workroom, thick briefcase in hand, Ben was standing at the printer, earnestly examining his document, which told him Green Bay was favored over Seattle by 2½ points, down from 3½.

"Still at it, Ben?" Mark said.

"Yeah, you know how it is. The work just keeps rolling in."

"Well, that's the way we like it. Say, Ben, you're still single, aren't you?"

"Yeah, still at large."

"Yeah, I remember putting in those crazy hours back before I married Margie. That's the time to do it, though. Gets a lot harder when you have a family. Speaking of which, I better get home before they lock me out. Don't stay too long."

"Nah, just finishing up a few things and I'll head out."

"Okay, see you tomorrow."

Crap, thought Ben. He's coming in Saturday. That means I'd better be in by eight or so. "See you in the morning."

He heard the front door slam shut as Mark left. He waited a few minutes to give Mark time to get to his car in the basement garage, a lot closer than Ben's spot in a neighboring lot. Ben had no particular reason to hurry home, so he took his time packing to go.

Ben shivered as he stepped out the front door into the street. The neighborhood of the firm's office in one of the skyscrapers of the business district was fairly deserted at this time of night, although he knew the bars and restaurants of the Power and Light District a few blocks to the south would be humming with people. Ben briefly contemplated heading to one of the bars for a few drinks, to listen to the music and mingle with people he didn't know. When he first came to Kansas City four years ago, he did so a lot. In fact, he met Melissa at one of the clubs there. He didn't go much anymore, since he and Melissa were dating regularly. Ben chastised himself for being so inhibited. You're not married, he thought. If you want to go have some fun, and she doesn't want to come along, that's her problem. God, man, you're turning into a house pet here. Woman won't even wait up for you, and you're still on her leash.

He remembered the evening they met, a year before last June. It was a Friday night, and then too he had just finished a bruising work week. Despite the long weeks he regularly joined some of the other young attorneys in his firm touring the bars and clubs. He was finishing a drink while his friends were dancing, and he spotted her at a table with a group of friends. As he stole glances at her, he realized she was looking at him as well.

He introduced himself, and learned that she recognized him. Working the desk in the sheriff's department, she saw him bringing some papers in, so she knew he was a lawyer. He listened attentively as she told him her story. She grew up in Sedalia, a small city an hour or so east of Kansas City, came to the city to attend the University of Missouri at Kansas City for a degree in criminal justice, and stayed in the city looking for a career in law enforcement or investigation. All she found was a job as a clerk typist in the sheriff's department, but she was still holding on to her dream. Ben played his lawyer card, encouraging her and sharing with her what passed, at least through the screen of the two and a half beers, as sound advice.

He had learned such solicitude was the shortest path to a young woman's confidence, and that insight led their evening to a most satisfactory conclusion in the small bedroom of his Grand Boulevard apartment. Many of the Friday nights since then ended the same way.

Ben thought back over his week. Sixty-eight hours, and another six or seven on Saturday. It's been a long week. Better to just grab a sub, head home, and collapse in front of the TV or something.

Ben turned into his parking lot and pressed his key fob to unlock his five-year-old Volkswagen GTI. As he climbed in, he thought about the pending partnership decision. If he made partner, car shopping would be one of the first things to do. He bought the used GTI as a graduation present for himself when he finished law school. It had served him well, but as a partner he should think about something more upscale to fit the image. Perhaps a Lexus or Acura, maybe even a BMW, a car people would respect. He would be able to afford it then, too. If he didn't make partner, the old GTI would have to do for a few more years.

He stopped by Grinders to pick up a sandwich for dinner, and headed home.

A few minutes later he arrived at his building, an old department store converted to apartments on Grand Boulevard, near Crown Center about a mile south of the office. Ben moved into a small loft apartment on the east side of the fourth floor four years ago, when he came to Kansas City to join the firm.

As Ben turned into the parking garage in the basement lot of the building, he noticed an ambulance with flashing lights parked in front of the main entrance on Grand Boulevard. He parked his car in the basement and bounded up the stairs to the lobby, rather than entering the elevator in the basement. Although he wasn't acquainted with many neighbors in the building, he was curious about what was going on.

In the lobby he saw Jim Purley, the building superintendent, sitting on one of the couches in the lobby, staring morosely at the flashing lights of the ambulance.

"Hey, Jim," he said.

"Hey, Ben," Jim replied. He was a wiry black man in his forties, with locks of curly, unruly hair, a collection of t-shirts with odd symbols Ben didn't understand, and a constant expression suggesting he wasn't quite sure where he was or how he got there. Ben made an effort to keep a friendly relationship with Jim, in part because it was always a good idea to be on the right side of the building superintendent, and in part because he liked Jim, who was a kind person despite his occasionally strange notions. Jim was a believer in spiritualism and New Age philosophies, which he explained at great length to Ben, oblivious to Ben's lack of comprehension of or interest in anything he said. Jim always looked a little beaten down, but there was a particular melancholy in his expression. His gaze remained fixed out the window watching the ambulance pull away.

"Jim," he asked. "What's with the ambulance? Is somebody sick?

"Mr. Shepherd. He's gone, Ben."

"Gone? Who's gone?"

"Mr. Shepherd in 1101."

Ben wished for a moment he paid more attention to his neighbors. He didn't recognize the name. "Shepherd? Don't believe I know him."

"Been there forever, like thirty years, longer than I been here. Can't believe he's really gone."

It struck Ben what Jim meant. "Gone? You mean, like, dead?"

"Yeah, he's dead. I found him."

"Wow, man. That's tough. That's really awful."

Ben put down his briefcase and sat in one of the chairs next to the couch. He looked out the window, following Jim's stare. Ben thought for a moment, but he was pretty sure he didn't know Shepherd. He knew an older man lived in one of the suites on the top floor, but he had never spoken to him.

"You okay?"

Jim nodded. "Yeah. I seen dead people before, but I never found one. Damn. And it was him."

"How did that happen?"

"The young lady called me. She looked after him. Called me when he didn't answer the phone, asked me to check on him. She asked me that before, I went in and always said I needed to do something. He was real private, but he never minded me. I think that's why she called me. He was always fine before, but this time, he was there in his chair, looking like he was asleep. I called him, then I tapped him, but he didn't wake up. So I called the lady and she came over. She called the ambulance. Went with him, though he was gone."

Ben ran through the people he had seen in the building, and recalled a man who might be the departed Shepherd. "Is he the older fellow? Kind of stocky, long white hair, Van Dyke beard? Dresses in flannel and jeans a lot?"

"Yeah, that's him. Was him."

Ben realized with a start why the image was fresh. "You know, I just saw him this morning. He was getting on the elevator when I was getting off. About 7:30. Had some coffee and the morning paper, I think."

Jim turned and looked at Ben in surprise. "You saw him this morning? Wow, you … you …"

"I what?"

"You must have been the last to see him. You know, see him alive."

The thought spooked Ben. "I was? Geez." He sat in silence a long moment, processing the thought. "I've never had much contact with death.

It's so weird to think that someone I just saw went up and, and died."

They sat in silence for several long moments. Ben wondered about the deceased man's life. "Shepherd, he was an older guy, right? This young lady – was she a daughter or what?"

"No, not a daughter," Jim replied. "A niece or something. Looked after him all the time. Real pretty lady, fine as a bee's wing. Business lady. All business, expensive suits, only talked to me when she wanted something done. She didn't even cry. But she was upset. Went with him in the ambulance, though there weren't nothing she could do."

Ben thought about the old man and his lonely last trek up to the top floor. The top floor ... the penthouse. Suddenly a thought seized Ben. "1101? Is that the one on the west side, with the bay window?"

"Yeah, that's it," answered Jim. "Been there thirty years. Always remembered my birthday."

1101 was the penthouse on the top floor, twice the size of Ben's fourth floor apartment. It was probably the best unit in the building, and it was coming vacant. I'm in the right place at the right time, thought Ben. No, don't say anything, it would be in bad taste. On the other hand, you don't want to stand by and let someone else grab it. Say something. After a moment's deliberation, Ben spoke. "So. That unit's going to be available, is it?"

Jim recoiled. "The poor man just died. Today. How can you think about that?"

"Sorry, I didn't know the guy," said Ben. "I know you're upset. I'm sorry about that. But seriously, could I take a look at the unit?"

"Man, that's cold," said Jim.

Ben shrugged. "Sorry. Occupational hazard. So when can I see the place?"

"Well," said Jim. "I guess thcy'll be putting it up for rent soon enough. Probably the estate's gotta get his stuff out, then we'll have to fix it up. He's been there a long time. I guess I could let you see it. But tomorrow, okay? The man just died. Have some respect."

Tomorrow morning, thought Ben. I figured I'd have to go in tomorrow. But it's the penthouse, it's worth it. "Tomorrow morning will be great. Eight okay?"

"Okay," said Jim. "Eight. Eleventh floor."

"Don't show it to anyone else till I've seen it, okay?" said Ben.

"No one else." Jim shook his head. "Cold, man, cold." He turned and shuffled toward the maintenance room.

Ben felt elated as he rode the elevator up to the fourth floor. The building was laid out with the east end of each floor divided into two smaller units, like Ben's. The west side, facing toward Grand Boulevard and Union Station, was configured as a single much larger unit. An extension over the entrance marquee also afforded each of the west side units a bay window extending out over Grand Boulevard. The eleventh was the top floor of the building; Ben figured the view from that unit must be spectacular. West side units didn't come open very often. He was delighted to have been in the right place at just the right time to get the first crack at what must be the best unit in the building.

Ben figured he really deserved some sort of upgrade in his life, which was why he found himself thinking about new cars so often. He had worked so hard for so long, kept his discipline and endured his modest circumstances. The reward of his labor was just a few tantalizing months away. If he made partner, a spacious new home would be a just reward for his efforts. As he stepped onto the elevator, he pumped his fist and let out a triumphant, "Penthouse, baby!"

He would get into work tomorrow soon enough, but he was looking forward with relish to eight o'clock.

Chapter 3

The doorman eyed Doug up and down, staring at his rumpled overcoat and scuffed shoes. "Sir, I am afraid you don't look like one who would frequent an establishment of this caliber," he sniffed.

"That's right, I don't," snapped Doug. "But under the circumstances I can't be picky."

-- David Shepherd, *Rib of Adam*

On Saturday morning, Ben was up before 7:00, and hit the elevator a few minutes before 8:00. When the doors opened on the eleventh floor, Ben could see immediately that the level of trim in the small elevator lobby on the top floor was more luxurious than on his floor. The carpet seemed denser and better padded, and the walls were trimmed in a gilt border speaking of an attention to detail modern developers rarely indulged.

Jim was standing in the hallway next to the door directly opposite the elevator door, marked "1101" in gold metallic numerals, unlike the generic signs fastened to the doors of the lower floor.

"You ready?" Jim asked.

"Let's have a look," Ben replied.

Jim unlocked the door and pushed it open. They stepped into a narrow foyer opening onto the main room. Ben immediately noticed the high pile and heavy padding of the carpet and the polished wood trim decorating the walls even in the foyer. He was determined to maintain a poker face, in case there should be negotiations about the rent, but he couldn't suppress a gasp when he stepped through the foyer into the main living room.

Ben was accustomed to living in a three-room apartment with a little over seven hundred square feet of living space. To him, the main room seemed to open into an expanse as large as his entire apartment. In fact, it was approximately sixteen feet deep and twenty-four feet wide, but to Ben it seemed immense. On the south wall of the room, to his left, a fireplace was built into a wall of stone suggesting to Ben the limestone bluffs that jut out of the landscape in many places in Western Missouri and Kansas. A couch, a loveseat, and two padded chairs were gathered around a low coffee table in front of the fireplace; clearly the space was planned around conversation. To the left of the fireplace was a small dining area with an expensive-looking six-seat table, and behind it the kitchen, separated from the living space by a half-height wall. The kitchen boasted stone counters and cabinetry in oak with glass doors, a far cry from the utilitarian finish of his own tiny kitchen.

He looked back toward the fireplace, and noted walls covered with bookshelves, packed with hardbound books of all sizes. The occasional gaps among the books were occupied by a collection of objects – a sextant, a jar filled with exotic nuts, a glass globe, a case containing a Civil War vintage single-action revolver. A long, half-height room divider extended out from the wall and separated the room into two zones. Its shelves were filled with more books, curios, and bins of old maps and magazines.

Ben stepped around the divider to look at the northern half of the room, configured into an office. A large, walnut topped desk dominated the space, on which sat, amidst piles of letters, papers, and books, a red IBM Selectric typewriter. Ben remembered seeing typewriters like it visiting his father's office as a boy. An Einstein Brothers takeout coffee cup sat on a pullout extension next to the typewriter. With a start Ben realized it was probably the same coffee cup the old man carried when Ben saw him at the elevator door the previous morning. The north wall of the room was covered with more bookcases. The bookcases were constructed of permanently fixed hardwood. These were not cheap add-ons, but the tools of someone who took his books seriously.

Ben's eye was drawn past the desk to the dominant feature in the room – a bay window extending three feet or so out of the room, about five feet wide. The bay looked out into a wide window, most of the width of the extension. On the other sides of the corner pillars, two smaller windows gave a panoramic view of the city to the west. Below the windows, built in cabinets topped with thick cushions created a three sided window seat, with backrests on the sides and a center cushion suitable for resting one's legs. Ben ran his hand over the plush velour of the cushions, and figured the side seats would be comfortable posts of conversation, or just for enjoying the view of the city.

Ben looked out the windows. To the north he could see much of the northeastern section of the city, including the distinctive pylons marking Bartle Hall, the convention center. The south afforded a fine view of Union Station and Penn Valley Park where the tower of the Liberty Memorial stood. He could hardly suppress a gasp of wonder; this must be one of the most spectacular residential views in the city. By the time Ben turned from the window, he knew he wanted this place.

A plush reading chair with a floor lamp and a side table sat next to the window, facing south toward the Liberty Memorial. Jim, who had been waiting in the foyer, wandered into the office space and gazed sadly at the chair.

"That's where I found him," he said. "Just sittin' there with his eyes closed and a book on his lap, as though he'd fallen asleep." He shuddered and retreated to the fireplace area, where he picked up a wineglass and carried it to the kitchen.

Ben continued his tour. On the other side of the bookcases on the north wall was the door into the master bedroom. Nearly sixteen feet deep and twenty feet wide, it seemed cavernous compared to Ben's twelve feet square bedroom. In addition to the unmade double bed, the bedroom contained two dressers, a console with a television and stereo, and a small settee positioned facing out a window on the north side. Two large windows on the west side flooded the room with light, even through half-drawn shades. Doors on the east wall of the bedroom opened into a small walk-in closet and the master bath, which offered far more room and more luxurious fixtures than Ben's cramped bath. After leaving the master bedroom, Ben turned left down a small hall containing a door to a second small bathroom and a linen closet. At the end of the hall was a second bedroom, about the size of Ben's bedroom, fitted with a sleeper sofa, a small writing desk, and more bookshelves.

Opposite the second bedroom was another even smaller room, no more than about six feet deep and eight feet wide. Clearly the old man used it primarily as a storage room, but on a folding table sat a tabletop photocopier, an old desktop computer, and an inkjet printer. Ben realized he had not seen a computer anywhere in the main office area. Apparently this was the old man's only computer, unless he stashed a notebook somewhere. Ben thought it odd that someone with so many books and papers about would have so little in the way of modern computer equipment.

His tour completed, Ben returned to the living room area, where Jim was kneeling by the fireplace sweeping up ashes in the hearth.

"I really like it," Ben said. "How much is the rent?"

Jim scratched his chin. He gave Ben a figure for Shepherd's rent, which sounded astonishingly reasonable to Ben. "They haven't changed Mr. Shepherd's rent in years," cautioned Jim. "He had a long lease, put a lot of his own money in the place. I 'magine they'll raise it. Won't know until the ownership runs the numbers, I guess."

"Well, I'm definitely interested," said Ben. "When will they be thinking of reletting it?"

"Well, the estate's gotta get his stuff out. Lotta stuff, as you see, lot of it been here for years, decades. Then we'll clean up, check everything out, get it ready, y'know. Maybe two weeks, three."

"I can be talking to the management in the meantime," Ben said. "Don't let them advertise the place until I've talked with them."

Jim shuddered a bit. "Man, it's like he's still here. I'll tell 'em you're interested, but it's still a dead man's place. Don't know why you're in such a hurry."

They left through the foyer and Jim locked the door behind them. Ben got off the elevator at the fourth floor and bid Jim good day. It was 8:45 when he grabbed his briefcase and headed for the elevator to go in to work. Mark would probably already be there, but this morning's exploration was worth breaking his usual practice. As Ben got out in the basement parking lot and headed for his car, he was thinking about what that view would be like at night, and smiling broadly.

Because he felt guilty about Friday night, Ben thought it would be a good idea to let Melissa choose the restaurant they dined at Saturday night. She picked Eden Alley, a vegetarian café at Country Club Plaza.

Melissa sat at the side of the table to his right, chattering away. Large round glasses framed blue eyes, their shape accentuating the wide oval of her face and prominent nose and wide mouth. Strands of shoulder-length blond hair periodically wandered across a broad forehead, brushed back with an unconscious stroke of her hand. She told him hair styling was an exercise in vanity. It may have been an exercise in futility, as her mane seemed to have a mind of its own. As usual, she was wearing an oversize cashmere sweater and jeans. Melissa often fretted about her weight, and Ben suspected she wore such baggy clothes as though to hide in them. Ben thought her figure was just fine, generous and attractive in a Rubenesque way. He made sure to praise her lavishly when she wore more stylish clothes, but he never criticized her choices, because he wanted her to be comfortable in what she wore.

She seemed to be in a good mood despite the misfire of the previous evening. They had not spent time together in three days, and they needed to catch up. She was extemporizing about some happenings in the sheriff's office as the server delivered their meals. Melissa chose a small berry salad, with dressing on the side. Ben ordered a large spinach loaf, because it appeared to be the item on the menu bearing the least distant resemblance to meat.

Melissa munched on a carrot stick. "So you worked again today? How late did you get out?"

"Oh, about three. It wasn't too bad."

"And you were there so late last night. I hope I didn't bitch out on you about that. But I was so hungry. I should be more understanding. You work so hard, and I admire that. I shouldn't complain. I'm not. I miss seeing you sometimes, but really, I understand."

"It's just a few more months, Lis. I just have to keep up my momentum until the partnership decision. If that goes well, it'll be better then." Of course, if it didn't go well, he would be taking a lot of time off.

"But that's more than six months. Ooh, that looks good. Mind if I try some?" Without waiting for an answer, Melissa reached over and sliced a golfball-sized piece off his spinach loaf. "Partners still work those hours, too, don't they?"

"Well, yeah, it's never going to be a life of leisure. Partners have to generate revenue. The spotlight is on them. But it'll be better, I promise."

"Hmm. Yes, better when you're a partner, like Mark. So, was Mark still there when I called last night?"

"Uh, yeah. But not much longer."

"And was he in again today?" Melissa could certainly handle a cross examination.

"Yeah, I know. But that's his choice. Sometimes I think he doesn't really want to go home. I'm not sure domestic life really suits him."

"My point is, I don't think we can assume you will have more freedom when you make partner. Oh, babe, I want to be supportive. I don't want to put you under any more pressure than you already have. But couples tend to get into these patterns early, and sometimes I think you really need to keep an eye on how your work life affects the rest of your life. It's important that there be more to your life than just work, you know."

"I know," Ben said. He tried to think of a way to steer Melissa back to talking about herself, off this subject. "So what did you do today? Apparently I could use some coaching on what normal people do when they're not working."

Melissa laughed. "Well, I slept in a bit. I wound up staying up pretty late – I thought I'd only read a few chapters, but I got caught up in this mystery and had to finish the damn thing. So I didn't get up until about eleven. I didn't want to get out from under the covers, my apartment was so cold. When I got up the thermostat said fifty nine! I had on two shirts, a sweatshirt, and a sweater and I was still chilly. I hate that place. I'd love to move, but I can't find anything else on the rent I pay. Maybe if Rob could come up with some more work for me, I could handle a little more." Rob Brock owned a private investigation firm in Westport. Occasionally Melissa did research for him, trying to make inroads into investigation, her career goal.

"When is your lease up?" Ben asked.

"September. Probably the air conditioner will break down again this summer, too. Maybe I could find a roommate somewhere."

Melissa carved another bite from his loaf and left that last thought hanging. Ben knew where the conversation was heading. Ben always deflected Melissa's probes into the delicate subject of cohabitation by pointing to the small size of his own apartment. If he moved into the spacious west side unit, their living arrangements would be the first thought in Melissa's mind. If he didn't mention the new place until after he made the deal, however, she would be upset about it. Besides, he wanted to talk about it.

"I'm thinking of moving myself," he said.

"Oh?" Curiosity and apprehension mingled in her tone. "What? Not ... away?"

"No, just within my building. One of the west side units is opening up. I thought I might take a look at it."

"Ooh! They're bigger, aren't they?"

"Yeah. They have two bedrooms, and a dining area. The living room is a little wider, too." More than a little, but that will do for now.

"Oh, I think you should! It would be so convenient to have more room and not have to move all your stuff too far. When is it available?"

"It just opened up yesterday. I'm going to talk to the management Monday before they advertise it. Maybe they'll give me a break if they can rent it right away."

Melissa stirred the salad with a fork silently for a moment. Then she said, "Do you think, if you have a bigger place, maybe we could talk about ... some other changes?"

Ben was ready for the challenge. "Well, you know, with the partnership thing coming up, I've been under a lot of stress. I thought I might go for the apartment because it's now or never. Those west side units don't come up very often. But you know what they say, too many life changes all at once isn't good for you."

"Oh, you're right. I have read that. Too much stress all at once ..." Her voice trailed off. Well played, Mr. Trovato. Must remember that one for future use. Too much stress, all at once.

"So, how did you find out about this?" Melissa asked, reaching for another slice of the diminishing loaf.

"I was just in the right place at the right time. The guy who lived there just, uh, passed on."

Her eyes widened. "The tenant died? Just yesterday?"

"Yeah. I got in just when they were taking him away."

Melissa shuddered. "He *died* there? In the building?"

"Yeah."

"In ... in the apartment?"

"Uh huh."

"Ewww. Doesn't that freak you out a bit? Living in a place where someone just died?"

"Not really. I mean, what do we know about the places we live in? Think how many people have passed through that apartment of yours over all these years. What are the chances one of them died? Pretty decent, I'd think."

"Oh, stop it!" Melissa cried. "You're creeping me out! My building is scary enough."

"Well, when you think about it, we don't know anything about all the people who have passed through the spaces we occupy, and we just live with their ghosts. Maybe a struggling artist lived in your place, who went on to do great things. Or a med student, who became a doctor and saved people's lives. Maybe people were conceived there, and are happily living their lives, completely unaware those lives began right there in your little bedroom."

Melissa rested her chin on a hand. "It's interesting to think of it that way. There could be some great stories in those kinds of ideas. I love it when you make me think of things like that. You do that really well, you know? You should work on it. Didn't you tell me once you wrote stories in high school?"

"Yeah. And they were high school stories, definitely. The world is better off without them."

"Well, so? You should work on that. You must hear all kinds of interesting stuff. Why not do something with it? You can be very creative, when you try."

"I have no creativity left. Law school baked it all out of me. I am a desiccated fruit, my inner plum turned to prune."

Melissa's laugh tinkled through the café. "Now that's funny. Creative and funny. See? You still have that side. I'm going to bring it out of you, whatever it takes."

"Oh," said Ben, "I suppose I could work on it, if I'm properly incentivized."

Melissa leaned close to him and looked up at him through the blond strands. "Oh, I think that can be arranged."

Three hours later, Ben lay in the bed in his small apartment, his fingers gently stroking her bare shoulder, her sleeping breath soft and regular on his chest. He watched shadows from the city lights to the east, tracing ghostlike patterns across the ceiling. What would he see in the darkness of his new bedroom?

Chapter 4

> The gorgeous blonde stood up and sashayed out of Doug's office. Doug and Barry stared openmouthed as she left, caboose swinging like a train on a rickety track.
>
> "Man," said Barry. "If I were her husband, you wouldn't have to look very far for me."
>
> "If you were her husband," said Doug, "she'd be trying to lose you."
>
> -- David Shepherd, *Rib of Adam*

Ben moved quickly to lease the apartment before the management could consider putting it on the market. He experienced a moment of doubt when the management named the rent; it was more than twice what he paid for his fourth floor unit. But Ben had lived frugally and saved his money, so he decided he could handle it until the partnership decision. If he made partner, the rent would not be a problem. If he didn't, he would have plenty of problems to keep it company.

By Wednesday, the realtor who ran the management company called to say his lease was ready. He left work about 3:30 and went to the company's office on 18th Street to sign the lease.

The manager told him the previous tenant had been in the unit for nearly thirty years, ever since the building was converted to residential units from its original use as a retail store and warehouse. His estate removed his property and furniture, but the company would need to replace the carpets, repaint, and recondition the unit. Ben could take possession in about two weeks.

Ben told her he would like a chance to inspect the apartment, to take measurements and plan for what furniture and other household goods he might need. She offered to call Jim Purley and arrange for Ben to pick up the key for a few hours.

About 4:30 he knocked on the door of the small utility room off the lobby Jim used as an office.

"Hey, Jim," Ben said when Jim answered the door. "I need to borrow the key to 1101 for a while."

"Yeah, they called," Jim said. "I got the key right here. " He handed it over to Ben.

"Okay. I'm just going to take some notes and measurements. Then my girlfriend is going to stop by in a while and look at the place."

"That the one with the blonde hair and bangs? Melissa?"

"Yeah, that's the only girlfriend I have."

"She's nice. I like her. You know, plenty of room for two up there."

"Uh, yeah, right. Well, we should be done in an hour or two."

Jim paused. "Hey, Ben. We gotta talk."

"Sure. What about?" Ben said.

"Okay. We known each other how long, three years?"

"Yeah, I moved in three and a half years ago."

"So it's not like you're some stranger. I like you, Ben. And I'm concerned about your welfare."

"Why? Is there something I should know about this place?"

"Well, it's about Mr. Shepherd."

"What about him?"

"Well, he, you know, *died* there."

"Yeah, I know. Last Friday. Remember, I was here when the ambulance took him away."

"See," said Jim, "the problem is, when I go in, I can feel him. I can feel his presence. I think he's still there. In spirit, anyway."

"Well, that's fine with me."

"No, no, you gotta understand. You don't want to mess with a spirit."

"A spirit? You mean, like a ghost?"

"I'm telling you, Ben, I can feel it. His energy is still there. I know you don't believe this much, but the energy don't care if you believe in it or not. You gotta take steps."

"Okay, what do I do about this ... this bad energy?"

"Oh no no, Ben. It's not bad energy. There's no such thing as bad energy. It's like ... well, it's like water, you know? Water's good. You're made of water. You need water or you'll die. But you don't want it in the basement, or coming over the levee. There's no good water or bad water, there's just water where it's supposed to be and water where it's not supposed to be."

"Okay, so I get your drift. The energy's like the water – there's no bad energy, just energy where it's not supposed to be."

"Exactly!" Jim said. "That's what spirits are. People – all of us – we got a certain energy, see? And sometimes when someone dies, especially when they die all of a sudden, sometimes the body leaves before the energy is done doing its work. So you got the person's energy, but it doesn't have a head to live in. So maybe it will want to use yours, you know, to get its unfinished business done. That's what you gotta watch out for. That's why you gotta protect yourself."

"Okay, so how do I protect myself?"

Jim reached into the drawer of his desk and pulled out a small purple cloth bag. "I got just what you need here, Ben." He handed the bag to Ben.

Ben opened the drawstring and shook a small object out into his palm. It was a small pink obelisk, with a point on one end and a silver cap on the other. "What is this?" he asked.

"It's a spirit crystal," said Jim. "It comes from a special quarry in Uzbistan."

"Uzbekistan?"

"Right. There's no quarry like it anywhere else in the world. The energy axis of the stone is exactly in line with the earth's magnetic field. They cut it special to keep the polarity lines running along the crystal. It has tremendous power as a spiritual channel."

"A spiritual channel?"

"That's right. Because it has spiritual lines running through it, see, you can use it to protect yourself if a spirit gets into your head. Like this." Jim took the pink crystal from Ben's hand and pressed the silver end against his forehead. He closed his eyes and squeezed his facial muscles tightly. He looked like a bay unicorn. "You have to think real hard and amp up your mental energy. That increases your brain pressure and squeezes the spirit's energy out through the spiritual channel."

"It goes out the pointy end?" asked Ben.

"Right. Always make sure the spiritual focus – that's the pointy end – is pointing out of your brain. That way the spirits have nowhere to go but out."

"You wouldn't want to jab the pointy end into your head," Ben said.

Jim looked alarmed. "Oh, no, no, no! That's the last thing you should do! That would give the spirits a path straight into your head. Never, never do that!"

"Well, I was thinking the point would hurt, but ... I see what you mean. Do you have to, like, direct it out the window or something? I mean, to get rid of them?"

"No, no. Once you get them out of your head, you're safe. They know you're on to them and you got defenses. Then they won't come back, at least not if you're careful."

"Okay, I think I've got it. I feel safer already. I'll keep it handy."

"You should put a chain through the base and wear it around your neck at all times when you're in the apartment. That way you'd be ready no matter when they find you."

"Um, okay, I'll consider that. Well, thanks."

Jim inserted the crystal back into the bag and handed it to Ben. "Uh, that's fourteen dollars."

"What?"

"Fourteen dollars. The crystal cost me fourteen dollars. Well, $13.95, but there was tax. We're even for fourteen."

Ben pulled out his wallet and extracted a twenty. He handed it to Jim and said, "Here, take this. That'll cover the crystal and a little extra for your advice. I mean, protection from spirits, priceless."

Jim took the twenty. "Thanks, Ben. I feel better knowing you're safe. Good luck now."

"Thanks, Jim. "

Ben left Jim's office, and after closing the door behind him, shook his head and dropped the bag into his pocket. "Spirits," he said. As he punched the up button for the elevator he wondered whether Melissa would like a pink pendant.

Ben bounded out of the eleventh floor elevator and slid the key into the lock. He was excited – it was his first time alone in his new place.

He felt a surge of euphoria as he walked into the living room. With all the furniture and clutter removed, the place seemed even roomier than he recalled. Fade marks on the carpet showed where furniture had been, and the walls, to the extent they were not covered by bookshelves, looked in need of paint, but all would be taken care of as a part of the preparation. The bookshelves them-selves looked to be in fine shape, no doubt because of the high quality of materials and finish used in their construction. Ben was elated with the possibilities of the place. He tossed his coat on the counter between the kitchen and the dining area.

He intended to take some measurements and draw sketches of the room layouts before Melissa came over, but the sight of the window seat, the only seating left in the unit, inspired him to sit down and check out the view. He eased into the luxuriant cushions at the right end of the seat, facing south toward the Liberty Memorial. The sun hung low in the sky over the buildings west of Grand, and the surfaces of the monument reflected its golden light. Ben generally had little time for sightseeing, but he relaxed and admired the spectacular view – his view, from his place.

He remembered Melissa was waiting to hear from him. He reached into his pocket for his cell phone, but he felt something soft and unfamiliar. Pulling the object out, he realized it was the crystal prism Jim sold him, inside its felt bag.

He pulled the prism out and examined it. Pinkish quartz, flat on six sides and turned into a point at one end, the size and shape of a stubby pencil. The texture of the glasslike stone felt soft to the touch, and the translucent material hinted at depth below the surface. It was an attractive object, Ben thought, but he didn't know what to do with it. He laid it on the windowsill, pulled out his cell phone, and texted Melissa that he was in the apartment. She responded, "b thr n 20."

Ben leaned back into the cushions. They were quite comfortable, and he could stretch his legs out on the window ledge between the seats, too narrow to be a seat itself. It's all coming together, Ben thought. The place, the firm ... the relationship? Ben wasn't sure about that part. But he closed his eyes and reveled in the moment, the view, the magnificence of the apartment, his general good fortune.

`heart of a creek`

Ben opened his eyes. He thought he heard someone say something. Probably in the apartment below. He realized he hadn't really checked out the noise transmission. His fourth floor apartment let him in on the neighbors' most intimate conversations and exhalations. Oh, well.

`heart of a creek`

Ben sat upright. The voice sounded like someone in the apartment, maybe a couple of rooms away.

"Hello? Is someone here?" he said.

He heard a floorboard creak in the master bedroom, just the other side of the wall to his left. Good Lord, someone was in the apartment. He stood up, took a couple of steps toward the bedroom door, and spoke in his most stentorian voice.

"Hey! Whoever you are, you are in my apartment. Come out here and show me your face! Now!"

He heard halting steps on the floorboards of the bedroom. A woman's shoe appeared in the doorway, and then she stepped out.

Ben would have gasped, but that required breathing, which was out of the question at the moment. She was beautiful, stunning. A swell of auburn hair undulated as she turned her head to reveal a perfectly symmetrical face, sculpted cheekbones and creamy skin framing large green eyes. She wore an expensive-looking ivory business suit, tailored to feature a lithe, gently curving frame over taut legs. Her small, immaculately lipsticked mouth formed an expression of surprise. "Who ... who are you?" she asked, in a tremulous mezzo mixing challenge and trepidation.

"Uh," stammered Ben, "I was just going to ask you the same question. I'm Ben Trovato. I just signed the lease on this place."

She raised a manicured left hand, touching slim, elegant fingers to her forehead. A quick glance revealed no rings on the third finger. "Of course, the new tenant. Already. I'm so sorry."

She took a few steps across the room toward Ben. She wore a necklace with a striking contemporary pendant, warm gold on matte skin. The vertical pleats of her stylish cream blouse curved gentle lines of longitude. As she stepped close, Ben sensed a wash of perfume, or perhaps pheromones. He felt slightly dizzy.

"I am Robin Atwater," she said. "I am vice-president of the publishing firm of Atwater and Bridges. We were proud to publish the books of Mr. David Shepherd, the late former occupant of this unit." She planted her hands on the slopes of her hips and looked into his eyes with emerald weapons of male distraction. "You are familiar with Mr. Shepherd's work, I assume?"

The correct answer, "No," was not an option. Quickly Ben searched his memory for all associations linked to "Shepherd." Jim said something, or was it Melissa? What was it? Buy time. "Oh, of course. I, uh, haven't read them all, but I certainly know his reputation, of course."

She turned to the window. The back side of the suit was well tailored, too, with a splendid infrastructure to match. "Perhaps then you will understand my situation."

She sat down on the seat cushion at the south end of the window. "This is very hard for me, I hope you understand. In addition to our professional relationship, I've known Mr. Shepherd all my life," she said. "He and my father, the late Stuart Atwater, founder of our firm, were lifelong friends since their college days in English lit at Mizzou. Publishing his works was my father's greatest pride, and is mine now. We lost my father a year and a half ago, and now this ..." Her voice caught, and she reached into her purse for a tissue.

Ben moved to the window and sat in the north end opposite her. He leaned over, close but not too close, and spoke softly. "I see ... this must be very hard for you."

"Yes," she said, her voice cracking slightly. "When my father lost his long fight, it was devastating for both of us, David and me. He meant to comfort me, I'm sure, but I think my father's death hit him even harder than it did me. He pulled away, stopped seeing old friends, rarely left this apartment. I took care of him more than the other way around. I was all he had, really, and I was here a lot, looking after him, trying to pull him out, trying to get him going again. Now that won't happen." She lifted the tissue to her eyes.

Ben said, "Jim – the super – he told me about you. He said you were always here, taking care of him. He spoke very warmly of you."

"Oh, he is sweet," she said. "Not very bright, but sweet." She stuffed the tissue in her purse, sat up straight, and tossed her head. Ben was struck dumb as the chestnut wave reformed in exquisite curves. At the moment he was sure he would carry that moving image in his head until his final breath.

"Anyway, about why I am here. As you probably know, Mr. Shepherd's most successful project by far was the series of Doug Graves detective mysteries. Unfortunately the eleventh episode we published four years ago left his loyal readers with something of a cliffhanger. Everyone expected the next Doug Graves novel would resolve that, bring the cycle to a more satisfying place. David told me he was hard at work on the twelfth story, and he was confident it would be the best of them all."

She stood up, crossed her arms, and wandered into the living room, looking around. "David had his, well, eccentricities, and one of them was an almost paranoid fear that someone was after his work. He kept each one completely secret until it was done. He always imagined someone would break in and steal his works in progress. So he developed a habit of hiding them various places in the apartment."

Ben stood up and strolled after her. "Wouldn't there be a computer file or something?"

"No, David was old-fashioned. He never used computers. Just sat at his desk right here and banged them all out on an old typewriter."

Ben remembered his surprise at not seeing a computer. What kind of writer doesn't use a computer? "A red Selectric, right?"

Her eyes widened. "How did you know that?"

Ben wondered whether he made a misstep. He decided to play it straight. "I was in here with Jim, after ... after he was gone, before they took the stuff out. I lived on the fourth floor, and came up here with Jim. I saw it on that desk."

"Then you probably saw how cluttered it was. He knew where everything was, but of course, he can't tell us now."

"Did you find any manuscripts when you took his stuff out?"

"We found some hiding places, little nooks and secret stashes where he hid a few pages or sketches here and there. We combed through everything, looked in every book – there were thousands – tested the floorboards, checked for false drawer bottoms, everything we could think of. But we didn't find the Doug Graves manuscript. It would have been the best hidden of all."

She fixed him with a piercing stare. She could freeze him pretty well with a glance, but this look welded him to the spot. "Hmm," she said.

He swallowed. "Hmm? Hmm what?"

She stepped toward the fireplace, then turned and pinned him with another stare. "If you are going to be the new tenant, you will have complete access to the apartment. You could bring a fresh set of eyes to the search."

She stepped toward him, lowered her head and gazed into his eyes. "Our firm has a lot tied up in this manuscript. We paid Mr. Shepherd a large advance, but more important, the world needs closure on the Doug Graves series. If that book is here, even in unfinished form, we want it, a lot. Our firm is willing to pay you a finder's fee, if you can locate the manuscript and bring it to us. We will make it worth your while if you can help us."

She pulled a business card out of her purse and handed it to him. After gawking at it for a moment, he reached for his wallet and gave her one of his. She studied it. "Block Stahl. Ooh." There was a distinct upturn to the "ooh," conveying "I'm impressed" rather than "how pathetic."

She extended her hand. He looked at it dumbly for an instant, then reached out and accepted her handshake. Her skin was warm, tender but not damp, and when she squeezed his hand a bolt of raw desire coursed through him like an electric shock. She released his hand and walked to the hall closet for her coat. As she slid her arms into the sleeves, she smiled at him, and the warmth of her expression flooded through him as though the summer sun had come out on this November day.

"So, I look forward to hearing from you. I think we can have a great and mutually satisfying relationship … working relationship. If you can find that manuscript." As she opened the door, she looked back at him and said in a musical voice, "Thank you." The door closed and she was gone.

Ben stumbled to the window seat and plopped down at the south end. He still clutched the card in his hand, and finally looked at it. It confirmed what she said: Robin Atwater, Vice President. Atwater & Bridges, publishers of fine books, with an address on Petticoat Lane downtown. Email and an office number, no cell.

Ben leaned back and exhaled. Occasionally in his fantasies he would come into rooms to find beautiful women waiting for him, but they never had business cards.

Chapter 5

Bertie pursed her lips and blinked at Doug. "Tell me, sweetie," she said. "How did a fish like you stay off my hook?"

"Good taste in bait," growled Doug.

-- David Shepherd, *Chest of Drawers*

Ben leaned back into the cushions at the south end of the window seat and sighed. With a stab of guilt, he thought of Melissa. She would be here any moment. Good thing she didn't arrive when Robin was still here.

Ben gazed north out the window toward the business district, eyeing the towers of Bartle Hall. He closed his eyes and brought Robin's image to mind. He was surprised how arousing he found it to be alone in the apartment with such a woman. In his mind he tasted the sweetness of those lips, felt the warmth of that ivory skin against his, imagined running his fingers over the silky fabric of the cream blouse, curving around the contours beneath. He was reaching for imaginary buttons when he stopped and shook his head.

Stop that. Do beautiful women know what effect they have on us? Of course they do. She knew exactly what she was doing to me. I'll bet she practices that hairflip in the mirror. She is probably involved. Has men crawling all over her. No ring, though.

He felt guilty indulging in such thoughts with Melissa on her way over. What to do about Melissa? He had deflected the living together issue once, but he knew it was far from over. Ben went through several relationships of varying intensity prior to meeting Melissa, but none lasted much more than a year. Maybe it was commitment phobia, but many of the relationships ended just because Ben got bored, just because the women he wanted always seemed more enticing than the one he had. He didn't feel this way yet with Melissa. As their relationship persisted past the first anniversary of their night in June, Ben didn't feel his usual restlessness.

He was quite fond of Melissa. She made him laugh, she was devoted to him, fun in bed, required less maintenance than most of his prior girlfriends. He had to admit she did as much to make their relationship work as he could reasonably expect, within her personal limits. Ben wondered whether he stayed in the relationship this long because he really cared for her, or because it was the path of least resistance. But now that path was curving upwards.

The timing is not great, Ben thought. In fact, the new place, the impending firm partnership, the pressure to make a decision about his relationship with Melissa, all made Ben feel he was arriving at a crucial juncture in his life. He wasn't a student with all the time in the world any more. He was a hard-working professional man, on the verge of a prominent place in society. He had a home rather than a place, a career rather than a job. His twenties ended with his next birthday. Well into adulthood, his future was taking shape quickly.

More and more, Ben thought of himself as a Block Stahl partner. Being a partner isn't just a job; it is an identity. It is one thing to drive an old beater and live in a closet when you are a struggling associate. When you are a partner, people expect more. They expect you to demonstrate good judgment and appreciation of quality. The solidity and prosperity of your place as a partner in a blue-chip firm should be expressed in the accoutrements of your life. The car you drive, the home you occupy, the suits and the watch you wear, all need to express the quality your position within a distinguished firm brings to your life.

That principle, Ben reflected, also applies to the partner you choose in life. Ben noticed certain common characteristics in the wives and lovers of the male partners he knew. Most were professional women, educated, sophisticated and successful in their own right. Even those who did not work radiated elegance, class, good taste. In their independent careers, their charity work, their artistic interests, their precocious children, they reflected the same passion for achievement driving their men. Ben considered a partner and his wife a team, both attuned to the environment of excellence and accomplishment the firm's culture demanded.

Maybe Ben's trepidation about escalating their relationship was not based entirely on his historic aversion to commitment. Maybe it was the opposite. Maybe for the first time, he was thinking about whether he should be looking for a long-term relationship, even marriage. He had to think about whether Melissa, as much as he still enjoyed her company, was really the right person for the long term. He wondered whether it was fair to her to thrust her into the role of a partner's wife. She didn't seem ready, as he was, to take on the style and demeanor of an accomplished, upwardly mobile professional. Would she be happy? Would she be able to make the changes she would need to? The fact that these questions occurred to Ben was not a good sign.

Now, Robin. Someone like her would walk into that culture as gracefully as she slipped into his life. Beautiful, poised, elegant, a successful business woman in her own right – she was ready for the life from the first day. She was exactly the kind of woman a rising partner needed by his side. Ben thought he felt some chemistry between them. That last smile as she turned to leave was more than professional courtesy. Was she interested in him? Did he have a chance?

Why not? Frankly, Ben was a pretty good catch. Reasonably good looking, with clean, symmetrical features, thick, curly brown hair, a charming smile. Trim and in good shape, without the vanity of a bodybuilder. He knew women found him attractive; sometimes he caught glimpses of them checking him out when they thought he wasn't looking. He was smart, easy to get along with, well versed in culture, art, entertainment. He knew a lot of bands, saw a lot of movies, read books – well, he would read more books once things settled down a bit. He knew how to treat a woman; his previous relationships ended only when he decided it was time. He was a future partner in one of the best law firms in town. He was in her class, definitely.

Ben closed his eyes, calling the breathtaking image back into view. Eyes, green, deep and mysterious. Gently sculpted cheeks, satin skin without a flaw. Chestnut hair, lustrous and undulant, sweeping over a slim, strong neck and delicate shoulders.

`Robin`

Ben sat up so fast he struck his head on the wallboard above the window cushions. Robin was gone, but he heard the voice again, and this time it sounded masculine. Was there someone else in the bedroom? He hadn't checked. Oh, God, was she here with a man? That so wrecked his fantasy. He hastened into the bedroom. No one. He checked the closet and the master bath; nothing. He quickly swept through all the rooms in the unit; no one else was anywhere in the apartment.

Before he could ponder it any more, the buzzer of his intercom sounded, and Melissa's sprightly voice came over the speaker. "Ben! I'm here. Are you going to buzz me in?"

Ben crossed the living room into the foyer and hit the button to release the ground floor door lock. Showtime.

He waited for her in the elevator lobby. A few minutes later the right elevator door opened and Melissa bounded out. She was still dressed in a yellow shirt with a khaki vest and navy skirt. She must have come straight from work. She was beaming broadly. She threw an arm around his neck and pulled his face to hers, bestowing a moist, energetic kiss on his lips.

"I've been getting excited all afternoon. I can't wait to see it! Come on, let me in."

Ben unlatched the door and gestured her into the foyer. She hurried in and stopped short upon catching a glimpse of the expanse of living room beyond. She took three steps into the doorway and stood, mouth open, looking around.

"Wow. Oh, my … wow. Just wow. Look at this place! I can't believe it. Ben, you gave me no idea how huge it is. How … how beautiful." She walked into the room, her gaze gyrating around. She looked for several long seconds at the stone wall around the fireplace. Then she turned and saw the bay window. She walked slowly to the window and looked out, her gaze sweeping from the pylons to Union Station.

"Oh, my. This is amazing. Why didn't you tell me how amazing this is? I can hardly believe we're here. And it's yours. It's amazing." She sat down on the window seat at the north end, looking out toward the Liberty Memorial, silhouetted against the last glow of the sunset. After a moment she said, "I may never move from here. I think this is where my life will end, just watching the sun come and go until I wither away. Seriously. I'll die happy. Do you think you could get a permit to keep my ashes here? Facing this way?"

Ben laughed and took hold of her hand, pulling her to her feet. "Come on, don't you want to see the rest of the place? We'll have plenty of time to look out the window."

Melissa's hands covered her mouth. "Omigod. That was a horrible thing to say. I just remembered how you got this. I shouldn't have said that."

"No problem. Come on, let's look at the rest."

Melissa looked around nervously. "Speaking of which, uh, where did he, you know ..."

"Where did he die?"

"Uh, yeah."

"Right where you're standing. There was a big easy chair looking out the window just a foot or two to your left. They found him in it."

She recoiled a couple of steps. "Ewww!" She looked closely at him. "That doesn't bother you? Not the least little bit?"

"Nope. I'm not superstitious. We've been over this."

"I know, I know. But still ..." She turned and paced toward the other end of the room, her mood dampened a bit. She studied the stone wall behind the fireplace. "This is so beautiful. I could look at it for hours." Her gaze swept over the bookshelves on the west wall. "So many bookshelves!" She stepped up to the shelf and ran a hand over the wood. "They're top quality, too. Real hardwood – walnut, I would guess. Beautifully finished. These shelves belonged to someone who owned a lot of books, and really cared about them."

"Yeah," said Ben. "He had a gazillion books. He was a writer, in fact."

Melissa looked at him, eyes wide. "A writer? Oh, that's so cool. Do you know what kind of writing he did?"

"He was a novelist, I understand. Wrote all kinds of stories, I guess, but mostly mysteries. Detective stories. He was pretty well known from what I'm told. Name was Shepherd. Mystery writer."

Melissa recoiled as if struck. Her jaw dropped and her eyes opened wide. "Shepherd? David Shepherd?"

"Yeah, David Shepherd. That was it."

Her hands rose to her cheeks. "Omigod! Omigod! David Shepherd lived here? *The* David Shepherd?"

Ben was startled at the intensity of her reaction. "Uh, yeah. David Shepherd. Wrote detective novels, the Doug something stories."

"The Doug Graves novels! I can't believe it! David Shepherd lived here? David Shepherd lived in this apartment and wrote the Doug Graves novels right here? I can't believe it!"

"Uh, you know him?"

"Know him? Omigod, David Shepherd is – was maybe the most famous writer in Kansas City! I knew he lived in the city, and I read on kansas-city.com that he died a week or so ago, but I never made the connection until now! David Shepherd lived here?"

She circled around the room for a moment, hands pressed to the sides of her head. "Okay, okay, let me explain. Yes, he was a great, great mystery writer. In fact he was a favorite of mine. He wrote a series of novels about Doug Graves, this down-and-out detective working in Kansas City in the fifties and sixties. I read all of them. He wrote other stories but the Doug Graves novels were his signature. I was so sorry he died. And then this – you're moving into David Shepherd's apartment?"

She dropped into the cushions at the south end of the window seat and looked at the place where the easy chair had been. "You're going to live right where he lived – and wrote – and, uh, died. I can't believe it. I cannot believe it. This is awesome and scary and exciting and sad all at the same time."

Ben thought for a moment of telling her about the manuscript. Then he thought about Robin and decided that was a bad idea.

Melissa looked up at Ben. "You saw the place furnished? Where did he write? Could you tell?"

Ben stood across from the window where the desk had been. "He had a big old writing desk with papers all over it and an old typewriter right here. He could sit at his desk and type and look out the window."

Melissa stood up, walked over and stood next to him. She closed her eyes and held out her hands, as if they were hovering over an imaginary keyboard. "He wrote right here. He sat here and he brought Doug and Barry and Mrs. Filbert and Zenobia and all those characters to life, right where we're standing. I can't believe it." She shivered slightly. "It's almost as if I can feel him here. I can feel the energy, the creativity. Oh, Ben, this isn't just an apartment. This is a magical place. I can't wait to see what it holds for us, uh, for you."

The room was getting dark. Ben stepped away from Melissa and flicked on the light switch by the bedroom door.

"Uh, continuing the tour, here's the main bedroom," he said.

Melissa turned and glided up to him. Her arms circled around his neck, and she pressed her body against his. "The bedroom, eh? Well, that is definitely on our list of areas to be explored." She pushed him through the bedroom door, but she wasn't looking at windows and furnishings anymore. Her lips covered his, searching and pliant.

He separated long enough to murmur, "Uh, there's no furniture."

"Live dangerously," she whispered. Dropping to her knees, she pulled him down with her. He separated the buttons of the yellow shirt as she loosened his tie and pulled it over his head. They stretched out on the hardwood floor, and as she reached for his belt buckle, he kissed her hungrily, and his fingers ran through her stringy blonde hair. But behind his closed eyes, in his imagination, they parted shimmering waves of chestnut.

Chapter 6

"So nice of you to drop in. Haven't seen you in a while," said Mrs. Filbert as Doug slung his coat onto the rack.

"I've been working," said Doug. "Paying the bills."

Mrs. Filbert picked up a stack of envelopes and fanned through them. "That's not what the mail says."

-- David Shepherd, *Mouth of the River*

Ben was in a good mood when he arrived at his office Thursday morning. Although it would be a couple of weeks before he could start preparing the apartment, he was looking forward to the change. He got off the elevator on his floor and turned down the hall toward his office with a spritely step. "Good morning," he said to Lesley as he passed her cubicle.

"Mornin'," she replied gruffly. Ben passed the cubicle, then stopped and looked around the partition. It sounded like Lesley was upset about something.

"Everything okay?" he asked her.

"It's all right," she replied, in a tone suggesting "it" was anything but.

Ben paused a moment. "Anything I can help with?"

"No, it's fine."

"Okay." Ben hung his coat in the hall closet and headed into his office. He wondered what the problem was. Usually Lesley was good-natured in the face of the pressures of the job. Her husband was a surgeon, and they lived in a prosperous section of Mission. She held a couple of graduate degrees, traveled, worked in all sorts of jobs. She was vastly overqualified for this work as a legal assistant. Surely she didn't need the job. Perhaps knowing she could walk away at any time made it easier for her to handle the frustrations. Or maybe it was just her maturity and good-natured personality. But something sounded wrong in her tone. Ben turned his computer on and was watching his emails come up when Lesley appeared in his door and sat down across his desk, her face fractured with stress lines.

"I'm sorry if I was snappish," she said. "Mark just bawled me out over something that was his fault. He gave me this tape of dictation just before I left yesterday and expected it to be done by the time he got in. Sheesh."

"Oh, sorry about that," Ben said. "Do you want me to talk to him or something?"

"No. no. This isn't your problem. I know how much you have on your mind. I just get so frustrated with Mark and some of the other lawyers around here. You'd think their title was

'God,' not 'Partner.' You're not going to turn like that when you're a partner, are you?"

"No, no. I depend on you for everything. The last thing I want to do is incur your wrath."

Lesley smiled at the joke. Ben's relationship with her was easygoing, and she appreciated the jest in his words.

"What is it about lawyers that they behave like such jerks? Is it something they teach in law school?"

"Yep. Assholicism I and II. Core curriculum in the first year."

"Sorry if I dump on you sometimes. I just feel like you're the only one I can talk to as an equal."

"No problem. I'm just sorry to hear you have these problems."

"Nothing I can't handle. Don't feel like you have to fix anything. I just use you to vent sometimes."

Ben paused a moment. "Look, Les, I know you don't want me to fix anything. And I don't mind hearing from you when you want to talk about something. But it seems recently things have been getting to you more often. Are you all right, really?"

"You're sweet, Ben. I'm good for now. I'll get through this."

"You know," said Ben, "Sometimes I really wonder why you stay here, if you don't like it. I'm not encouraging you to go. I'd be lost without you. But you could do so many things. Sometimes I don't know why you stick it out."

"I have to stay. You need me."

"Oh, it's charity work then? It's an honor to be the object of your philanthropy."

They both laughed. "Seriously," she said, "I don't know how long I will be around. Every now and then I get the urge to look around. Don't you? Are you sure this is where you belong?"

The change in direction in the conversation caught Ben by surprise. "Oh, gee, thanks a lot, Les. I deeply appreciate your confidence in my prospects."

"No, I don't mean your ability. You're as good as anyone here. You're just not like these other people. You're the only lawyer here I could possibly have a conversation like this with. Are you sure you want to spend your life as a partner here?"

"Oh, no. I've just been working seventy hour weeks for three and a half years out of casual interest. Of course it's what I want."

"I don't know, sometimes it just doesn't seem like you really fit with the culture. That's not a criticism; I don't feel that much at home with it myself, and I sense you're more like me than them. What about Melissa? From what I've seen of her, this doesn't seem like her kind of people, either. Do you think the circle here is right for her?"

Ben must have made a face. Lesley pulled back and said, "Oh, sorry. Did I cross a line there?"

"No, no. I just ... she'd probably agree with you. We'll both have to work it out, I guess."

"I'm sure you will. Oh, well, I'd better let you get back to work before your billables fall into the upper stratosphere. Thanks for listening to me. We cranky old ladies need that." She disappeared out the door.

Ben stared at his computer. Was it that obvious? Lesley may have met Melissa three or four times when she stopped in the office for short visits. They might have conversed for five minutes or so. Now Ben wondered whether others at the firm harbored such impressions of Melissa. Ben probably needed to figure this out, but it wasn't a distraction he needed or wanted at this point.

That afternoon, Mark Masters scheduled Ben for a conference in Mark's office. Ben guessed it was about the partnership, and he was right.

Ben gave Mark a rundown of his cases and where things stood. Ben saw printouts of his time records piled on Mark's desk. Mark leaned back in his chair and smiled.

"Some pretty impressive hours you're putting in, Ben. I probably shouldn't tell you this, but I'm pretty optimistic about your prospects in this year's partnership vote. You've done the hours, you've brought in clients, you work is first rate, and nobody can top your billables. I was kind of surprised they didn't give you a tender last year, and your case is even better this year."

"Do you have any idea what the reservations were last year? Anything I still need to work on?" Ben asked.

Mark crossed his arms. "Well, you know I can't really disclose anything from the discussions. But whatever concerns there were, you're well on the way to answering them. But the next six months are critical, Ben. You're on the right path, but you have to keep your focus, keep your eye on the goal, and keep up the pace. Now is no time to take anything for granted. If anything, you need to make the next six months the best of your time here."

Ben wondered if he should broach the topic of personal life. "I don't know if you can advise me on this, but do an associate's, uh, personal circumstances enter into the calculation? Does it help if one is, you know, committed, on the personal level?"

Mark chuckled. "Do you think your prospects would be better if you were married or something? No, that would probably be an illegal consideration. I certainly wouldn't get married just for the occasion. But if you're leaning that way, don't feel you have to put it off. I wouldn't take an extended honeymoon a month before the partnership vote, but the partners understand, life goes on. You got something to share here?"

"No, no. I'm just getting to the point, you know, where you start thinking about such things. And my girlfriend is definitely thinking about them. I just don't know whether this is the time to be making any major changes. I mean, before the decision."

"Well, it would be a great way to celebrate if you make it. Marriage is a great institution. That's why they call it commitment." Mark chuckled at his own joke. "Seriously, when it's time, you'll know. But above all else you want to keep your focus for the next six months. That's really the only advice I can give you. Just stay on the path and give it your best."

Mark picked up Ben's records and stuffed them back into the folder on his desk, a clear signal the meeting was over. Ben rose and thanked Mark for his time and advice. "Any time," Mark lied.

After he was out of Mark's sight, Ben pumped his fist in celebration. It was going to happen. He was more determined than ever to put off the Melissa decision until June, at least.

Ben returned to his office. He sat at his desk and spent a few moments in thought, then pulled out his wallet and extracted the business card tucked into a well-concealed pocket. He picked up his telephone and dialed the number on the card. A recorded voice answered at the other end, "Atwater and Bridges, Publishers. Please listen carefully as our menus have changed. If you know the extension of the person you are calling, please enter it now ..."

Ben hung up the phone and shook his head. Six months. Focus.

Chapter 7

The voice on the phone was terse. "The alley off 38th and Prospect. One hour."

"I don't take directions into dark alleys from voices on the telephone," Doug said.

"You will if you want to see the dame again." Click.

Drat, thought Doug. 38th and Prospect it is.

-- David Shepherd, *Belly of the Beast*

A week later, the building manager called and told Ben the painting was done, and new carpet installation was scheduled. He could take possession on December 1. Ben asked if he could begin moving some of his property into the unit, and the manager agreed.

The next day, Ben took the afternoon off and obtained a key and a hand cart from Jim. He packed several boxes with books, dishes, clothing, and other items he could move without placing them on the floor. Ben figured the more he could get into the unit before his actual move, the easier the move would be. He spent much of the afternoon storing kitchenware in the cabinets, hanging up seasonal clothes in the hall closet, and transferring books, CDs, and videos to the shelves around the fireplace.

By 5:00 Ben finished the task. He sat down at the south end of the window seat to catch his breath, and reflect some more on his good fortune. He stretched out his legs on the center cushion and felt a deep relaxation. Being in the window seat reminded him of Robin. He closed his eyes and summoned up the vision of those graceful curves and enchanting green eyes, still as vivid as the day he met her, maybe embellished a bit. As he did, he heard a gentle hiss, like muffled static.

`Robin?`

Ben jumped up and sat bolt upright, eyes wide open. He heard the word spoken as if by someone nearby, clearer than the voice he heard on the day he met Robin. This was not coming from downstairs or over the intercom.

"Hey!" he shouted. "Is someone in here? Come out here right now. You are trespassing! Show me your face!"

`Robin there?`

The voice was even more distinct now, as if spoken by someone in the room. He could tell it was a man's voice, deep and resonant.

Ben leaped up and quickly checked all the rooms, even opening doors and looking in closets. He was certain no one else was in the apartment, but he heard the voice again.

`Who are you?`

"Who am I?" shouted Ben. He then realized he did not want his new neighbors to hear him shouting, and lowered his voice. Still, he spoke with urgency and growing anger. "Who am I? This is my apartment. Who are you? What is going on here?"

`Your apartment? My apartment. Oh, my.`

The voice was as clear now as if the speaker was standing next to him. Ben's head was swimming. Nothing like this ever happened to him before. He sat down again on the left window seat. He spoke out loud, but to himself.

"Okay, calm down. This is not happening. There must be a rational explanation. Just calm down, and this will go away."

`Not going away. My apartment. Don't understand.`

"You don't understand?" Ben exclaimed. Then he realized he was talking to the voice, although no one was there. "There is a rational explanation. There is a rational explanation."

`Rational explanation. Must be rational explanation.`

Ben realized the unseen speaker was agreeing with him. It was bad enough to be going crazy, but having company in insanity was too weird.

"I am Ben Trovato," he said. "I am now the tenant in possession of this unit. I am a rational human person, and I am not insane, and I ... I ... I am talking to a disembodied voice. What is going on here?"

`Let me think. Must figure out. Will be`
`back.`

"You will what? Who ... what ... what the hell?"

Ben listened but heard no response. All he heard was a soft noise like static, or white noise. Then it faded out.

He leaned back on the window seat, wrestling with a disturbing thought. Robin said the former occupant was obsessed with security. What if microphones or speakers were planted somewhere in the apartment? He would have to ask Jim about the security system. Would Jim even know?

Ben picked up his empty boxes and headed back down to his fourth floor apartment, but he couldn't stop thinking about the incident. It bothered him that he had heard the voice twice. Jim was superstitious about his moving into the space where a man died. Ben wasn't superstitious, but he needed a rational explanation. Should he hire a security firm to sweep the unit? If there were speakers, who was using them, and why? Did he know for certain the old man was really dead? He saw the ambulance, but he didn't see a body. Was this some weird elaborate hoax to fake the old man's death? Was Jim in on it? Was Robin? Could he find a way to talk to her about it without appearing completely bonkers?

December 1st was only a week away. All of a sudden Ben's step up in life seemed a lot more complicated than it did earlier in the day.

Chapter 8

> "Here, take this," the dame said, holding out a small velvet sack.
>
> Doug opened it up. It was a prism of clear glass, about the size of a pea.
>
> "They're going to release your daughter for a piece of costume paste?" asked Doug.
>
> "It's not paste," she said. "It's a real diamond, worth $20,000. Try not to lose it."
>
> -- David Shepherd, *Finger of Fate*

About noon on December 1, Ben took off work and went to the management office on 18th Street to sign the papers. He hesitated for a moment before signing the lease, pondering the commitment it represented, but then scrawled his signature with a firm hand. The manager handed him the keys, and he left with a mounting feeling of excitement.

He drove down to Grand and parked in the underground garage. He was still assigned the same parking space; apparently the old man did not even own a car. He didn't even bother stopping at his old place, but took the elevator directly to the eleventh floor.

As soon as he opened the door, he noted the immaculate new carpeting in the subdued green shade he chose. The walls were freshly painted in ecru, also of his choosing. Actually, the word "ecru" was not part of Ben's working vocabulary. Melissa did most of the color shopping, because she had more of a sense for such things, but the final choice was his, and he thought it worked out quite well. The place looked fresher, even more opulent than when he first saw it.

Ben dropped his coat and briefcase on the center cushion of the window seat and plopped down on the north seat. Here I am, he thought, hanging out in my place. My new place. Delivery of some new furniture was scheduled between two and five in the afternoon. On Saturday, Melissa and a couple of his friends from work would come over and help move the rest of his possessions from the fourth floor. He reveled in the stillness and silence of the room, so much quieter and more peaceful than his old apartment. Against the background of silence, he suddenly became aware of a soft hissing sound.

`Hello`

A pulse of dread shot through Ben. He heard the voice again. He had rationalized away the previous incident. But now the voice was here again, intruding on his moment of celebration.

`I know you hear me. You might as well say something.`

Ben swung his head around wildly, but he couldn't pinpoint the location of the voice. He called out, "Who are you? Where are you? What are you doing in my apartment?"

`I was going to ask you the same question, but I suppose I know the answer.`

"What do you mean? This is my apartment. What are you doing here? How are you doing this?"

`Calm down, please. You don't have to shout. I can hear you as well as you hear me.`

"Calm down? I've got a voice coming from nowhere in my apartment, and you want me to calm down? Come out, wherever you are!"

`Believe me, I would if I could, but this is how it has to be.`

Ben sat down on the window seat. "I'm going insane. This is what it feels like to go insane."

`No, you are perfectly lucid. I understand your consternation. This is a new experience for me as well, but we'll have to make the best of it. We need to talk.`

"Talk?" Ben didn't have any better ideas, so that was what he would have to do for the moment. "Who are you? Where are you? What are you doing in my apartment? What do we have to talk about?"

`I'm glad you're ready to listen. I am David Shepherd.`

It took Ben a moment to absorb what the voice was saying. "David Shepherd?"

`At your disposal.`

"If you were at my disposal, I'd have disposed of you by now. The writer? The *dead* writer?"

Alas, that seems to be the case. I am David Shepherd, I am a writer, and I lived in this apartment for many years. Well, in fact, I still live here, but obviously my property rights are not what they used to be.

The voice was as clear now as if the man was standing next to Ben. His head reeled. Bizarre as it was, he decided the best option was to play along until he figured out what was going on. "So ... so you're ... what, a ghost?"

I prefer to think of myself as involuntarily incorporeal, but you could put it that way. My base of operations has been transferred to the other side of the divide, but I have the ability to visit here and communicate with you, obviously.

"Then ... Jim was ... Jim was right? The apartment is haunted?"

Our mutual acquaintance can rarely be described as "right," but he does occasionally have some comprehension of things supposedly more clever people overlook. What exactly did Jim tell you about the apartment?

"He said you ... you may still *be* here. He gave me this crystal ... the crystal ..." Ben frantically tried to recall where he left Jim's pink stone.

A crystal? Is that what it was? I saw
this converging path and followed the
direction it pointed in. The next thing I
knew, I was seeing the apartment through
someone's eyes. Your eyes, it appears.

Ben remembered setting the crystal the
window sill, where it pointed directly at his
forehead as he sat in the window seat. Slowly he
turned his gaze to the window sill. The crystal lay
on the sill where he left it the day Jim gave it to
him, still pointing toward his forehead. Moving
quickly, he seized it and ran to the apartment door.
He opened the door into the hall and slapped the
blunt end of the crystal to his forehead. Fortunately
neither of his neighbors was in the hallway.

What are you doing?

Desperately, Ben closed his eyes, tensed his
muscles, and concentrated with all his might, as
though he could squeeze the unwelcome visitor
out of his brain through physical effort.

Do you have any idea how silly you
must look?

"It's supposed to channel you out!" Ben
wailed.

Too late for that. Now I know how to
get here, and I'm staying until we talk.
So you might as well close the door, put
that thing away, and hold a decent
conversation with me.

Ben closed the door, dropped the crystal into his pocket, and plodded to the window seat. He collapsed into the south seat and sighed.

"Okay, how does this work?"

As near as I can tell, I am located somewhere between your sensory organs and your consciousness. I can see what you see, hear what you hear, feel what you feel, etc. But I don't seem to have a window into your consciousness, so we still need to converse to communicate our thoughts to each other.

"Oh yeah?" Ben decided to test him. "What am I looking at?"

Those dreadful pylons at Bartle Hall. Damn, they ruined the skyline when they put those things up.

Ben gulped. He reached into his pocket. "What am I feeling?"

That crystal thing. Keys, coins. At least two quarters, some dimes or pennies, I can't tell. And lint. Don't you turn your pockets inside out when you wash your trousers?

Ben opened his briefcase and pulled out the first paper he touched. "Okay, read this." He scanned it.

"Rule 84.13. Allegations of Error Considered - Reversible Error - Review in Cases Tried Without a Jury or With an

Advisory Jury. (a) Preservation of Error
in Civil Cases. Apart from questions of
jurisdiction of the trial court over the
subject matter and questions as to the
sufficiency of pleadings ..." Oh, my God,
what language is that in? Don't tell me
you're a lawyer.

All of a sudden the apartment felt very
confining. "How long have you been in there? Are
you there all the time?"

No, this is only my third visit. I
have very little sense of how time is
unfolding on your side, so I can't really
say how far apart my visits have occurred
from your point of view. But trust me, I
do not have a voyeuristic interest in
your life. I am here for a specific
purpose, and I assure you I will only
come when I have a reason to do so, and I
will let you know when I am here. It
seems only fair.

"Fair? Fair? You're invading my head, and
you're talking about fair? Okay, so you're a ghost.
What are you trying to do? Are you trying to scare
me away? It won't work."

Not at all. I have something very
specific in mind. As you know, I am ... I
was a writer. I spent many years developing a series of novels. I put a great
deal of thought into the next volume of
that series, but unfortunately I had to
leave before it was finished.

Ben remembered his conversation with Robin. She said something about an unfinished novel. In fact, she thought the manuscript was somewhere in the apartment. So it was true.

"An unfinished novel? Robin said something about that."

Ah! You know Robin? I recall seeing Robin on my first visit, momentarily, like a flickering image. At first I thought I was seeing through her eyes. How do you know her?

"She was here, the first day I came to the apartment. She was looking for a manuscript. She thought it might be hidden somewhere in the apartment." He decided not to bring up her mention of a finder's fee for the moment. "She was your publisher? She seems young for that role – about my age."

She is the daughter of my lifelong friend and longtime publisher, Stewart Atwater. I've known Robin since she was born. She's the closest to a daughter I ever had.

Ben summoned up his most vivid erotic fantasy of Robin, but the voice did not react. Ah, apparently it couldn't read his mind. That was good to know. "So, there is a manuscript? Where is it?"

There was a manuscript. Unfortunately, I burned it.

"WHAT?"

`I burned it, in the fireplace, while`
`playing Mozart and sipping a fine Caber-`
`net. I had a bad habit of impulsively`
`destroying manuscripts when I thought`
`they were going astray. I meant to start`
`retyping it immediately, but unfortun-`
`ately fate intervened.`

Ben's spirits fell as his fantasies of the finder's
fee and of impressing the lovely Robin withered
like a punctured balloon. "No manuscript."

`So. Robin was here looking for a manu-`
`script. That means she believes there is`
`one, and that you might find it at some`
`point. This is working out better than I`
`hoped!`

"Better? There is no manuscript to find for her.
So what are you doing here?"

`That is where you come in, my young …`
`roommate. I have a business proposition`
`for you.`

"A business proposition? What kind of business can I do with a ghost?"

`I am sensing a triangle of congruent`
`interests here. The lovely Ms. Atwater`
`earnestly desires my manuscript, and`
`believes you may be able to produce it.`
`My goal is to provide her with that manu-`
`script, which is complete in my mind and`
`only needs a material manifestation in`

your world. That is where you come in. I
need your help.

"My help? For what?"

I need you as my amanuensis.

"Your ... what?"

I need you to type my manuscript. From
dictation, so to speak.

"Type your manuscript? What do you think I
am, a secretary? How is this a business proposition
for me? What incentive do I have to do that?"

Well, you have some incentives.
Robin's firm already has a substantial
financial investment in this manuscript,
not to mention the future revenues it
would offer. If I am not mistaken, she is
probably willing to pay you for it.

Ben thought, can he read my mind after all?

And she is, of course, a most attractive young woman. I would guess you have
at least a little interest in gaining her
attention.

Cripes, I hope he can't!

Then, there is also the deterrent
interest for you. You would probably
prefer to spend a few hours performing
this small service for me than to have me
lobbying you to do so at, say, three in
the morning.

"Are you threatening me?"

No, I have every intention of leaving you alone and allowing you to go back to a normal existence as soon as possible. But I really need to get this done, and for better or worse you and I are in this together. I need your help. Please.

Ben's mind reeled with the sheer strangeness of it all. "I don't know. Can I think about it?"

Certainly. I will check back with you shortly. I haven't worked out this time business, so I can't say exactly when, but since I can see through your eyes I can assure you I will do my best to minimize the inconvenience to you. Farewell, I shall return.

The hissing sound faded away. Ben slumped back in the south seat of the window and stared out, dumfounded. What had he gotten into? What kind of madness was this? Could he really believe this crazy nonsense?

He didn't know how long he sat and mulled it over, before the buzzer sounded announcing the arrival of his furniture. The distraction was welcome, but the excitement of his big day was killed. Now he was sure the voice would be back; the only questions were when, and what crazy demands it would make next. He didn't bargain on having a roommate, especially in his own head.

Chapter 9

> She tailed him through the store, yammering away the whole time. Doug couldn't stand another minute, so he ducked into the only place he could find some peace – the men's room. She followed him in, still yakking.
>
> "Lady!" Doug exclaimed. "Look where you are!"
>
> She cast an appraising glance around. "Oh, good," she said. "Your office."
>
> -- David Shepherd, *Finger of Fate*

Ben, Melissa, and three friends from the office spent much of Saturday moving his furniture up from the fourth floor apartment. Between the new furniture and Ben's furnishings from the old apartment, the place was set up the way Ben planned it. Ben and Melissa spent the evening ferrying several boxes of small possessions up from the fourth floor. After they moved the last of them into the hall to load onto the elevator, they walked through the empty apartment, Ben's home for more than three years. He planned to turn in the keys on Monday, as he was paying rent by the day.

"Remember that first night?" Melissa said.

"Of course," Ben said. He was not sentimental about places, and he was ready to move on. But he knew Melissa was thinking about it. Their relationship had begun and developed here, and now he was leaving this part of his life behind.

After locking up the old place, Ben and Melissa went up to the new apartment and spent the rest of the evening unpacking and putting in place the remainder of his personal possessions. They finished about midnight. Exhausted, they headed directly for bed. Ben took a shower, and by the time he returned to the bed Melissa was already fast asleep. He crawled in next to her and slipped his arms around her. He was ready to drop off too, but she stirred in response to his touch and turned her face up toward his. Due to fatigue, their lovemaking was more perfunctory than recreational, but when they finished, she nestled against him with a gentle intimacy, and he drifted off to sleep with deep contentment.

`Psstt. Hello? Hello? Wake up!`

Ben awoke with a start. He looked around the dark room, confused. Did he hear something in a dream?

`Yoo hoo. We need to talk. Can you disengage?`

He realized Melissa was asleep, snuggled against his chest. Turning his head away from her, he hissed, "Get out of here."

Melissa stirred and looked up. "Mmmm. Did you say something?"

"No, I just woke up with a start."

Well played. Seriously, can you get free?

Ben stiffened. Surely Melissa would hear the voice. But she murmured, "Mkay," and lowered her head to his shoulder.

She can't hear me. Excellent. Bathroom, now.

It was true. Melissa was awake enough to react Ben as slid his arm out from under her head. "Gotta go," he whispered.

He hastened into the bathroom and shut the door. For good measure he turned the water on in the sink. In a low, urgent whisper, he said, "What the hell are you doing here?"

I'm still waiting for an answer to the proposition I presented to you. You asked for a couple of days and as near as I can tell they have passed.

"What the hell? You come into my bedroom, while I'm with my girl ... I mean, really? Is this your idea of persuasion? Dropping in on my private life like ... like ..."

Now calm down. When I come to call, I have no way of knowing you are inconvenienced at the moment. I know nothing of your situation until I find myself inside your senses.

"I mean, you could have had the decency to leave, when you realized I was ... we were ... hey, just exactly how long were you there before you woke me up?"

You were asleep when I arrived, so I wasn't getting any sensory information, and I had to wake you up before I realized you, ah, had company.

"That's what I mean. If you had any human decency you would have left then."

Well, I see your point of view, but it takes no small effort for me to get here, and having made the trip, I at least needed to find out about my proposition. So, have you thought it over?

"Now just a minute. This is not, I repeat, not all right. You can't reasonably expect to drop into the middle of someone's life and expect them to engage in polite conversation."

Look, I don't want to intrude on you any more than necessary. I just need to know, are you going to help me or not?

"Help you? Are you crazy? I don't even know if you're real, or some kind of weird hallucination, but if you think I'm going to help you ..."

"Ben?" Melissa's voice came through the door. "Are you okay?"

"Yeah, yeah, just fine. Out in a minute," Ben called. Covering his mouth, he hissed, "Now see what you've done? I can't do this. You have to go. Now."

`Very well. I see we won't accomplish`
`anything tonight. As you wish, I shall`
`leave, but I assure you, I will be back,`
`again and again. I urge you to think`
`carefully about my proposition.` The background hiss faded away.

Ben turned off the faucet and opened the door. Melissa was standing outside.

"I woke up and you were gone. Then I heard talking in the bathroom, and the water running and running. Were you ... were you talking to someone?" Her expression was apprehensive.

"No, no," Ben said. "I was just, um, I was just muttering to myself. I seem to have developed a habit of talking to myself recently. Have to remember to keep that under control."

"Are you sure?" Melissa looked past him into the bathroom. "It sounded like you were saying something and pausing while someone else spoke. And you had the water on for so long. Is your phone in there?"

"No. Look." Ben pointed to the charging station on his dresser. His phone was plugged into the charger. "See? My phone was right here all the time."

"Well, all right. I just ... I thought it seemed strange."

"Nothing to it," said Ben. He slipped his arm around her waist and steered her toward the bed. "Nothing to worry about. Let's get back to bed."

He wrapped his arms around her, and since they were both naked, he quickly thought of a way to distract her. But as he lowered her to the sheets, he couldn't dispel a thought from the back of his mind. *I wonder how I would go about finding a psychiatrist.*

Chapter 10

> "Doc," said Doug, "What can you tell me about cause of death?"
>
> "That's easy," said the coroner as he set about examining the next stiff, "Cause of death is shot in the head."
>
> "Yeah, I know," said Doug. "But what if he was already dead when he was shot? You think you could tell?"
>
> "What do you want me to do? Ask him?"
>
> -- David Shepherd, *Neck of the Woods*

Shopping for a psychiatrist did not turn out to be as easy as Ben assumed it would be. The firm offered an employee assistance program, but despite assurances of confidentiality Ben didn't want to take a chance. He checked for psychiatrists on the firm health care plan, from his home computer, and collected a list of names. When he started calling them, he was surprised at how hard it was to get an appointment. Either they limited their practices to some kind of specialty, or they had no appointments available until after the New Year holiday, or there was some other problem. Finally, on his tenth call, a Dr. Menon offered him an appointment two days later. He was a solo practitioner in a medical building in Mission, and it was in the middle of the day, so Ben would have to leave work. Nonetheless, he took the appointment. He was in a hurry to get rid of the voice.

He arrived fifteen minutes early for his appointment, and a receptionist, who evidently served several doctors in the building, gave him forms to fill out. Medical history, insurance, contact persons. Who should he list as a contact? He certainly didn't want Melissa to know, nor his parents. Finally he left the space blank.

After about fifteen minutes Dr. Menon came out and introduced himself. The doctor looked to be of Indian ancestry, perhaps in his forties, with an easy smile and relaxed manner. He reached for Ben's hand. "I'm Dr. Menon. Come in, have a seat. Would you prefer Mr. Trovato, or may I call you Ben?"

"Ben's fine." They sat in two upholstered armchairs, the doctor's pad on an end table by his chair, a coffee table with a box of tissues between them.

"So this is your first consultation, Ben?"

"Yeah, I never, you know, never felt the need before. My mental health has always been pretty good. I'm a take care of yourself kind of guy."

"So what brings you here?"

After explaining he never experienced any kind of mental health issue before, Ben said, "I don't know if it's some sort of syndrome or something, but I thought I should have it checked out. I thought maybe some sort of therapy or medication or something might get rid of it." He then explained in as matter-of-fact a tone as he could muster his experience hearing the voice of Shepherd.

The doctor, a cool customer, maintained a poker face throughout Ben's improbable story. After asking a few questions to bring out some details, he moved to what Ben assumed was diagnostic information. Any head injuries? Nope. Any travel abroad? No. Unusual stresses or traumatic experiences? Other than working in an inherently stressful occupation, none. Any adverse effects on work? Nope, averaging seventy hour weeks, boss just said he's doing fine. Anyone in his family with similar problems? Certainly not that they told him. His parents and sister and most of his aunts and uncles were healthy as horses. Very healthy horses. Substance usage? Occasional social drinking, no drugs. Any infections, severe colds, periods of illness? Nope, haven't used a sick day in years. Smell any strange odors, experience funny taste in the mouth, or feel sensations on the skin? No. Withdrawal from family, friends, and social activities, reduced energy, lack of motivation, loss of pleasure or interest in life, moodiness or mood swings? No's all around. None of that.

After a long round of questioning, Dr. Menon said, "I would like to refer you to a neurologist for some testing, perhaps a CT scan or an MRI. Experience such as this can result from some physical conditions, such as a brain injury or tumor. I don't have any reason to suspect that, but the neurological would be useful to rule it out."

That was a blow, but Ben gathered his nerve and pressed for more information. "And what if a physical cause is ruled out? What would you look at then?"

Dr. Menon was noncommittal about any kind of diagnosis. Eventually he said, "Hearing voices, or auditory hallucinations, as we call them, are often a sign of schizophrenia. However, your presentation is very logical and orderly, and you seem to be adjusting very well in all other areas of life, which is not something we would expect in a person experiencing the early onset of schizophrenia. Schizophrenia is a very disabling condition, and it doesn't seem you have any other issues beside the voice, so I would be very hesitant to make any kind of diagnosis."

Ben didn't want to ask any more questions, as he was afraid of the answers. But he persisted. "What if it is an early onset of schizophrenia? What effect ... what does that mean?"

"I really don't think you should worry," Dr. Menon said. "Given all you've told me, I would be very surprised if our examination leads to a diagnosis of schizophrenia. But even if it does, there is much we can do with medications. It is very possible to live a nearly normal life with proper medication. But you shouldn't worry, really."

Dr. Menon gave him a referral sheet for a neurologist and asked him to have the neurologist send him a copy of his report. But as Ben took it, he felt numb. All he was looking for was a fix for a small problem. But suddenly a very large cloud darkened his previously clear horizon.

Ben sat in the south end of the window, staring blankly at the pylons.

Brain tumor. Schizophrenia. Words he read about other people. Never young, healthy, vigorous people like him, with a bright future, a great new apartment, and a partnership coming up.

Granted, Dr. Menon didn't say he had a brain tumor, only that it was something to rule out. The only other possibility he mentioned was schizophrenia. Apparently hearing voices screams "schizophrenia" to psychiatrists. Dr. Menon's assurances notwithstanding, Ben felt the foundations of his world growing soft.

Ben picked up his laptop computer and typed "brain tumor symptoms" into Google. The first link led to an authoritative-looking medical website. He ran down the list of symptoms. Headaches, uncheck. Seizures, uncheck. Mental and/or personality changes. Well, other than the normal reactions anyone would have to a hostile takeover of one's own cranium, uncheck. Mass effect – what's that? Has to do with IICP – increased intracranial pressure. Sounds pretty normal in the practice of law. Symptoms include nausea and vomiting, drowsiness, vision problems such as blurred or double vision or loss of peripheral vision, headaches, and mental changes.

An eye exam is recommended. Well, that beats a CAT scan. Uncheck. Focal, or Localized, Symptoms: hearing problems such as ringing or buzzing sounds or hearing loss, decreased muscle control, lack of coordination, decreased sensation, weakness or paralysis, difficulty with walking or speech, balance problems, or double vision. Uncheck, uncheck, uncheck ... okay, this is good. Nothing here about voices. Or dead mystery writers.

Now for the next alternative. With a deep sigh, Ben went back to Google and typed in "schizophrenia symptoms." He read the definition: schizophrenia is characterized by profound disruption in cognition and emotion, affecting the most fundamental human attributes: language, thought, perception, affect, and sense of self. Geez, thought Ben, that's pretty dramatic. My main problem is I can't watch a movie without some old fart bothering me to type his stupid manuscript. Other than that I'm fine.

He read on. Symptoms, while wide ranging, frequently include psychotic manifestations, such as hearing internal voices or experiencing other sensations not connected to an obvious source (hallucinations).

Yikes. That's hitting close to home. He read further on down:

> *Hallucinations - Hallucinations can take a number of different forms - they can be:*

1. Visual (seeing things that are not there or that other people cannot see),

2. Auditory (hearing voices that other people can't hear).

Houston, we've got a problem. He read on to discussions of a large number of symptoms, none of which sounded anything like him, even allowing for a degree of cognitive dysfunction enough to render him unable to recognize his own illness. So we have one very specific voice with one very specific request, and a diagnosis based on that alone. About then he heard the hiss.

```
Ah, computer out, I see. May I con-
clude you've thought it over and decided
to cooperate on our joint venture?
```

"Go away," said Ben. "You are a hallucination, possibly a manifestation of a serious life-threatening condition. I really don't need this right now."

```
What are you talking about? You're
young and healthy. Trust me, I can tell
you a bit about life-threatening condi-
tions, and this isn't that.
```

"I went to see a shrink. He says I may have a brain tumor."

```
What, because of me?
```

"I could be dying."

```
Good Lord. That's ridiculous. You do
not have a brain tumor.
```

"The other possibility he mentioned is schizophrenia."

I can't speak to whether you are schizophrenic, but if so, it has nothing to do with me. Listen. I am real.

"Oh, I see. My hallucination is trying to convince me of its reality. What is the saying, the devil's greatest trick is convincing mankind he doesn't exist?"

What, now you believe in the devil?

"Well, no."

It's amazing how people will put some foolishness in quotation marks, and it becomes received wisdom. So how does this help?

"I don't know, it's just ... I just want to be my normal self again. I don't feel crazy. Except for you, I am perfectly healthy and functional. I don't know."

Look. This is a normal, unremarkable paranormal relationship. I know, you are a skeptic like me, so this is new for both of us. But trust me. You can stick your head in a CAT scan machine or poison a perfectly good brain with psychotropic drugs, but there is one and only one way you are going to get rid of me, and that is by helping me get done what I need to do. Really, is that so terrible?

Ben didn't answer. The voice was actually starting to make some sense. That was the scariest part of all. Schizophrenia is supposed to be madness, but what if your delusion spins a pretty persuasive argument?

Of course, there is always the side benefit. If you have a manuscript, you get to deliver it to the lovely Robin. If I'm not mistaken, that part of the deal works for you, doesn't it?

Now he really had a point. The image of Robin rotated through Ben's mind for a moment. Then he said, "Okay, assuming I go along, how exactly do you see this working?"

The way I figure, I just dictate my text, and you type what you hear. I can see your screen, so if you make any mistakes I can stop and correct you. You just need to relax, clear your mind, and type whatever you hear. I'm sure with practice we'll get a smooth routine down.

"Practice? How much practice? How long will this take?"

Well, I estimate this title will be somewhere between 90,000 and 100,000 words. How many words per minute do you type?

"I have no idea. But I type all the time, so I guess I'm pretty fast."

Let's see. My typing speed was 65 words per minute. So say you are half as fast as I am, or about 30 words per minute. That's 1800 an hour, let's say 1500.

At 90,000 words, we're talking 60 hours.
Give me an hour a night, and we'll be
done in two months. Three, tops.

"And then you'll be gone?"

Forever. Of course, we will also need
to transmit the completed manuscript to
the lovely Robin. I'll oversee that process as well, but she will be delighted
to receive the product and should make
that stage very easy for you. Then you
sit back and enjoy the proceeds. She did
promise you money, didn't she?

Ben ignored the question. The prospect of
having this over with in two months seemed
attractive, particularly in contrast to the alterna-
tives. He picked up his computer, carried it to his
desk, and plugged in the power cord. "You're on.
Let's do this."

Chapter 11

> Doug ran a sheet of paper into the typewriter and rolled it into position. He searched the keyboard and pecked a key. Then another. And another.
>
> "Oh, this won't take long," said Barry.
>
> "Lay off," said Doug. "Every now and then I even miss old Filbert."
>
> -- David Shepherd, *Palm of God*

Ben opened up his word processor. "Okay, let's get going. You have an hour. Shoot."

Right now? Excellent. Now, let me see. How does this thing work? I never used one. Hated the damn things, in fact.

"Just imagine it's a sheet of paper. I'll do the rest. My time is worth $335 an hour, so don't waste it."

Good heavens, that's obscene. Very well. Understand, this is new for me, so it may be a little choppy at first ...

"Time's wasting. What font do you want? What margins? Single or double spaced?"

Uh, double spaced, one inch margins. Font? Let's see, I used the Courier 10 ball on my trusty Selectric. God, I miss that machine. I have no idea what computer font that is.

Ben checked his font list. "Courier New is the only Courier font I have. 10 would probably be size

12. He selected the font and hammered out a random series of letters. "How does that look?"

`That will do. Indent the first line of each paragraph a tab.`

Ben opened the paragraph control and chose "First Line Indent 0.5".

`Dang! This thing requires you to be a typesetter. How do you get any creative work done?`

"You stop fiddling and start writing. Go."

`All right. Title, all caps, center on first page. Heart of a Creek.`

"*Heart of a Creek*? That's the title?"

`Yes, that's the title.`

"What the hell does it mean? That's a weird title. Doesn't the title make a difference in whether people pick up the book in a bookstore?"

`It's a very significant title. The meaning becomes clear on the last page of the book. And people will pick it up if it has my name on the author's line, thank you very much. Now would you stop distracting me with questions and type what I tell you?`

"All right, all right. I'm just saying. Your book, your call."

`First paragraph.` His voice rose into a sonorous, dramatic pitch. `"They found her in`

```
the heart of a creek, in the heart of
America."
```

Ben snorted as he typed.

```
What?
```

"Don't mind me. Your book, I'm just the typist."

```
Maybe I should explain what we're
doing here.
```

"Typing your novel."

```
But it's important for you to
understand the bigger picture. This is
the twelfth and final novel in a series I
wrote about a detective named Doug
Graves.
```

"Yeah, I remember Robin said you left the readers in a cliffhanger with the last one."

```
Yes, that was Belly of the Beast. At
the end my doughty hero was unfortunately
in a coma, to which he came as a result
of the negligence of his friend and
frequent employer, the shady lawyer Barry
L. Grounds.
```

"Sure, make the lawyer the bad guy. It figures."

```
So in this story, Doug has emerged
from the coma and is in desperate need of
funds, so he accepts a proposal from
Barry to investigate the death of a young
socialite, found murdered in a creek in
```

rural Kansas, far from her Kansas City home.

"And this is your big finale, I assume?

Indeed. I have a magnificent plot in mind leading to Doug's redemption from the abyss in which I left him.

"So, you aren't expecting me to stick around for Volume Thirteen, I hope?"

Given my current incorporeal state, I won't be in a position to extend our collaboration, however successful it may be. I don't think you could claim to be discovering hidden manuscripts on a recurring basis. In addition, I am operating under certain strictures.

"Strictures?"

You see, what we are doing here is far from standard procedure for this side. I was allowed to visit with you only by persuading the Powers that Be of the urgency of bringing my life's work to a conclusion.

"So you're only here for this, to get this book done? I'm not living in a haunted house on a permanent basis?"

Generally the Powers are quite parti-cular about the division between the world of the living and the world beyond. However they do allow certain exceptions. Have you read many ghost stories?

"I don't get to read much fiction, and when I do I'm certainly not interested in ghosts."

If you did, you would realize that in most ghost stories some unfinished business binds the restless spirit in this realm. It turns out there is some truth to this, although the reality is much more complicated.

"So you are a ghost, and this book is your unfinished business?"

In my case, that unfinished business is very specific, and I have been put on a tight schedule in getting it done.

"Tight? How tight? Is that where the two months comes from?"

Well, no. You see, the way time operates in your world bears very little relation to the passage of events on this side. So I may not always have a precise grasp of how much time has passed from your perspective. Rather, I have been given a limited window of opportunity to complete this project, and I will not have the luxury of my customary preference for rewrites.

"So, no Cabernet-fueled conflagrations this time?"

No, no. Alas, the incomparable feeling of a fine Cabernet settling in is one of those cherished memories I will know no more.

"No wine in heaven? Sounds like paradise isn't what it's cracked up to be." Ben paused. "Say, while we're on the subject, really, what is it like to, you know, go through the gate, so to speak?"

Uh, that brings us to another of the conditions of my participation in this enterprise. I have been firmly instructed that under no circumstances am I to reveal anything to you about the transition process or the beyond.

"What? I have a window into the mysteries of life, death and eternity, and I can't get any information? Not even just a little hint?"

Not at all. There is concern that if you have privileged knowledge of such things, it may disrupt the intended flow of life. You might go start a religion or something. The Powers seem to think there are quite enough of those.

"Aw, come on. Nobody would believe me if I told them anything anyway. I just want to know for my own curiosity. Maybe it would make me more religious or something. Isn't that a plus on their books?"

No, rules are rules. You've heard of the Old Testament, haven't you?

"All right, all right. Just type." Ben peered at the screen of his laptop. "Okay, they found her in the creek. What next?"

He forgot to keep track of when the hour was up.

Chapter 12

> Barry pressed his face against the car window. "They doing it? Are they going at it?"
>
> "I imagine they are," said Doug, twisting the telephoto lens onto his camera."
>
> Barry was breathing faster. "Should we get closer? Maybe look in a window?"
>
> Doug gave him a withering look. "I need a photo, not a broken nose."
>
> -- David Shepherd, *Rib of Adam*

A few days later, after having his fourth floor apartment cleaned, Ben dropped off the keys to the old unit with Jim. It's official now; the penthouse was his place, his only home.

That Friday Ben and Melissa entertained some of their friends in the new place. Melissa wore Ben's favorite dress, a bright blue number showcasing her generous curves, the neckline revealing a lovely cleavage that scooped up Ben's imagination and funneled it into the rolling terrain to the south. She was an effervescent hostess, giving impromptu tours, showing off the apartment's fine finish and clever features, and making sure everyone in the room was having a good time. Some of Melissa's girlfriends teased her as to when she would be changing her address, to which she responded only with shy but knowing smiles. The evening was a rousing success, and several bottles of wine gave their all for the cause of the general merriment.

After the last guests bid good night and staggered out the door, Ben and Melissa stood at the picture window and gazed out contentedly at the lights of Kansas City scattered before them.

Melissa rested her head on Ben's shoulder. "I think we're going to be very happy here."

Ben was a little alarmed at her casual use of the first person plural, but this was absolutely not the moment to debate the issue.

Melissa turned toward him and pressed against him. He looked down into her adorable and adoring face, and beyond it down the passage through to the valley of delights. "I think the dishes can wait," she said in a husky whisper.

His arms circled around her waist and signaled his assent by reaching upward for the blue zipper.

Some hours later, Ben awoke to the realization that the wine had undertaken its voyage to the sea, and was gathering in the harbor of the port of exit, recently occupied with commerce in other goods. Carefully he extracted himself from Melissa's warm damp embrace. She settled into the covers with a contented sigh.

Ben made his way through the dark to the bathroom, closed the door and lifted the seat. He surrendered to sweet release.

`Well, that was nice.`

Ben's startled response produced a most unfortunate reaction, to the detriment of the wall and floor by the toilet.

"What ... what ... what are you doing here?"

The usual, of course. I didn't realize you would be occupied.

"What ... You have no right –"

Melissa's voice called out from the bedroom. "Ben? Is everything all right?"

"Fine, fine," Ben said. He turned on the spigot.

She is really quite a lovely young lady. Very enthusiastic.

"Listen," he said in a low whisper. "I can't stop you from coming and going, but when I'm with Lis, that's off limits. Absolutely off limits."

Well, I didn't plan it that way. I don't know what your situation will be when I get here. And it's no small effort to get here, so I thought I'd just wait until you were done. You are done, aren't you?

"Look. This is my apartment, my home. You have no right to ... to –"

Well, I suppose you have a point legally, but as a practical matter, as long as we are working together on this it's my apartment, too. As it has been for years.

"Okay, but look. Even people who live together, even roommates have boundaries. There have to be boundaries. If I'm going to help you, if we're going to do this, you have to respect my privacy. You have to give me some space, you know?"

Fair enough, roomie. I just thought you should realize what a good thing you have here. That's advice from someone who has, shall we say, been around the block a few times.

"Well, thanks but no thanks. I don't need your advice, and I really don't intend to talk locker room with you about my love life."

You know, there's no reason to believe it would be any better with Robin.

"Robin?" He paused and lowered his voice to an urgent whisper. "What does this have to do with her?"

Beautiful women aren't necessarily better lovers, you know. I haven't observed any correlation, and my sample size is significant. Beautiful women tend to be self-absorbed.

"You can just forget about that. I have no interest in that woman."

Oh, please. I am inside your mind. I see what you see, I hear what you hear, I feel what you feel. Don't try to tell me the very thought of Robin doesn't send cascades of lust coursing through your system like the Hwang Ho in flood season. Oh, my, what's that happening down there at the mention of the subject?

"What's this got to do with Robin? Wait a minute. Were you and Robin ... oh, my God. That's disgusting!"

Absolutely not, young man. Put that notion out of your mind this instant! Robin was the daughter of my dearest friend. I've known her since birth. The only time I ever touched her was when I bounced her on my knee as a toddler.

"So that's what this is about. You're upset that I see your precious baby as the grown woman she's become. Let me tell you, a woman who looks like that is no –"

That's enough! That's quite enough! My point is that this project I have undertaken with you is an artistic charge of the highest order. I expect you to approach this effort with a degree of seriousness and professionalism appropriate to the responsibility.

"This from the guy who just tuned in on my ... my ...?"

I will not tolerate you using this as a tool of seduction! Given the fact that I may enter your consciousness at random, you should consider seriously the consequences of abusing the trust I have placed in you. I suggest you appreciate

what you have, and do not put that at
risk for an adventure that can only turn
out badly.

"Are you ... are you threatening me? Are you?"

No, I just hoped we might accomplish
some work this evening, but I can see
from your frame of mind and, um, state of
engagement that that is unlikely. It
appears I have wasted my time, and unfortunately time is not something I have to
waste. So I will leave you to your
activities. You should attend to that
young lady you have and not cast our eyes
elsewhere. Good night.

"Oh yeah? Listen, it's my life, okay? Do you
hear me?" No answer.

"Ben?" Melissa's voice was at the door. "Are
you in there?"

"Yeah, I'll be out in a sec."

"Are you talking to yourself? Are you okay?"

"No, no. I'm fine."

Ben turned off the water and returned to the
bedroom. Melissa was back in bed, looking up at
him. He thought of reaching for her to initiate a
second act in the evening's recreations, but he
paused wondering whether Shepherd was still
present in his head. This wasn't an experience he
really wanted to share. But when he looked at
Melissa, her face bore an expression of concern in
the dim light.

"What's going on?" she said.

The question startled Ben. "Nothing." The answer sounded completely unconvincing even to him.

"Are you seeing someone else?"

"No, no! Why would you think that? You're my one and only. You know that!" He caressed the side of her head and started to lean in to kiss her, but she pulled back.

"I know, I know, and maybe I'm just being insecure and needy. But it seems you've been distracted lately – looking around or not listening, not really here. And you go into the bathroom and stay there after we make love, and I hear you muttering in there. It makes me feel like you aren't really happy with me."

"Of course I am, of course I am. It's just a weird time for me, with the partnership and all."

"Yes, I know, and I want to be supportive when you need it. But I was reading this article about signs of an affair, and some of the things that have been happening began to bother me. If you … if you were feeling restless or something, you would let me know, wouldn't you? Would you talk to me about it?"

"Don't even think about that. There's no one else for me. We're fine. You're my only girl. Here, let me show you."

He pulled her to him and kissed her enthusiastically, and their bodies responded to the emotion of the moment. But as they say in the theater, the first time with an audience is the toughest.

Chapter 13

> The hotel registers left no doubt. Doug didn't look forward to telling Mrs. Miggleman that her husband was entertaining more than clients all those evenings.
>
> Why would a man want two dames? One was too many.
>
> -- David Shepherd, *Neck of the Woods*

Ben was spending a snowy December Saturday going through boxes of papers, while Melissa perched in the window seat, doing something with the curtains. She stood up and crossed her arms with pride.

"There!" she exclaimed, in a tone that commanded his attention. "That looks much better!"

She had tied the drapes back at the middle with a belt of fabric, made from the same materials as the drapes.

"What looks better?" said Ben.

"The curtain ties. They were there all the time, hanging behind the drapes. They were all dusty. They probably haven't been used in years."

"Why use them?" Ben said. "If you want to close the drapes, you have to take them off. More effort."

"No, you need the tiebacks," Melissa explained. "The curved lines of the drapes add drama."

"I hate drama. I avoid it wherever I can."

"Nonsense," she said, walking toward the kitchen brushing off her hands. "The window is the natural center of attention in the room. The curved lines showcase the window much better. That's why you need me, to help you with these things."

The door buzzer sounded. "Who's that?" Melissa asked.

"I have no idea," Ben said. He pressed the speaker button. "Hello?"

"Ben!" a melodious voice came over the speaker. "It's Robin. I'm in the building. Can I come in for a minute?"

There are moments in human existence when the certainty of doom becomes clear, as the wheels slide irreversibly toward the cliff, as the balance shifts and the fatal plunge begins. Ben never experienced such a moment, but he imagined it would feel something like this. He also discovered another quirk of the human condition: at the very moment when one needs the brain to be working at peak efficiency, it ceases to function.

"Sure, come on in," he heard himself saying to the speaker.

He went to the door, casting a sidelong glance at Melissa and seeing her transfixed with an expression of curiosity. At the sound of a knock, he opened the door, and Robin sailed in with the majesty of a winning yacht claiming the regatta.

She was dressed in a stylish and obviously expensive leather jacket, a patterned blouse revealing an ornate handcrafted jewel necklace and just a suggestion of cleavage, and designer jeans seemingly designed for her hips. An elegant wave of chestnut swept out from under her chic beret.

"Hi," she said. "I was just in the neighborhood and I thought of you. I thought I'd stop by and see how you were doing in the place."

"Uh, hi," Ben said. "Well, it's coming together, as you can see."

Ben became suddenly aware of Melissa, standing motionless at the kitchen divider, struggling to close her mouth, without success.

"Oh, Robin, this is my ... friend, Melissa Sturgeon. Lis, Robin Atwater."

"Hi, so nice to meet you," Robin said in a polished cadence, appropriate to an extra with no speaking lines in the script. She wandered into the apartment, casting an assessing gaze around.

"Oh, it looks so different. That's to be expected, of course. It's your place now, and you'll be making it your own." She stopped by the window seat.

"Oh, my," she said. "I see you tied the drapes back. Hmm, I rather liked the strong, masculine lines they had before. Oh, I shouldn't say, it's up to you."

Ben glanced at Melissa, who looked as though she expected to be struck by a large truck.

Robin's gaze ran up and down the built-in bookshelves. "I don't imagine you found what we were hoping for, did you?"

"No, sorry," said Ben. "I've been keeping my eyes open for it, but I haven't found anything."

Robin glanced toward the master bedroom. "Say, did you check whether any of the planks of the wainscoting in the bedroom are loose? That would be a possibility."

Ben glanced at Melissa. Her eyes burned him like sunlamps.

"Umm, no," Ben said. "I'll look at them."

"Well, if anything does turn up, you know where to find me."

"Yeah, I, uh, I have your card, somewhere."

"Hope to hear from you then," she said turning to the door. "So nice. Bye," she said to Melissa, with a tone of vague acknowledgement that Melissa was more sentient than the furniture. The door thumped behind her and she was gone.

Melissa looked at Ben. "Friend?" she said. That slender syllable crushed Ben under an infinite mass of questioning, insinuation, accusation, and desolation.

"Uh, she's just a casual business acquaintance. I just didn't feel she was entitled to any more information."

"Um," Melissa replied. This syllable, as void of emotion or communication as the previous one had been charged, hung in the air like a black hole of expression, giving out nothing, yet bending the entire fabric of local space with the immense gravity of all it held within. "Business acquaintance." It was a simple statement of fact, yet it struck with greater power as an interrogation, indeed, a denial of the very fact asserted.

"Yeah, she's with the publishing firm that published the Shepherd novels. She was over a lot when Shepherd lived here. She … they seem to think there might be a manuscript stashed somewhere in the apartment, and she keeps pestering me to see if I've found it. But I haven't found anything."

With that single stroke, Ben reversed the tide of the conversation and seized the upper ground.

"Oh?" Melissa's voice rose by a major fourth within the bounds of that short syllable. Ben was learning that invoking the mention of the Shepherd legacy was good for whatever ailed their relationship at the moment. Melissa's hero worship still outweighed her suspicion or jealousy. "There might be a manuscript? Here? That nobody's read?"

"Well, they think it's possible. Apparently the old man had a phobia about someone stealing his work and sometimes hid his works in progress in the apartment. But I haven't found anything."

Melissa's eyes were sweeping the apartment. "A hidden manuscript! Oooh, the master mystery writer left us a mystery! Where it might it be?"

Ben ran a quick mental inventory as to whether there was anything in the apartment he wouldn't want Melissa to see if she started poking around. "I don't think there is one," he said. "I haven't torn the wallboards off or anything, but I really doubt a manuscript is stashed anywhere. I wish it was. From what she said, there may be money in it for me if I find anything."

Melissa was walking around examining the seams of the walls and floorboards. Ben felt a moment of relief. That could have turned out much worse, he thought. I seem to have escaped the Robin encounter in one piece.

"By the way," Melissa called out, "she's very pretty, isn't she?"

"I suppose," Ben answered. He was sure that sounded as lame to her as it did to him.

"You have very good taste in business acquaintances. Very good. Hmmm."

Dammit, thought Ben. Women are a minefield.

Chapter 14

> "I want the truth!" thundered the police
> chief. "The truth, the whole truth, and
> nothing but the truth!"
>
> "You need a new mouthwash," said Doug.
>
> "Don't insult me, you two-bit gumshoe!"
>
> "Oh, so you don't want the whole truth
> after all?"
>
> -- David Shepherd, *Belly of the Beast*

The following Thursday, Ben worked all day drafting, researching, and revising a huge motion for protective order, as mind-numbing as it was complex. He was exhausted when he arrived home about 9:30. He popped a frozen dinner into the microwave, opened up a beer, and dropped into the cushions of the couch in front of the television. Surfing through the cable guide, he found a rerun of an action movie based on a superhero graphic novel, with not much plot but spectacular special effects. He had seen it already, but it seemed the perfect mindless occupation to while away an hour or so before crawling to bed.

The villain had just kidnapped the police commissioner's daughter while the protagonist was walking the street battling his demons, when Ben heard the hiss.

Are you ready? I came up with a great
ending for this chapter and I want to get
it down while it's fresh.

"Oh, God, not tonight. I am totally beat. I can't
help you tonight."

Come on. We don't have time to waste.
Let's just finish this one chapter. An
hour and it's done.

"I can't. I just worked twelve hours worse than
any you ever did. Leave me alone."

We need to do this. What is this
nonsense you're watching? It looks like
something out of a comic book.

"It is. It's based on a superhero comic. You
don't have to watch."

Neither should you. You lose brain
cells with every minute you spend on this
garbage.

"I have only five or ten brain cells left to lose.
Not tonight. Go away."

An explosion doesn't make bodies fly
up in the air like that, unless it
happens right under them. Don't these
filmmakers know anything about physics?

Ben could tell he would not get to relax
tonight. He switched off the set with his remote
and pushed himself to his feet. He shuffled over to
his desk and opened up his notebook computer.

"All right, all right. An hour. Then I'm going to
bed."

Wonderful. Where were we?

Ben studied the bookmarks in his document. "Chapter Nine. Barry is trying to talk Doug into breaking into Boswalt's office to steal back the letter Barry sent by mistake. Last line – 'I'll owe you,' said Barry. 'I'm good for it. Have I ever let you down? Wait, don't answer that.'"

David dictated several paragraphs as Ben typed.

"You know, this Barry character is completely unrealistic. A lawyer who did half the things he does would be disbarred."

Nonsense. My readers love Barry. He's the character you love to hate.

"Well, he's not at all credible. I know a lot of lawyers, but no slimeballs like him."

Then you don't know enough lawyers. Everybody loves to hate the sleazy lawyer. Hey, how do you tell when a lawyer is lying?

"His lips are moving."

Oh, you heard that one?

"I might have thought it was a little bit funny the first hundred times I heard it, but that was so long ago I can't remember."

Well, it's a classic. Never gets old.

Ben's fatigue wore off, and he was ready for an argument. "Now wait just a moment. I always treat you and your profession with respect. You are here in my apartment, taking up my time, depending on me to do your work. Is it asking too much for you to give my profession a little respect, as well?"

You need more of a sense of humor. People laugh at lawyer jokes because of the truth in them.

"Well, I think your stereotype of the lying lawyer is false. In fact, I think it is harder for a lawyer to get away with lying than it is for other professions. We have this little thing called the adversary system. If I tell a lie, there's somebody on the other side being paid very well to catch me at it. Who are you to talk? You wrote fiction. You told lies for a living."

Now wait just a minute. Fiction is not a lie. Fiction is a special form of truth telling. As Picasso put is, "Art is a lie that makes us realize the truth."

"See? You admitted it, it's a lie."

Well then, bring some of your lawyerly logical powers to bear. What is your definition of a lie?

"Uh, a lie is a false statement. A knowingly false statement."

Hmm, so if your beloved tells you, "My heart belongs to you," is she lying then? Because she certainly still needs her heart, and you have no use for it, do you?

"Well, that's a metaphor. A lie is ... I guess you'd have to add the element of intent to mislead.

A lie is a false statement, that you know is false, by which you intend to mislead someone."

Aha. So an essential part of a lie is that the audience believes it to be true. Tell me, did any of my readers reasonably believe Doug Graves actually existed? That my descriptions of his misadventures were true accounts of facts I observed?

Ben was stumped. "Okay, no, so fiction isn't technically a lie. But still, you get to make up whatever you want. Those of us who work in the real world have to deal with truth we can't control."

So if you and your august opposing counsel are both truth tellers, then, may I assume you stand up in court and pro-vide an agreed upon statement of the facts of the case?

"Well, no, obviously. I'm going to stress the facts that serve my client's argument, and they're going to talk about the ones that support their client's. The judge or jury decides who has made the better argument. But we both have to work with the real facts."

So you are both storytellers. You both select the facts that serve your theme, and you craft the narrative that most effectively presents it.

"Now wait a minute. We tell a story, yes, but it's a true story. We can't make anything up, although we can build some facts up and leave others out."

My point exactly. You must realize the point of storytelling is not truth or falsity. It is what facts we choose to present. We select the facts that illuminate the truth we have to tell, and we emphasize them as eloquently as possible. Those that do not, we leave out. You ask witnesses to tell the whole truth, but that itself is a lie. You don't want the whole truth. You don't want to hear facts which, while true, are not meaningful.

"Yeah, we would say they have to be relevant."

Exactly. And that is the essence of storytelling. The storyteller, be he a lawyer or a news reporter or a writer of fiction, tells you the facts that matter. That is what I mean by a story. A story is selection, out of the universe of available information, of the facts that tell us something meaningful about our world, about our existence as human beings. The art of storytelling, in fiction as in law, lies in the skillful selection of the facts that matter, and the skillful omission of those that don't.

"But when you're writing fiction, you're still making facts up, not telling us what's true."

You're not seeing my point. Tell me, young man, what is the opposite of "truth"?

"The opposite of truth? Uh, that would be a lie, I guess."

Wrong. Is not a lie a form of truth?

"You're driving me crazy. How is a lie a form of truth?"

Think about it. As you said yourself, a moment ago, a lie is a false statement that the speaker hopes his audience will believe. The intent to mislead is essential to a lie, did you not say that?

"Well, yeah."

So in that sense, must a lie not be composed mostly of the truth? A lie must have enough truth in it that the recipient of the lie will believe it. Say a man comes home at midnight, still radiant from the blandishments of his mistress, and his wife asks, "Where have you been?" What is he going to say?

"I suppose he would say something like, 'I had to work late. My car wouldn't start. I forgot to call. Sorry.'"

Exactly. If he were to answer, "I was abducted by aliens and had to hijack a starship to return from Alpha Centauri," it would accomplish nothing for him. His story about working late must be plausible enough for his wife to believe it, or at least admit its possibility. It must have enough truth in it to pass for the truth. In that sense, a lie is not the opposite of the truth, but a variation on the truth. So it is with fiction, humor, sarcasm, metaphor, all of our deliberate departures from literal truth.

"All right, so if a lie is not the opposite of the truth, what is?"

You see? The opposite of truth is not falsehood, but meaninglessness. We struggle against the idea that there is no meaning or point to our existence, that we are mere machines of protoplasm, eating and sleeping and avoiding pain and seeking pleasure until we stop, and then it's over. This is the power and the importance of the story – the idea that the events of our lives have a meaning, that there is an arc and a direction and a beauty to our lives.

"Unless the truth is that there is no great big meaning. Then your stories are just lies and self-deception. The ancients looked up at the stars and saw what they thought were pictures, so they made up stories to fit the pictures. Only the pictures weren't real. They were random juxtapositions of stars. People just projected stories they wanted to believe onto a reality that had nothing to with them."

Yes, the word for that phenomenon is "pariedolia," but it's not necessarily wrong. Do you know anything about the constellations?

"A little."

But not enough to understand them, apparently. Go out on a winter night – tonight would do nicely – and find Orion. Are you familiar with Orion?

"Of course. The one with the belt."

See? Just now you used the story to give meaning to a pattern you observed. Anyway, if you read astronomy you will know that the stars of Orion are not a random pattern, but actually represent something real. All but one of the bright stars are similar – they are huge, young, immensely bright stars, all in the same stage of development, scattered further out along the spiral arm of the galaxy we live in. In essence, when we look at Orion, we are looking at the booming suburbs at the outer edge of the city we live in.

"Okay, I'll take your word for that."

Then turn your head in the opposite direction, and you will see Cygnus, which looks like a giant cross, and Lyra, a parallelogram next to a very bright star, Vega. This region is full of star clusters, nebulae, closely packed fields of stars – an older, more stable part of the galaxy. To follow the metaphor, we are looking back into the dense, aging city core. You can sweep your head from Orion to Lyra and see the whole history of the galaxy, laid out before you on a winter's night. When we look at Orion, we see our past; when we look at Lyra, we see our future. That's a magnificent story.

"So your point is ..."

My point is the ancients were right. There are stories in the stars. They just didn't have the information to know the right ones. Do you know much about quantum physics?

"Uh, the barest idea. I read a couple of books, but the more I read the more I get the sense that if you think you understand it, you probably don't."

Then you understand more than many of the people who write books about it. I don't pretend to understand either, but one of the things they do tell us is that matter itself, everything you are made of and think of as solid and permanent, is itself just a highly structured form of energy. Energy in the process of becoming, not just being. An event is merely one scenario from many possible ones, the one we observe. In other words, the reality we experience is a process, a selection, a story. The great poet Muriel

Rukeyser once wrote, "The universe is made of stories, not of atoms." From what I understand of science, she appears to be right. Literally.

"Now you have my head spinning. So what does all this have to do with this detective story of yours?"

What we do as storytellers is to draw on the vein of experience we all have, and tell people those things they know to be true. We use a fictional setting, but our fiction only works to the extent we identify truths people know from their own lives, and show them how those truths have meaning in our world. We might stretch their understanding of the world, but we must maintain enough of the truth they know our alternate world is credible under the logic of the one they know. That is what the story does for us. The story affirms that there is purpose in our lives, there is meaning to be found, there is a reason why we are here. We live our lives to act out our stories. And those of us privileged to write tell those stories. We keep people going, by reminding them that the universe has meaning. That it is, in fact, made of stories.

Ben paused a moment. "It occurs to me that you are telling me this from the situation you are in now. Is there something you can tell me, based on what you've seen since ... since ..."

```
No. I can't tell you anything about
that. Those are the rules. We discussed
that.
```

"All right, all right. Well, one meaningful fact in my story is that I have to be at work seven hours from now. So if you want this chapter typed, we'd better get to it."

```
Very well. What is the last line you
have?
```

"'So you want me to break in and get it back,' said Doug. 'And if I'm arrested, then what? Think they'll let me go because you told me to do it?'"

```
All right. Next line: "Not to worry,"
said Barry. "I'll represent you for half
price. Hey, free; you're a buddy."
```

"Oh, Jesus Christ."

```
Just type, okay?
```


The next day found Ben at a law office on Grand, questioning a safety expert in a deposition.

"Now, Dr. Bergquist," asked Ben, "Do the records you reviewed reflect whether periodic maintenance had been performed on the crane at the time of your inspection?"

"Objection," said the opposing attorney. "Lack of foundation, calls for a conclusion, hearsay."

"Objection noted. You may answer," said Ben.

"I'm not sure," said the witness. "Which records are you referring to?"

Ben examined his papers. "From what I see, the crane was scheduled for periodic maintenance in June ... "

`Hello, are you ready to get down to work?`

" ... uh, three months before the accident, I believe. Is that correct?"

"Objection, lack of foundation, hearsay, conclusion."

"Answer."

"You have the records, I don't know," snapped the witness.

"Well, Dr. Bergquist ..."

`Where the hell are we?`

"... would you please look at the packet in front of you and direct your attention to Exhibit ..."

`What are you talking about? What packet?`

"Yes? Exhibit what?" said Dr. Bergquist.

`I have an important idea I want to get down. Can you please get to your computer before it slips away?`

"Not now!" said Ben.

"I beg your pardon?" said Dr. Bergquist.

"Let the record reflect that the witness was not told what exhibit to examine," said the attorney for the other side.

"Excuse me, Exhibit 45-G," said Ben. "Now, looking at this exhibit – do you have the exhibit?"

`I don't know what you're exhibiting here, but we really need to get to work. Which room are we in? I don't recognize it.`

"We're not ... I'm sorry, Dr. Bergquist, do you have the exhibit?"

"I do."

"Now, would you look at the maintenance log for June ..."

"Objection, foundation not laid," said opposing counsel.

"Would you look –"

`Look at what? I have to say your behavior is very strange. Who are you talking to?"`

"... at the maintenance log and tell me when the scheduled maintenance for June was –"

"Objection, hearsay, foundation not laid, asked and answered," said opposing counsel.

"What was the question?" said Dr. Bergquist.

`Something is clearly wrong here.`

"You're telling me!"

"What?" said opposing counsel. "Are you concurring in my objection?"

"Wait, where are we?" said Ben. "Did I finish the question?"

`I don't think you even asked me a`
`question.`

"Would you read back the question?" said opposing counsel to the reporter.

"Wait, wait, withdraw the question," said Ben. "Uh, excuse me. Can we take a five-minute break?"

"Are you all right, counsel?" said the other attorney. "Shall we reschedule?"

"Absolutely," said Dr. Bergquist.

"Absolutely a break or absolutely reschedule?" asked the attorney.

"Five minute break! Five minute break!" said Ben. He stood up and headed for the door.

"When ya gotta go, ya gotta go," said Dr. Berg-quist.

"Off the record!" Ben barked to the reporter. He hurried out of the law office and to a secluded corner of the hallway.

"What are you doing here? I'm at work. I thought you only bothered me at the apartment."

`I don't know where you are when I`
`arrive. All I know is what I detect`
`through your senses. I've never seen`

anywhere but the apartment before. This
is a new development.

"New development? What? That you can
follow me anywhere?"

Apparently. My guess is that the
connection is growing stronger, and is no
longer confined spatially to the apartment. This complicates matters.

"You're telling me. Now you can see and hear
anywhere I go? I have no refuge from your
meddling?"

Now, I have no interest in intruding.
Just understand that I have no way of
knowing where you are or what is
happening until I get here. Since it is
no small matter for me to make the
journey, I really do not want to waste
any opportunities to get work done.

"Don't you understand I have a job? A very
demanding job that commands all my attention
when I am at work? I can't type your damn novel
when I'm in the middle of a deposition."

The attorney on the other side appeared at the
end of the hallway. "Mr. Trovato? Can we
continue? Are you all right?"

"One moment," Ben answered. He returned to
an urgent whisper. "I gotta go. I mean, now. Come
back later. I'll try to type for you tonight, but now I
absolutely have to get back to work."

Very well. But rather than return and
try to get back again, I guess I'll tag

along for a few hours. I have all the time in the world. You can barely imagine.

"I suppose I can't stop you. But keep quiet. I have to concentrate."

Oh, believe me, I'll have nothing to say. I'd be bored to death, if I wasn't already dead.

Ben headed back to the conference room. It's enough to be haunted, he thought. But by a bad comedian?

Chapter 15

It was just an ordinary ride to Abilene.
He'd done half a dozen times before. Two
days, maybe three.

-- David Shepherd, "Three Days Ride,"
The Winterset Formation

A few days later Ben and Melissa decided to check out a new café a coworker recommended, just off Southwest Trafficway on the western border of Westport.

Ben picked up Melissa at her place about 6:30 and turned left onto Mill Street. Melissa was chatting about her day, when suddenly she stiffened. "Stop the car!" she cried.

Ben jammed on the brakes and the car stopped with a screech. As an afterthought he glanced in the rear view mirror; fortunately, nobody was behind him at the time.

Melissa gestured toward the curb. "Pull over! Pull over and park!"

Ben swerved the car into the next available space and looked around to see what was wrong. Melissa grabbed her purse and sprang out of the door. Ben shut off the car and bolted after her. "What's wrong, what's wrong?" he called.

"Nothing," said Melissa. She pointed to a nearby storefront, with a hand painted sign saying

"Well Read." "It's this new bookstore. It looks like it's finally open. We have to check it out!"

"I thought there was some emergency. And I thought you were starving," said Ben.

"I am. But first things first!"

Melissa barreled through the front door, and Ben followed. The bookstore was small. Mismatched bookcases crowded the floor space. They were packed to capacity with secondhand books. Toward the front, a couch and five or six assorted chairs surrounded a coffee table. A young woman with glasses and braided hair smiled behind the counter. "Welcome to Well Read," she said. "I'm Eve. May I help you with anything?"

"Where are the mysteries?" said Melissa.

Eve gestured toward the right wall. "Along the wall in the corner," she said. Melissa headed straight to the spot and began an intensive examination of the spines of the books crammed onto the shelves.

"May I show you anything?" Eve said to Ben.

"Ah, no. I'm just kind of following her around." He glanced toward a section with sports titles. Eve turned away, and Ben paused. "Wait a minute. Do you have anything by David Shepherd?"

"Oh, yes," she replied. "A lot of people have been asking about him since we lost him so tragically last month. We will miss him so much.

Of course the Doug Graves mysteries are very popular. They're over where your friend is looking."

"I think we have them all. There are eleven, right?"

"Yes, and what a wonderful series. A lot of us were left wanting more after the last one, but I guess that was where he will leave us."

Ben couldn't resist playing with the earnest proprietor. "Oh, yeah, the last one ended with a cliffhanger, didn't it? Doug was in a coma, right?"

"Yes, that's right. All his fans were sure he would write another volume to bring Doug out of there, leave us in a more satisfying place. But I guess that won't happen now."

"How do you know? The last one was, what, three or four years ago? Maybe he wrote another that hasn't come out yet."

"We could hope. But I hear that after his best friend died, he went into a shell and stopped writing. It's very sad, really. We'd all be thrilled if there was another one, but I don't see how that could happen."

Ben decided the game had gone far enough. "Didn't he write other stuff? Do you have anything besides the Doug Graves stories?"

Eve's face brightened. "Oh, I'm so glad you asked. Most people never look beyond the usual, the mysteries and the histories. But there's so much more. Let me show you something."

She led Ben to another part of the store, pulled a volume off the shelves, and handed it to him. It was an older hardbound volume in a maroon cover, with no jacket. Ben saw the A&B logo on the spine. He examined the cover: *The Winterset Formation: Stories from the Heartland*, by David Shepherd.

"This is a real treasure," she said. "It's a collection of short stories, all set in Western Missouri and Kansas. There's quite an assortment. Some historical tales, and some crime stories, as you'd expect. But he also wrote several on more general themes, some in a unique style I call 'prairie noir.' They really display his mastery of character and setting. I think you will really enjoy this set."

"Sounds great," said Ben. "Short stories. Just what I was looking for."

"Feel free to browse," Eve said. She went back to the counter.

Ben carried the volume to the sitting area in the front of the store and started reading the first story, a historical tale. Shepherd dropped the reader right into the point of view of a man riding a horse through the deserted landscape of Kansas. Ben marveled at the sensory detail of the experience Shepherd provided. He felt the emptiness of the man's stomach, the dry scratching of thirst in his throat, the heat of the sun and the stillness of the air, the sound and smell and feel of the horse rocking beneath him. He could see the colors and feel the textures of the brush and grass and trees growing all around, the turns of the path as it wound through unnamed hills, each with its own character, scattering dust and clacking rocks of the trail beneath the horse's feet. Slowly he was drawn into the man's journey, alone in a silent country-side, the way before him stretching out in vast and perilous gulfs of distance. Ben thought of driving through that same countryside at 70 miles per hour, thinking of it as empty and dull, even though he knew an exit with convenience stores and fast food chains always lay half an hour or less ahead of him. For the traveler, the voyage was infinitely richer in detail, yet perilous in the lack of sustenance and resources it offered him. Ben read on, as the urgency of the drama increased. Darkness fell and fatigue and hunger and thirst distorted the narrator's perspective, until the story wound to its devastating and brutal closure. After he finished, Ben sat stunned. In a few moments he became aware of his surroundings again, sitting in a plush chair in a warm and lighted store, the throbbing life of a city just beyond the glass pane next to him, even as the man whose senses and soul he had inhabited for the last 40 pages lay dying, alone on a dark and desolate plain.

Melissa came over to him, four books clutched in her arms. "Well, it looks like the next couple of weeks are shot for me. You done? We should probably get going."

Ben glanced at his watch. Over half an hour had passed since they entered the bookstore. He had completely lost track of the time. "Yeah, I'm done. Let's check out."

Melissa looked at his book. "What's that?" Ben showed her, and her face lit up. "Oh, that's wonderful! I never read that one. Are you getting it? Can I borrow it when you're done?"

"Sure." Ben thought he should probably warn her about the wallop awaiting her in the first story.

They turned to the counter. Melissa set her books down, and Ben told Eve to ring them all up on his card. As she was doing so, Melissa picked up a sheet of paper on the counter and read it. "Oh, Ben, look at this."

The green sheet of paper was a flyer for a writer's group meeting at the store, on the second and fourth Thursday of each month.

"We're really excited about that group," said Eve. "It's led by Josh Ryder. He's an instructor in creative writing at Longview Community College, and writes wonderful poems and stories. We have four or five people signed up. Are you interested? Do you write?"

"Ben, you should go," said Melissa.

"Are you a writer?" asked Eve.

"No, I don't write."

"But he should," said Melissa. "He's really good with words."

"You don't need to be a writer," said Eve. "You can bring as much or as little as you want to the group. It's all about helping people find their voices and develop their craft."

"This could be fun," said Melissa. "Maybe it would help you get back in touch with your talent. You could use a diversion that doesn't have anything to do with work. Maybe it would even help your legal writing."

Under normal circumstances Ben wouldn't have given the idea a second thought. As busy as he was, the last thing he needed was a new pastime. But he thought again about the story, about the power Shepherd's words assumed over him. It wouldn't hurt to go a session or two, see what it was like. He could always stop.

"Okay, maybe I'll try it."

"Great!" said Eve. She pulled out a tablet and handed it to him. Five names with emails and telephone numbers were written on it. "Just sign up here. We'll look forward to seeing you Thursday!"

Later at the café, Melissa bubbled on and on about the bookstore and how pleased she was with her new acquisitions. She enthused about his intention to attend the writers group. Ben wondered whether it would be as easy as he thought to get out of it, since Melissa seemed to have more invested in it than he did.

After dinner Ben dropped Melissa off at her place and headed home. He got ready for bed, but when he slid under the sheets, he noticed the book on his bed stand. It wouldn't hurt to read another story before bed. Perhaps it would help him get to sleep. It wouldn't take more than a few minutes.

He was wrong about that.

Chapter 16

> The writer's lot is lonely. He picks his perilous way over the mountain path of words that will not come. He straggles through the gulch of the blank page. He shivers alone in the dark valley where inspiration fails. At last he arrives in the green pasture, a friend by his side who was not there when the journey began.
>
> -- David Shepherd, The Writer's Journey

Ben thought he might read more stories when he got home the next night, but before he could settle in, Shepherd arrived primed for a work session. Ben opened up the work file on his computer and dutifully typed in what Shepherd dictated to him.

"But why would Heinclaw start the fire?" said Doug. "It's not even his property. No insurance company would write him a policy on it."

"Because he owns it through a shell company," said Barry. "I traced the company back to him through records in the county court."

"Circuit court."

What?

"Circuit court. Barry is a Missouri lawyer. He'd call it the circuit court."

Excuse me. I have developed these characters through eleven novels, and I think I know exactly how they'd speak.

"Well, then, you've been getting it wrong for eleven novels, because most lawyers I know would call it the circuit court, not the county court."

Let's be clear here. I am the writer, and your role is to transcribe what I give you. I never intended this to be collaboration.

"That's odd. I recall the word 'collaboration' being used on multiple occasions, and not by me."

Look, I do not mean to dismiss your contribution, which I appreciate. But I have never had a co-author. My work has always been my own, and I am not about to change that now.

"I'm not stealing your thunder. I'm just trying to help. Maybe I know a few things you don't, and maybe I have some ideas you might want to hear out."

Oh, really? So we're all writers now? You think successful writing is something you can just start to do anytime you feel like it?

"No, I'm not claiming to be a writer. I just have some ideas. I used to do some writing, by the way. My creative writing teacher in high school thought I was pretty good. I'm just out of practice."

Oh, wonderful. I am tethered to a high
school writer.

"Look, this is your project and it makes no
difference to me whether it's any good or not. I just
think you might be a little open-minded about con-
tributions I can make."

This is the contribution I need from
you. I need for you to type what I tell
you to type, without distracting me or
wasting our time with comments. You want
to get this over with, right? You can
accomplish that by carrying out your
assignment as efficiently as possible and
not distracting me from my train of
thought.

Ben decided to let it go. He typed what
Shepherd told him to and finished out the hour.
After Shepherd left, Ben saved the file and closed
his laptop. As he did, he noticed a sheet of paper
under the computer. It was the flyer from Well
Read, advertising the writers group.

Hmm, thought Ben. High school writer, huh?
Maybe we'll see about that.

Ben arrived at Well Read a few minutes after
seven. Eve smiled at him behind the counter, and
he nodded in return. He saw a group of four
people sitting in the chairs and couch by the front
window. Ben paused a moment, then rounded the
counter and took an empty folding chair. "This the
writing group?" A young man with curly, unruly
hair wearing a sweatshirt under a sports coat

looked up to greet him. "Ah, a new arrival. I'm Josh Ryder, organizer of the Well Read Writers' Circle. I teach writing and I write, well, all kinds of stuff. I'm here to become a better writer. "

The other participants introduced themselves. A woman named Dolores with unnaturally red wavy hair in a brightly colored wrap wrote poetry to capture her mystical visions. Eric, a nondescript, bespectacled fortyish man in a jacket and turtleneck, working on a novel. Leila, a serious-looking young woman in a jersey decorated with owls, was writing a "YA" novel. Ben must have looked perplexed, as Eric leaned over and whispered "Young Adult."

They all looked at Ben. "Your turn," said Josh.

"I'm Ben Trovato. I don't really write ... well, I write all day, but none of you would want to read what I write."

"So what brings you here?" asked Josh.

"Uh, my girlfriend pressured me to come." Eric and Dolores chuckled, but a grimace flashed across Leila's face. "Seriously, I used to write some when I was in high school and college, but I haven't tried since I went to law school. But some recent events got me interested again, so I thought I'd check this out."

"So if you haven't been writing, what do you like to read?" said Josh. "That can be a guide to where your writing interests may lie."

"I haven't had much time to read, but lately I've been checking out some, uh, some mysteries."

"Hope we can help. Let's get started. Usually we begin with a read and comment. Anyone who's ready reads some of their work, and we discuss our impressions. Anyone ready to read?"

Dolores produced a notebook with several pages of handwriting in purple ink, illustrated with drawings in the margins. Dramatically, she declaimed a poem that, as far as Ben could tell, tracked a voyage through several emotional states in the course of a rainstorm. Ben listened with mounting apprehension, wondering what he was getting into. After she finished, the others offered comments about structure, meter, imagery, and choice of words. Finally Josh looked at Ben and said, "Ben? Any thoughts?"

"Uh, that was intense. And personal. Obviously." Obviously.

Eric read next. He said his selection was from a novel he was working on, a thriller. Ben would not describe the passage as "thrilling." It had something to do with tensile and torsional stresses on bridges, with a side discussion into beam types and bolts. It was pretty rough sledding, but it held Ben's interest more than Dolores's emotional travelogue.

When Eric finished, Josh shook his head and said, "Wow." He paused for words and didn't find any, so he looked around the room. "Anyone?"

No one spoke, so Ben decided he might as well. "It's really technical," Ben said. "I followed it pretty well, because I work in a technical field. But how are you fitting this into a novel?"

"Ben raises a good question," Josh added. "Who is your audience? What level of expertise are you assuming?"

"That's my problem," said Eric. "My protagonist is a structural engineer who works with bridges. The story, called *The Bridge*, is about how he discovers a main bridge into the city is structurally unsound and may collapse when it is under strain. My problem is that I have to give readers the background why the bridge is unsound, so they see the situation through my protagonist's eyes."

"Okay, I can see your challenge," said Josh. "You have to bring the readers up to speed on the technical issues, but you also need to avoid overwhelming them with an information dump about the science. That exposition is going to take a lot of skill. You need to get that information across without losing the reader on the way."

"Well, he lost me!" exclaimed Dolores. "I mean, really who cares?"

"Please, Dolores, let's keep it constructive," said Josh.

"It sounds like you've done a lot of research," said Ben. "I know a little about that stuff, and everything you said sounded solid to me."

"I should know it," said Eric. "I've been a structural engineer working on bridges for MODOT, twenty-four years now. You know the Heart of America Bridge? That's one of mine."

"Let me get this straight," said Leila. "You're a bridge engineer, writing a thriller about a heroic bridge engineer?"

"Well, you know what they say," replied Eric. "Write what you know."

They discussed Eric's work for a while longer, mainly trying to come up with ways to convey his scientific information more simply and make the language more readable.

After they finished discussing Eric's work, neither Ben nor Leila offered to read anything. Josh looked at the clock and said, "We still have about forty-five minutes left. How about an exercise?"

Ben didn't remember to bring any paper to write on, so Eric pulled out an extra tablet and gave it to him. Josh said, "Let's do a dialogue exercise. Take about fifteen minutes and write out an argument. A discussion between two people with differing views. No tags, no narrative. Just use the dialogue and see how much you can develop the two characters and give us an idea of their different viewpoints."

For a moment Ben sat confused and embarrassed as the others began scribbling furiously. Then an idea came to him. He wrote out a rough recreation of the debate he and Shepherd held the night before, with a few changes to disguise the nature of their relationship. When his turn came, Ben read from his pad with great apprehension. When he finished, however, the other participants complimented him on the quality of his dialogue.

"What is your premise?" asked Josh.

"Well, the one character is a writer, who's been very successful. Only he has developed arthritis in his hands, so he can't write or type any more. So his nephew gets pressed into service to take dictation. Only the nephew has aspirations of being a writer himself, and he's got a bit of an attitude."

Eric laughed. "A *bit*?"

"Intriguing premise," said Josh. "You've already given us a feel for the characters, and set up a conflict between them you can milk for comedy or use for character development. How do you see using this – short story, novel, screenplay?"

"I haven't really thought about it. I've just been playing with the idea a bit. I don't know where this goes."

"Well, good work. Stay with it," said Josh.

Ben left the meeting brimming with triumph. He could do this. Welcome back to high school, Mr. Shepherd.

Chapter 17

"I know what you're thinking," said Barry.

"How do you know?" said Doug.

"I can read your mind."

"Read my mind? You can barely read the morning paper."

-- David Shepherd, *Chest of Drawers*

Melissa wanted to make Ben a home-cooked dinner. Ben wasn't sure how this would turn out, as Melissa's previous culinary adventures revolved around setting the microwave. Her mother was an excellent cook, though, and Melissa promised she had learned something from the master.

Melissa emailed Ben a shopping list about 4:00 that afternoon, so on his way home Ben stopped at Cosentino's to pick up what she requested. Melissa arrived at the apartment about 6:30, bearing a shopping bag. Before heading for the kitchen, she pulled three books from the sack and handed them to Ben.

He examined the books, two paperbacks and a hardbound. They were all by David Shepherd. He read off the titles – *Eye of the Storm, Neck of the Woods, Hand of Kindness.*

"Those are the first three Doug Graves novels," Melissa explained. "You really should read them in order."

"I don't have much time for recreational reading," said Ben.

"I know how busy you are. But I thought you might enjoy these as a break. Really, reading something non-work-related would be a great release for you."

"Hey, I read."

`No, you don't.` Ben was startled. He hadn't noticed the telltale hiss telling him Shepherd was listening in.

"Do you?" asked Melissa. "Tell me, what was the last fiction book you read?"

"Uh, how about that one about the cyber detective – what was the name? Bytes Webster. I read that."

Melissa cocked her head at him. "I gave you that one in March, almost nine months ago."

"Well, it's been a really busy year."

"Anyway, you might really enjoy these. Shepherd has an analytical mind, like yours, and his sense of humor reminds me of yours. That's beside the fact he wrote them right here!"

"Well, thanks. I'll get to them at some point," Ben said, putting the books down on the end table by his sofa.

Melissa carried the shopping bag into the kitchen and set it down on the counter. "So, you are going to love this dinner. I'm making steak diane, a specialty my mother taught me."

She's right, you know. You should read more.

"Not now!" hissed Ben.

"What?" called Melissa from the kitchen.

"Oh, nothing. I didn't say anything."

"I thought you said 'Not now.'"

"Uh, I meant, I'm not hungry just now. I can wait."

"Well, good thing. This will take half an hour or so."

Knowing the series would be excellent background for our work.

Ben cupped his hand around his mouth and turned toward the fireplace. "Not tonight. I am not working for you tonight."

Oh, I don't expect that. I just thought it might help to spend some time together. What is it you young people call it – hanging out?

Ben whispered louder. "I am not 'hanging out' with you!"

Well, you don't have to be rude about it.

"Did you say something?" Melissa called. "I have to be in the kitchen. If you want to talk you have to come in here where I can hear you."

"No, no, I'm just muttering to myself. I'm ... I'm ... rehearsing something."

"Oh?" said Melissa. She took a couple of steps toward him, smiling brightly. "Is there something you want to say to me? Something you have to rehearse?"

"Uh, no, no, not that. I mean, it has nothing to do with ... I mean, it's just some, it's work stuff, you know."

"Oh," said Melissa, sounding disappointed. "You know, you work so hard, it would really help you, I think, if you could just forget about work for a while, and just relax and enjoy this dinner. I really think ... well, I don't mean to tell you how to manage your work, but I really think it would do you good to let it go, just for a while."

`She's right, again. You're going to get old very fast if you can't set work aside. Oh, wait, you consider our collaboration work, don't you?`

"Uh, right. You're very right. Both of you."

Melissa's mouth dropped open. "Both of us? You mean you and me?"

"Both ... I mean about both things. What you just said, and ... what you said before. Would you excuse me ... for a moment?" said Ben.

Melissa looked hard at him. "Are you okay, Ben? You seem a little distracted tonight."

"I'm fine, I'm fine. I will be just a moment."

Ben bolted into the bedroom and shut the door. For good measure, he retreated into the bathroom and shut that door as well.

"Look," he said in a low but urgent voice. "We have to set boundaries here. I am not your friend. We are not hanging out together. You have expropriated my mind and my time, without my permission, and I have agreed to tolerate that for the limited purpose of helping you get this stupid novel done. But I need my time off as well. I am having a nice evening with my girlfriend, for which I have a reasonable expectation of privacy. Leave me alone!"

Well, excuse me. I just thought I'd look in, get to know you a little better, in order to better understand how I can make this relationship work for you as well. I know you're not going to be doing any typing tonight, so I'll be leaving soon. Believe me, I have no voyeuristic interest in your love life. I must say, though, you are very lucky to have such a discriminating lady friend.

"I want you to leave now. New rule: when I am with Melissa, I am not with you. I do not think that is unreasonable."

Oh, come now. I will respect your boundaries, of course, but I must say I enjoy the company of your young friend as much as, in fact more than I do yours. I promise I will not interfere in your anticipated intimacy, but I would apprec-

iate a little time with the two of you.
What's the harm?

More like, what choice do I have, thought Ben.

Yes, there is that, too.

"There is what?" asked Ben, startled.

The matter of choice. I do want to
respect your privacy, but of course the
choice really is mine, isn't it?

I didn't say anything about choice, thought Ben. *I just thought it. I didn't say it, did I?*

I believe you did. You acknowledged
you had no choice, but I really don't
want you to think of our relationship in
those terms.

Ben was certain he had not said anything. He concentrated on directing his thoughts toward the ghost. *Are you hearing me? Can you hear this?*

Certainly I can hear you. Is the young
lady correct? Are you feeling all right
tonight?

Ben leaned against the wall, stunned. The ghost could hear not just what he said, but what he was thinking. Did he have any secrets? Any refuge? Is this what madness feels like?

Are you all right? You seem upset.

Ben focused his thoughts on the ghost again. *What did I just think?*

How should I know? It seemed we were
communicating until I asked whether you
are all right. I am concerned, really.

As Ben contemplated this development, the horror he was feeling vanished and a sense of elation swept in. Shepherd could hear his thoughts when he intended, when he directed them toward the ghost, but could not hear his thoughts to himself. He focused on the ghost again, projecting his thoughts out. *Can you hear this?*

Of course I can hear you. You know
that. What is wrong with you?

Jubilation filled Ben. He could control what Shepherd heard or didn't hear. He could carry on a conversation in total confidence.

Melissa tapped on the bathroom door. "Ben, are you okay?"

"I am fine," he called out. He opened the door. Fortunately it opened inward, or it would have struck Melissa, who was leaning next to it. Ben bounded out. "I am beyond fine. I am excellent, bordering on superb."

Melissa looked at him quizzically. "Well, dinner will be ready soon. I could use some help."

"Help you shall have." He took her elbow and led her back toward the kitchen. *We are going to enjoy a very fine dinner. Those of us who can eat, that is.*

Oh, don't rub it in.

"Perhaps I should build a fire," he said. "A nice, roaring fire, which we can enjoy with a fine cabernet."

You're having fun at my expense, aren't you? Well, enjoy yourself.

I am, thank you very much.

Melissa said, "A fire would be nice, but you didn't get any firewood yet."

"Oh, I am sure there is something here that is flammable. And disposable."

Now you're being gratuitously cruel. Not classy at all.

Melissa cast him a confused look. She opened the cupboard where he kept his stock and looked in. "There's no cabernet. There's some zinfandel, and some chablis. The zinfandel is probably better – the chablis has a screw cap."

Echh. Swill.

"Only the best for my lovely and me," Ben said. He pulled out the wine and poured two glasses. He handed one to Melissa, took the other, and dropped into the couch.

Melissa held her wine glass in both hands and sat next to him. "Something is bothering me," she said, "and we need to talk it through."

Ben stiffened. To any man, those three little words are the most terrifying a woman can utter: "talk it through."

"You have to admit," Melissa said, "You have been acting a little funny tonight."

"I'm fine," said Ben. "You know, crazy week at work, I just have trouble slowing down."

"I know, you work so hard," said Melissa. "But you always do. Tonight was different. Just not like you at all."

"I'm sorry. Really, it's okay. Just don't worry."

"Well, this is bothering me," Melissa said, shifting her wine glass from hand to hand, untasted. "While you were in the bathroom for so long, I got to thinking. Maybe overthinking, I know, I overthink all the time. But I got to thinking maybe this whole thing – the apartment, the dinner, the conversations we had earlier – maybe you started feeling like it's all coming down on you, that I'm pushing too hard."

"No, not at all," Ben protested. This was spiraling out of control rapidly.

"Really, I just wanted to make you a nice dinner. I just wanted to give you a nice evening in your new home. I didn't mean to pressure you." A tear formed in the edge of her eye and began a slow-motion trek onto her cheek.

Damage control, damage control, screamed the centers in Ben's brain.

"No, no, it's fine. Really, I appreciate it. Really, you were right earlier, I'm going to get old fast if I can't set work aside."

Melissa shook her head. "Did I say that?"

No, you idiot. I said that.

"Not that, but something like ... no, no. You were right, relaxing would be good for me. Let's just ... relax ..."

Just then the stove timer went off in the kitchen. Melissa looked up. "Well, the steaks are done. I guess I better get them ready. Can you set the table while I fix them up?" She got up and headed for the kitchen. Ben sighed and leaned back into the couch. Saved by the bell.

Chapter 18

> Doug was making love to his scotch and soda when he heard the bar stool next to him creak. Then he heard the voice. Not just any voice – that voice. A velvety purr, sexy and menacing at the same time. "Well, there's some wildlife in its native habitat."
>
> -- David Shepherd, *Hand of Kindness*

The following Monday, after a frantic morning, Ben escaped to the food court at One Kansas City for lunch. As he headed into the sub shop, he noticed a woman sitting at one of the tables with her back to him. A rich mane of auburn hair flowed over lovely shoulders above a slim frame, dressed in an expensive-looking jacket. Ben hoped to get a look at her face from the exit to the sub shop.

Ben picked up his sandwich and turned toward the tables in the food court. He glanced toward the woman. The front view was every bit as enticing as the rear – sculpted cheeks, a perfectly symmetrical face, eyes cast down toward a sheaf of papers she was studying. Ben felt a surge of recognition. After a moment to gather his courage, he walked up to the table where she sat.

"Hello, Robin," he said.

Her eyes, startled, rose and quickly surveyed his face. Ben knew she was trying to place him outside the context of the apartment.

"Ben Trovato. From the Shepherd apartment."

Her face brightened with the memory. "So, how are you? All settled in?"

"Yeah, I'm starting to feel at home," Ben said. He paused, debating whether to ask if he could join her.

She saved him the decision. "Have a seat," she said, beckoning to the chair on the other side of the table. "I'd love to catch up." Thus far her expression and tone communicated more a professional connection with a business contact than any stirring of personal interest. Nonetheless, she invited, and Ben gleefully accepted. He sat down on the chair. He quickly scanned the contents of the table – a tray of sushi with a few bites taken, gourmet coffee, a stack of double-spaced, computer printed pages appearing to be a manuscript.

"So," she said, a momentary pause indicating she was trying to think of polite but noncommittal conversation, "How do you like the place?"

"I'm really enjoying it," Ben said. "Well, at least the time I get to spend there. My work is always busy so I don't get a lot of time at home."

"I know the feeling," she said. "I have the same problem. Not much time at home when you're married to your work."

Married to your work, he thought. Very promising choice of words. People married to a person do not describe themselves as married to their work.

"I don't suppose you have found anything," she said, her voice rising with an implicit question at the end of the sentence.

"No, but I'm keeping my eyes open for any sign of a hiding place," Ben said. All of a sudden he wished very much that he had something to stir her interest. He wondered whether he should use Melissa's line about feeling Shepherd's presence, and quickly decided against it.

"Being in the apartment has revived my interest in Shepherd. I've been reading some of his stuff. I just picked up *The Winterset Formation* last week and I'm halfway through already. Knocks me right over."

Robin smiled and her manner became more animated. "Oh, I'm so glad you found that! Most people never get past the Doug Graves stories, but there's so, so much more."

"I find myself thinking about him a lot. Sometimes I stand near the window where his desk was and imagine that old Selectric, picture him hammering away, turning out those stories about Doug and Barry and Zenobia and ... and all those other great characters." Ben made a mental note not to go much further, lest he say something to betray the fact that he never actually read those stories.

Robin was clearly warming to the subject. "Oh, yes, so many memories," she said. She paused, a winsome smile on her face. "Did you ever meet him, living in the building?"

This required some finesse. "I recall seeing him, said hello once or twice in passing. We never held a real conversation, didn't exchange names. I didn't put the face together with his pictures, so I never realized the man I knew was him. Now I feel like kicking myself. If I'd known, maybe I would have banged on his door. He would probably think I was a stalker." Robin laughed. Obviously, her memories of the man were pleasant, and she was enjoying the conversation. Time to take it up a notch.

Ben looked into her eyes pensively. "How are you doing? I know this must be a very hard time for you."

Bingo! An expression of nostalgic pleasure swept over her face, a complex expression, her cheeks rising, her eyebrows knitting somewhat, her mouth twisting into a wry, asymmetrical half smile, her eyes cast up as she reviewed her memories. He had forded the moat of professional distance, scaled the parapet of privacy, and stormed into the courtyard of her emotions. He was no more a contact; he stood in a position to become a confidante, a comforter, a companion. There was far to travel, but the path lay open.

"Oh," she said, her voice slightly grainy, "I am doing better. You're right, it's been a very hard time. But life goes on."

"You mentioned memories," he said, leaning a few millimeters closer. "Tell me some of them. I'd really like to know what the place was like when he lived there."

Robin's green eyes locked on his. Then they rolled up as she ventured into the past. She was not avoiding his gaze, she was summoning memories to share. "Oh, I have so many," she said. "I don't know where to begin."

"Did you visit often in the apartment?"

"Yes, I can remember it from my earliest childhood. A couple of times a week, at least. He would host salons, back then. My parents would bring me, and I would play while they discussed their grown-up matters. When I was older, in my teens, I came to appreciate what an amazing group of people he had there. All the brightest, the most creative people. For a young girl just discovering literature, it was magical." She closed her eyes and smiled warmly, clearly reveling in the memories.

"It must have been fantastic," Ben said. Anything to keep her talking.

After a moment she looked at him again and smiled warmly. Then she glanced at her watch. "Oh, my, it's getting into the afternoon. I have a meeting soon, I have to get back." She began gathering up her purse and coat. Ben felt all his progress slipping away. He needed to act fast to preserve the mood of the moment.

"I'd love to continue this conversation and hear more of your memories about him. Could I maybe buy you dinner sometime?"

She cast an appraising glance at him. Ben realized she heard this proposal as a pass, which in truth it was. She was checking him out now, not as a sensitive confidante but as a man interested in her company. He guessed she had a lot of experience at that.

That mischievous elfin grin of hers stole across her face. "Sure," she said. "Why not?" She pursed her lips in thought for a moment. "Tonight is pretty good, actually. Let's do the American. Pick me up at my office about seven. You remember where it is?"

Ben managed to contain his exhilaration and keep a pleasant but calm face. "Yeah, I have your card." He was tempted to pull out his wallet and show her where he kept it, but that would be too obvious. "Pick you up at seven, then."

She flashed a flirtatious grin that sent a shock wave through his system. "See you then." She slung on her coat and turned toward the exit. As she walked away he watched the auburn hair undulate, admired the confident sway of her walk. When she was out of sight he slumped back in his chair, stunned. Be careful what you ask for – make sure you can handle it.

As soon as he got back to the office, Ben called the American Restaurant for reservations. Although the restaurant atop Hall's at Crown Center was less than half a mile from his building,

Ben had only eaten there once. His frugal lifestyle didn't have much room for fine dining, but for Robin, only the best would do.

About an hour later he received a text from Melissa: "2nite?" Ben felt a stab of guilt. He texted back, "Probably tied up late." She responded, "OK. :-(CU 2moro. <3u." Now Ben felt like a cad. Just for the record, he thought, we never actually agreed on exclusivity.

Ben left his office at a quarter to seven and drove his car two blocks to park right in front of Robin's building. He took the elevator to the sixth floor, and opened a glass door to the left in the elevator lobby, bearing the legend "Atwater and Bridges, Publishers." A receptionist behind a nameplate saying "Natalie" patrolled the desk. He walked in and said, "Ben Trovato, for Ms. Atwater. She's expecting me."

The receptionist pressed an intercom button, and a moment later said, "She'll be with you in a moment." From the office to the left of the reception desk, Robin's voice sang out, "Almost ready."

She wasn't almost ready, though. The receptionist beckoned toward one of the chairs in the center of the room, but Ben stepped away and looked around the office. It was well appointed, with thick pile carpet, and opulent leather furniture, its bookish smell summoning up memories of hours Ben spent in school entombed in the library. The walls between offices were covered with well-stocked bookshelves. In a space between two of them stood a glass display case containing a red typewriter. Ben leaned in to examine it, and realized it was the same red Selectric he observed on the desk of Shepherd's apartment on the Saturday he first visited the apartment. Indeed, a brass label affixed to the front of the case confirmed his impression:

> On this typewriter, famed novelist and writer David Shepherd wrote the Doug Graves mysteries and many of the works in the Atwater and Bridges library that countless readers have enjoyed.
>
> On loan from the Estate of David Shepherd, Howard Bridges, Executor.

Ben's inspection was interrupted as Robin emerged from the office, and once again Ben was struck foolish with the sight of her. After an eleven-hour day, she looked fresh and perfect, as though she had spent hours preparing for their evening. She smiled, melting Ben on the spot. "I'm hungry," she said. "Let's go."

Ben led her out to the car and held the door as she climbed in. As he drove over, he could feel her proximity acutely. Although she wore a long coat, he cast several glances at the brief stretch of calf he could see between the hem of her coat and her stylish boots.

He left the car with the valet, something he never did on his own, and they took the elevator up. The hostess led them to the window table he requested when he made the reservation, offering a sweeping view of the skyline, from the illuminated Link crosswalk over Grand Boulevard out to the buildings of downtown. Impressive, Ben thought with a note of pride, but not as good as mine.

Ben had studied the menu online, which gave him a chance to look up several food names he didn't recognize. The 32-page wine list was even more intimidating; Ben never realized it was possible to spend $4000 on a bottle of wine in Kansas City. He wondered whether Robin would expect him to order for her, never a problem with Melissa. Fortunately, Robin knew exactly what she wanted and dictated her order to the server with scarcely a glance at the menu. Ben ordered a ribeye, mainly because he recognized all the elements of the entrée. She also knew what wine she wanted, so Ben just ordered a glass of the same.

When their meals were served, Ben eyed her plate with curiosity. "What is that side dish you ordered?"

"It's stinging nettles with risotto," Robin said. "Have you tried it?"

"I have to confess I didn't even know stinging nettles were a vegetable. I would have guessed was some kind of jellyfish."

"It's a flowering herb. It grows naturally with barbs that do actually sting. They contain formic acid, which also gives fire ants their sting. I understand they can be quite painful if handled raw, but when they are boiled, the toxins cook out and you're left with this delicious, highly nutritious vegetable. Here, try some."

She separated a portion of the dish out and placed it on her bread dish, which she slid over to Ben. He tasted it and found it quite palatable, with a rich spinach-like flavor.

"You're very well informed to know all that," Ben said. "Would I be correct in guessing you are a pretty voracious reader?"

"That's pretty much a prerequisite in my business. But yes, I have always been a reader. Growing up in my dad's house, that's no surprise. I laughed when I read *To Kill a Mockingbird,* and got to the part where Scout describes her father as always reading, because that was my dad, too. "

"I read a lot in high school and college," said Ben, "but I'm afraid I got out of the habit in law school, as I had to study so much. And since then I've been working too hard to reestablish the habit. But I've heard so much about Shepherd since I moved into the apartment, I've started rereading some of his mysteries. And exploring his other stuff, as I mentioned at lunch."

Robin's face formed a bemused smile. "It's strange to me to think of him as the literary giant he was, because to me he was always Uncle David. Then later he was such a large part of my business, I came to think of him as both a person and a product."

"You seem young to be in such a position of responsibility," said Ben. "I mean, vice president of an established publishing house, and you can't be more than five years or so out of college."

"Eight, actually, thanks very much," she said. "But I have to be honest. This was my dad's firm when he was alive. His and David's, in a way. They were lifelong friends since their college days in English lit at Mizzou. When they graduated, my father took a job with a publishing company here. When David completed his first novel, my father persuaded the house to publish it, and a long and beautiful collaboration began."

"That wasn't Atwater and Bridges, was it?"

"No, that came later. About twenty-five years ago, my father and his partner, Howard Bridges, decided to go out on their own. David wouldn't dream of working with anyone else. We have published all of his works since, and it has been ... was a very mutually beneficial arrangement."

She took a sip of wine. "I joined the firm directly out of college. When my father became ill, I took over his work, more and more, so I became the firm's main liaison with David. We are a very small operation, a family shop, almost. My partner Howard handles the business and production end, as he did when he and my dad founded the firm. I handle the content, the talent."

"Well, that's a pretty important job."

"It is. There is a lot of pressure, trying to figure out what will sell in a very competitive market, yet provide the kind of quality we have always prided ourselves on. We're kind of a niche company, built around the kind of books David was good at – mysteries, crime stories, historical, character and setting pieces. David provided our flagship, so to speak, but we attract attention from a lot of writers and agents who work in those genres as a result of the reputation he built us."

Ben thought it a good idea to keep her talking about herself as long as possible, both so he could gather information and so she would sense he took an interest in her work and ideas, not just her beauty. She was probably used to men hitting on her, so it was important to develop a line of communication on the intellectual plane. "So now you'll need to develop the next generation of writers, I guess."

"Exactly!" she said. "David's passing is the end of an era for us, but that means we find ourselves in a new era, and I have the chance to really put my own stamp on the company's profile. It's an awesome responsibility, but an opportunity, too."

"You must get a lot of manuscripts in. Do you read them all?"

"Oh, heavens, no. We mainly work off query letters from writers or proposals from agents. If we're interested enough to ask for manuscripts, we have a crew of editors I farm them out to for reading. I wind up spending most of my time trying to find titles that will sell and figuring how to market them, what with ebooks, the collapse of the bookstores, all the changes in the business."

"That's too bad. There you are spending your days in a publishing house, and you don't get to read?"

"You know what, though? Much as I love to read, after spending most of my waking hours on the job, I find myself not wanting to read on what time I do have for myself. Instead of losing myself in the story, I find myself doing a market appraisal. What's working here, what isn't? What potential does this author have? Can I sell this? Can I find someone who can write like this? I can't read a book any more without it turning into work."

"I can understand that," Ben said. "I used to love to argue. I was always in debate in school and college, I'd get into Internet debates, I was always taking the contrary position in every discussion. But now that I work seventy hours a week in contested litigation, I just want to avoid conflict as much as possible in my own life. That's the peril of doing what you love. That's why I'm enjoying getting into reading again. I used to write in high school. I was thinking I might try it again."

As soon as he said that, Ben regretted it. She cast him a sly smile and said, "Say, you don't have a manuscript you were hoping I'd read, do you?"

Ben hastened to recover. "Oh, no, no. I haven't written anything. I have all I can do just to keep up with my own job. I do wish I had a manuscript to give you, though."

She sent him a searching look. "Should I give up on that last Doug Graves novel? I would think you would have found it by now if there was one."

"Don't give up yet," said Ben. "It's only been a couple of weeks now, and I haven't really had time to search for it. I've been so busy. Maybe over the holidays I will have time to put some effort in. Or in January." Damn, better get going on that dictation project. Shepherd said two months, but they were way behind schedule.

"He had a lot of hiding places, so don't give up. Be careful what you cover."

"Tell me more about your time there when you were growing up. Were you there a lot?" he asked as he put his card down to pay the check.

"Constantly," she said. "My father would drag me over and they'd sit all day, going over books or talking about this subject or that. I'd perch in the window seat and read all afternoon. I felt bored at the time, but how I miss it now. What I'd give to be ten again, curled up in that window lost in Jane Austen as they argue about Bret Harte in the background."

When she said this, Ben felt a stab of inspiration. He debated whether he should say it. Would his intentions be obvious? Was he overplaying his opportunity? He decided to take the chance. "I was still setting up when you stopped in before. Would you like to come over and see the place now that it's finished?"

She looked at him with a cool and knowing gaze. "Hmmm." Ben felt a wash of humiliation. She had read his thoughts, seen a move ahead of him, she knew what he would do before he did it. Finally she said, "Sure. It might be nice to see what you've done with it." Glee surged through Ben. She fathomed his intentions, and accepted his invitation anyway. This could really happen.

Chapter 19

> Her lips drew close to his, and Doug's gaze
> fixed on that blossom of lipstick, parted
> ever so slightly to reveal the pearly white
> below. He felt his head spin, and closed his
> eyes to lean in. Just as he did, the mouth
> pulled away, and whispered, "You can
> dream, lover boy."
>
> -- David Shepherd, *Eye of the Storm*

Ben heard himself and Robin speaking in muted tones as they walked back to his car, as though Ben was watching a scene in a movie. During the block-long drive to his building, Ben felt as though he could sense the warmth of her shoulder under the winter coat, less than a foot away from his.

He escorted her up in the elevator. As he unlocked the door, she giggled. "This feels weird," she said. "I've known the way he had it for thirty years. It is strange seeing it arranged by someone else. But the way you approach it tells me about you."

"I'm no interior designer," said Ben. "It's not something out of *House Beautiful*."

He took her coat and hung it with his in the hall closet, pushing his coat into contact with hers. She stepped into the living room, folded her arms and looked around. A wave of insecurity swept over Ben – why didn't he do more to fix the place up? What if his new furniture was hopelessly uncouth? Melissa thought it was okay. Don't think about Melissa!

"It's so different," Robin said at last. "I remember it as always being cluttered, but with such a clean, spare decor, the character of the place comes out more. It's like seeing it for the first time." She likes it!

She glided around the room, examining the various features. She glanced across the kitchen and dining area. She stood by the fireplace, as if studying the stonework for some time. She walked past the bookshelves, running a hand across the oak, scanning the titles of the scattered books and CDs and videos he shelved in place of Shepherd's immense library.

At last she stood at the window, looking out over the lights of the city. "Oh, this brings back so many memories."

She still wore the expensive business suit he noticed at lunch, the well-tailored jacket framing her square shoulders, an ivory collarless blouse displaying the elegant curves of her neck, a rich patterned skirt giving way to lean, shapely legs. Ben couldn't resist moving close behind her, close enough to see the strands of her auburn hair and the texture of her skin, to sense the aroma and the warmth and the nearness of her.

She turned to face him. Nine inches separated his face from hers, inside the perimeter of casual acquaintance, within the zone of intimacy. The situation was unstable; either he had to step back, embarrassed at his faux pas, or commit himself and move in toward contact, incurring grave risk if he miscalculated. He could not stay in that zone of tension, but he did, frozen in the moment.

Before he could decide between fight and flight, she decided for him. She gazed up at him with a serene, knowing smile. Then she took the slightest step toward him, laid her right hand on his chest, and turned her face up to his. He closed his eyes and lowered his mouth to hers. Her lips molded to his, warm and moist and soft. He lost himself in the taste of her, the fragrance of her breath, and the warmth of her skin. He hung suspended in time, tethered to a gently moving creature encircling him with invisible chains. Every cell in his body stood on alert as the electricity radiating out from that conquered center surged through them.

Eventually – Ben had no idea how much time passed – she slid her lips off his and leaned back a few inches. Her green eyes locked on to his, lips curling into a subtle curve of triumph.

Ben raised his right hand toward her cheek, but with the same hand whose gentle pressure on his chest took control of him, she gently pushed off from him and stepped away. She walked to the window and sat down on the south seat, folding her legs up next to her, leaving no possibility of Ben attempting to sit next to her.

Ben took the north seat opposite her, leaning forward to be as close to her as he could without obvious awkwardness. She did not speak, but fixed her gaze on him with her Mona Lisa smile, revealing nothing and inviting all revelation.

Ben's mind fell empty, blank. He knew he needed to say something. What could he say now to reach her? Chitchat would never do. It must be something powerful, meaningful, but he had no idea what to say. He stared back dumbly, quite certain the grin on his face looked completely foolish. What to say, what to say?

`Ask her about her father.`

Given his considerable state of distraction, Ben was not surprised he failed to notice the hiss announcing Shepherd's presence. He felt a surge of indignation at Shepherd's intrusion into this extraordinary moment, and Ben certainly didn't want Shepherd as a witness to whatever escalated entanglement with his niece-figure might occur over the next couple of hours. Then Ben realized Shepherd knew Robin well, and he had to admit Shepherd's advice was better than anything he could think of at the moment.

Thanks, but get lost!

Ben returned Robin's gaze with a carefully constructed expression he hoped would convey comfort and sensitivity. "Tell me a bit about your father. What was he like?"

She leaned back and her eyes widened, as though she did not expect him to say this. Turning her gaze out the window, she smiled wistfully. "Oh, he was a wonderful man. So brilliant, so talented. Yet he was a people person. He listened to people. He cared about people. He was loyal – loyal to David, too, right to the end."

"They were friends since college?"

"Oh, yes, inseparable ever since college. My dad was a wonderful writer, too. He thought he would be a writer as well. But he recognized David's brilliant gift, too, before anyone else did."

"But he went into publishing, instead?"

"Yes. He married my mom right out of college, couldn't do the starving artist lifestyle. He had to earn a living. He took a job as an editor in a publishing house here. When David got out of the Army and finished his first novel, my dad helped him by editing and polishing it up. Then talked the company into publishing it. It sold well, and David was on his way."

"So they worked together all those years?"

"Yes. After about ten years, Dad got tired of the company getting all the benefit of the work he and David were doing. He joined up with Howard Bridges and formed Atwater and Bridges. David went with them, of course, and ever since his books have been the foundation of the company's reputation. Dad never did get to write his own novel, but he was proud and happy to be part of David's success. That was the kind of man he was."

This is going well, Ben thought. But it's time to get her talking about herself again. "Was it always the plan for you to join the company?"

Her eyes rolled up, summoning the memory. "No, in college I wanted to be a singer. I was good, I studied opera. But it's tough to find work in music. Plan B was a minor in English lit as well, just in case. As it turned out, the music career didn't happen. When I graduated the job at the firm was waiting for me. That was eight years ago, and I guess there's no going back now."

"So this is where you see your future?"

"Well, like most young people, I thought there was no way I'd spend my life under my dad's watchful eye. But he was a great teacher, and he showed me everything I would need to know to take over his work when he was gone. As if he knew he would be leaving." Her voice trailed off.

Ben didn't like this turn in the conversation's direction, but he had to hang in. "Well, it seems you were well prepared when ... when it ... when it happened."

Her smile faded. "It's all coming back. My father's illness ... it was terrible. He was in such pain, but even then, as he was dying, he told me ... he told me ... I needed to take care of David. He was counting on me. Even as his own life was slipping away, he still could think only of others. And when he was gone ..."

Her voice broke and her hands covered her face. For several minutes she said nothing. Ben sat riveted, with no idea what came next. Say something. Do something. Think of something. He rose up and tentatively reached out to touch her shoulder, to do something to comfort her. But she shook off his touch, stood up and clutched her purse. "I'm sorry, I'm sorry. I have to go. I thought I had it under control, but I guess ... I'm sorry." She rose from the seat and bolted toward the coat closet.

Ben leaped up and followed her. "Can I help you? Get you some water, or some coffee, or –"

"No, no. I have to go." She raised her head, her voice controlled and pleasant now. "It's been a very lovely evening. Thank you for dinner, and for showing me the place. I really must go. I'm sorry if I got a little out of control. May I have my coat, please?"

"Ah, sure," Ben said, trying to mask his disappointment as he retrieved her coat and held it as she slipped her arms into the sleeves. "I'll drive you back ..."

"No, thanks, I'll get a cab." She walked briskly into the hall and pressed the elevator button. When the door opened, she stepped on and turned back toward him, leaving no room for him to follow her. "Thank you so much for your kindness, and I do apologize for spoiling such a pleasant evening. Good night." The elevator door closed between them.

Ben walked back into his apartment and slammed the door. He plodded to the window seat and sat numbly on the south end, watching until a taxicab pulled up to the lobby and then drove up Grand Boulevard. Ben stood up and paced the room.

"I don't believe it," he barked. He waited for an answer, but heard none. He said again, louder, "I don't believe it!" Still no answer. "I know you're there. I know you hear me."

`Well, you don't have to shout.`

I know what you did. You know what you did. You sabotaged me!

`What?`

You knew she would get upset and leave! You sabotaged me!

`You were floundering, so I just gave you some advice. It seemed you needed it.`

You just can't stand it, can you? You can't stand the thought that your darling little niece is a grown woman with grown-up desires. And that I might be the object of those desires.

`Nonsense. She has been a grown up for a long time. And you were deluding your-self if you thought you would get her into your bed on such casual acquaint-ance. You were struggling to make simple conversation, and you needed rescue from an embarrassing situation.`

Ben folded his arms and resumed pacing.

Okay, new rule. If you get here and you find I am with a lady, whether it's Robin or Melissa or anyone else I choose to be with, you turn around and go back where you came from. That's non-negotiable.

As if you have any control over the matter. We've been through this before. But your little tantrum is distracting you from the real issue – your behavior.

My behavior? My behavior? Of all the nerve!

Yes, your behavior. You are behaving like a cad towards two young women, both of whom I care about.

It's none of your business!

Indeed? Bear in mind that if it were not for me, you would never even have met Robin.

Ben wrapped his hands over his ears, even though it did no good. Not only did Shepherd interfere in his evening, now he was preaching to him. Was there no way to get rid of this infestation?

Oh, that's right. There's only one way. You have to give him what he wants to get him to go away.

All right, let's settle this. I want you gone, and I understand I have to finish this damn book. We have to make more progress, but I can't do this tonight. Not after what just happened. Come back in a couple of days, and we will work on it, get it done and go our separate ways. Deal?

Very well. I think you're right. I have an idea for how we can make better progress, but you're not going to like it. We can discuss it next time. Good night.

The hiss faded out quickly. Wait a minute, thought Ben.

Hey! Hey! Come back here! What do you mean? What are you suggesting?

But Ben heard only silence. Next time. Ben guessed Shepherd was right – he wasn't going to like it.

Chapter 20

The Christmas lights blazed all along the lines of the Spanish style buildings of the Plaza, and the streets overflowed with cheerful, bustling shoppers. Doug cast his eyes nervously in all directions as he elbowed his way through the crowd. No better place for true evil to hide than there amid all that merriment.

-- David Shepherd, *Belly of the Beast*

Ben invited his parents to come visit over the Christmas holiday. They had only visited from their home in Chesterfield, near St. Louis, twice since he moved to Kansas City. Since he finally had room to host them, Ben looked forward to their visit.

He set up the second bedroom as a home office, but put in a double sleeper sofa, nightstand, and dresser, so the crowded little room could also double as a bedroom when needed. Ben's parents planned to spend Christmas Day at his sister's house in Columbia, but they accepted his invitation to come stay the night of December 23.

Melissa was even more excited than Ben over his parents' visit. About a year earlier she accompanied Ben to Columbia for one of the family gatherings, but they only spent a few hours together, and Melissa met many people that weekend. She expressed delight at the prospect of spending extended time getting to know his parents.

For the one evening his parents were in town, Ben planned to treat them and Melissa to dinner at one of the better restaurants in Kansas City, and then tour Country Club Plaza viewing the Christmas lighting displays that community is noted for. But Melissa volunteered to prepare them a home-cooked meal in Ben's well-appointed kitchen. Ben liked his plan better, but she insisted. Because Melissa barely scraped by on her salary from the sheriff's office, Ben offered to buy the groceries. She refused, relenting only to allow Ben to buy the roaster turkey.

On the afternoon of the 23rd, Ben left the deserted office and arrived home shortly after 1:00 pm. Melissa bustled in shortly later, two grocery bags in her arms. She commandeered his kitchen and set out busily preparing the dishes. Ben did a final cleanup. He set up a small, recently purchased artificial Christmas tree in the corner of the bookshelves near the fireplace.

Around 3:00 Ben's cell phone rang. He headed for the front of the building to guide his parents into the underground parking garage. Melissa, deeply immersed in her pots, pans, and casseroles, remained in the apartment fixing dinner.

Ben waited under the marquee in front of the building, until his father's maroon Ford pickup appeared up Grand Boulevard. He flagged them down and directed them to a parking space borrowed from a neighbor away for the holiday.

Ben's mother Mary jumped out of the passenger door as soon as the truck stopped, and threw her arms around Ben's neck. She was still slender in her late 50's, with round glasses and braided hair past her shoulders. Her reddish hair was beginning the transition to silver. Ben's father Bob followed her out of the truck and gave Ben a firm handshake; he was not a hugger. Solidly built and nearly six feet tall, he still bore a residual tan even in the depths of December, earned in the many hours he spent outdoors during the peak season. His thinning hair, also turning gray, was cut close to his scalp. He had the look of a man comfortable either in a worksite or a boardroom.

"Don't keep us in suspense," said Bob. "Let's go see this penthouse of yours."

"And that girl of yours," Mary added. "Is she here?"

"Oh, yes," said Ben. "She is whipping up something in the kitchen for you. It's an inherited condition. I understand her mother is quite a chef."

They took the elevator up to the eleventh floor. "I ordered a drumroll, but apparently all the musicians are off today," Ben joked as he opened the door. As he escorted them into the foyer, Melissa came rushing out of the kitchen, a plaid Christmas apron over her sweater and jeans. She looked eerily domestic. She threw her arms around Mary's neck and they hugged as if they had known each other all their lives. She then repeated the gesture with Bob, who flashed a startled expression.

"Oh, we're so happy to have you visit!" Melissa exclaimed, and Ben flinched at the expression. The first person plural felt a little too matrimonial. Technically, he thought, you're a guest here, too.

"Uh, does Melissa, uh ..." Bob said to Ben.

"Melissa lives down in Westport, about three miles south of here," Ben said. He watched his mother's face for relief or disappointment, but didn't see either.

Ben led his parents into the living room, where they reacted in much the way Ben and Melissa did when they first saw the living room. The rooms of their Chesterfield home were certainly larger and better decorated than his, but somehow the narrow apartment building amplified the effect of the large space. He swept his arm to show them the rock wall fireplace, but stopped short. "What on earth ...?" he muttered.

Four lumpy red felt stockings hung from the mantle of his fireplace, each with the initials of one of them neatly drawn in green marker. Melissa lifted her hands to her face in mock surprise. "Oh, my!" she exclaimed. "Santa Claus must have sneaked in early. I didn't even notice him!"

They took down the stockings and examined the contents. Each contained an assortment of candy, dried fruit, and nuts, along with a paper-back copy of one of the Doug Graves novels and a

Christmas tree ornament in the shape of a Kansas City landmark. Ben's ornament was a small gold frame containing a photograph of the bay window, with a gold tag showing the year.

"Oh, this is so sweet!" said Mary.

"Yeah, Santa's good that way," said Melissa. Ben smiled at her and shook his head. She responded with an impish grin.

Ben lit his first fire since his Boy Scout days. Remarkably, the flames took hold. Melissa proudly served up the repast: green bean casserole, corn pudding, mashed potatoes, cranberry sauce, and biscuits. After they finished the dinner, she brought out a homemade pumpkin pie.

After eating their fill, they retired to the couch and chairs in front of the fire flickering on gamely when Ben fed it as generously as Melissa fed the guests.

Mary sighed in pleasure. "Ben, this is wonderful. We are so proud of you, son."

Ben shrugged. "Wait until June before you say that."

"Why June?" asked Mary.

"The partnership decision. Then we'll know whether there is anything to be proud of."

She folded her arms. "They are entitled to their opinion, we are entitled to ours."

After dark they toured the Plaza in a horse-drawn pumpkin carriage, admiring the holiday lights. They dropped Melissa off at her apartment and returned home. Ben invited his parents to sleep in the master bedroom, and retired to the convertible sofa bed in his den and guest room. He stretched out on the thin padding of the bed and stared for a while at the nondescript view of a neighboring building out the window. Just when he thought he might drift off, he heard the hiss.

Nice people, your folks.

Thank you. Can't work tonight – I need to let them sleep. They're heading out early tomorrow.

Oh, I don't expect you to work. I give holidays off. I'm a demanding master, but not a slave driver.

What I'm doing isn't involuntary servitude?

Oh, relax. Your folks seem fond of Melissa, and she of them.

Too fond. Don't you get started. I'm getting a little claustrophobic here. I'd like to think I still have some say about this cozy little domestic arrangement.

Ah, you will always have your say. I'm just observing. Although this room was much more comfortable under my steward-ship. Did I ever tell you Tony Hillerman once slept in this room?

No. I was kind of hoping I would, too.

Very well, then. Enjoy your holiday. Good night.

The hiss faded away. Ben was glad to be alone for a while. Claustrophobic, indeed.

Bob wanted to leave early for Columbia, as the weather forecast predicted snow after noon. They set out for the Classic Cup at the Plaza for breakfast, and stopped on the way to pick up Melissa.

The aroma of eggs, sausage, and syrup blended with the pine scent of holiday decorations. As the robustly scented coffee was served, Ben asked his parents, "Will you be going to Hawaii in February?" Bob and Mary usually took advantage of the slow construction season for a midwinter vacation on the Big Island.

"Not this year," Bob answered. "We're going down for a week on the Florida Panhandle coast, near Panama City."

"Oh, I hear the beaches at Panama City are lovely," Melissa said.

"Not Hawaii?" Ben asked. "You usually enjoy going so much."

"Well," said Bob, "Business has been slow. Making payroll is more important than going to Kealakekua. Besides, we have to think about retirement five or ten years down the road. Can't afford to indulge the way we used to."

The prospect of his parents retiring caught Ben by surprise. Another sign of passage, with so many already hanging over his life. Maybe he could send them to Hawaii next year from his partnership bonus.

"What kind of work does your business do?" asked Melissa.

"Engineering, retail and office building, mostly," said Bob. "I do the civil, my partner does the mechanical and electrical. We've got two young assistants, but until the building picks up in the spring, we don't have much for them to do."

"I wish you didn't have to worry about it. I know how much you looked forward to Hawaii," Ben said.

"It's fine," said Mary. "We have a lot of great memories of Hawaii. It will be fun to try something new."

Ben stirred his coffee. "Do you ever think about ... do you ever regret –"

"No," said Bob firmly.

"Not at all," added Mary. "Everything has turned out for the best. I believe that completely." Melissa cast a glance at Ben, one eyebrow raised.

"I just worry a little," said Ben. "It bothered you for a long time, I know."

"You get over it. You move on. I have no regrets," said Bob. "It's better on my own, really."

"Don't you worry about us, darling," said Mary. "We're just fine. You just keep your eye on your own bright future."

"Okay," said Ben. "I just want the best for you, that's all."

After breakfast they returned to Ben's building. Ben and Melissa accompanied his parents down to their truck as they prepared to leave. Melissa hugged both of his parents vigorously.

Mary said to Melissa, "Are you seeing your family, dear?"

"Oh, yes. I'm heading out for Sedalia in a little while. Christmas at my folks' house is always a very big deal. Lots of people. My mother has probably assigned my kitchen duties already."

"Well, thank you for the lovely dinner and for your company." They hugged again. Even Bob gave Melissa a quick squeeze.

The truck backed out, and Ben and Melissa watched it pull away up Grand Boulevard.

Melissa turned to Ben and inserted herself into the crook of his arm. "I just love your parents to death," she said. "With my family, there are always so many people and so much going on. You and your parents have this relaxed, easy intimacy. It's not the same in a big family."

"Yeah, they're great," Ben said.

As they walked toward the elevator, Melissa asked, "What was that about at breakfast? Around the Hawaii thing? Something was going on, but I couldn't tell what. The regret thing."

"Oh, it's a long story," said Ben.

"I'm not in any hurry," Melissa said.

"Well, earlier in my Dad's career, he was with Wright and Mehlman, this huge engineering firm. They have offices all over the country. Big projects, major players. Dad was a rising star, the number two guy in their St. Louis office."

"What happened?"

"About fifteen years ago, when I was in junior high, the company landed this big deal contract, for the engineering on the Holtzmann Towers building. Big office building on the riverfront."

"In St. Louis?"

"Yeah. Dad was in charge of the structural engineering. It was a high pressure project. So, anyway, the owner wanted a change of plans, but Dad thought it wouldn't be strong enough, and it was cutting corners. He was under a lot of pressure to go along, but he refused to seal it. They couldn't build it without his seal, and he figured if he just stood tough they would back off."

"Did they?"

"No. They took him off the project and another guy sealed it, and the building went up with the design change. After that, his days as a rising star were done. They didn't fire him or anything, but it was clear he wasn't moving ahead. He didn't get the important jobs anymore."

"Wow. That's awful."

"So a couple years later, he and a friend went out on their own. They've made a go of it, doing strip malls and medical offices here and there around St. Louis. But it hasn't been the same. Every downturn, they struggle. Meanwhile, Holtzmann is still standing."

"Umm. Knowing what you know, would you take a job in that building?"

"I don't know. I'll never have to decide."

Melissa was silent for a moment as they walked to his car. "They sounded sincere when they say they don't regret it."

"Now, yeah. But it's been fifteen years. For a long time he didn't handle it well at all. It's hard on your pride, taking a blow like that."

"Whose pride are you talking about?" asked Melissa, "His, or yours?"

Ben recoiled. "What do you mean? I'm proud of my dad. If I have any heroes, Dad is one of them."

"Okay, okay," said Melissa. "I understand. Just clarifying."

They drove down to her apartment without saying much more. Ben let her out in front of her building and gave her a perfunctory kiss. "You better leave soon. It's supposed to snow."

"I'll be fine. Merry Christmas!" she called as he slipped back into the car.

He said, "Merry Christmas. See you Friday." She turned and disappeared into her building.

Ben decided to go by the office and get some work done with few people around.

As Ben tucked his access card back into his wallet, he reached into the hidden pocket and pulled out the business card again. He fingered the deckle texture of the card, studied the fine engraved print. Should he take a card to her office? Would it be too soon to call her with holiday greetings? Surely, after the sparks between them on Monday she would expect him to call. Would she be interested in a Christmas Eve dinner, perhaps? What if she was alone, needing some company on a holiday evening?

When Ben got to his desk, he picked up the telephone and dialed the number. When he reached the receptionist, he said, "Hi, is Robin in?"

Chapter 21

"Have I got the perfect job for you," said Barry.

"No," said Doug.

"How do you know? I didn't tell you about it yet. You have just the right experience."

"That's how I know," said Doug.

-- David Shepherd, *Palm of God*

The receptionist answered in a practiced voice "I'm sorry, Ms. Atwater is out of the country until after New Year's. May I take a message, or transfer you to her voicemail?"

Ben masked his disappointment in a casual tone. "No, thanks, I'll catch her after the holidays." He hung up with his hopes dashed. He visualized Robin lounging in an abbreviated swimsuit on a Caribbean shore. That certainly worked for him, but he did not care to visualize who might be with her.

Ben returned to his apartment about seven. He figured he would watch television for an hour or two, then turn in and start out for Columbia early. But as he settled in front of the TV, he heard the hiss heralding Shepherd's arrival.

I thought you were going to leave me alone until after Christmas.

Is the holiday over? It's hard for me to tell time on your side. It doesn't look as though you are otherwise occupied.

Don't I even get a few nights off?

Since I'm here, and you're not busy, why not see what we can get done? I thought you wanted to get this over with.

All right, all right. Ben went to his desk and turned on his notebook. He opened the novel document and moved the cursor to the end. *Here we are. Chapter 13.*

How many words have we completed? Don't you have a way to tell on that thing?

Ben looked at the document statistics at the bottom of the page. *Page 38. Words: 11,462.*

Ugh.

What?

I have mixed feelings. On the one hand I am amazed at the precise quantification of our output this technology gives you. On the other, I am disappointed at our progress. 11,000 words is barely an eighth of the way through. I am afraid we will have to revise our estimate of the duration of this project upwards. Unless
...

Unless what?

Ben remembered their conversation on Monday, when Shepherd meddled into his evening with Robin. Shepherd said something about a new approach Ben wasn't going to like.

Is there something you're trying to tell me? Something I'm not going to like?

Now that you mention it, I did have an idea for how we could move this faster. Didn't I hear somewhere that the young lady is a secretary?

Young lady? You mean ... you mean Melissa?

Yes, of course. She is a secretary, am I correct?

She's an admin assistant. I suppose you would call that a secretary. Wait a minute – what does she have to do with this?

I was thinking that the typing part seems to be something of a limiting factor on our transcription process. Perhaps we could hasten our progress by bringing in some reinforcements.

Are you thinking ... are you suggesting ... oh, no. No, no, no. We are not getting Melissa involved. Not going to happen.

I would imagine her typing skills are excellent. Much better than yours. Plus,

she knows the books, which would bring
the error rate down. In addition,
collaborating on this would probably help
your relationship.

*Our relationship is none of your damn business!
You can't be serious. I am not telling my girlfriend I am
hearing a voice from a dead writer!*

My guess is she would be quite
delighted to help, after initial incredu-
lity, of course.

*Look. This is my life. This is my relationship, not
some plaything for you. Talk about boundaries – this is a
boundary we are not going to cross.*

You're afraid to ask her. That's it,
isn't it?

No.

But you've found invoking her fascina-
tion with me an excellent path to getting
your way with her, haven't you?

I have not ... where did you get that idea?

It has, hasn't it?

*Well, all right, sometimes. Just how much have you
been snooping into our life when I don't know it?*

I will take your attempt to change the
subject as confirmation. Now, we both
want to get this done. We're not doing
very well up to this point. The lovely

`Melissa is a devotee of my work. Don't`
`deny it, I know. Do you not see the`
`congruence of interests? Believe me, it`
`would expedite the process considerably`
`to get her involved.`

Ben paced the room, stewing. He knew Shepherd was right – Melissa would be thrilled to help. But how would he tell her? Would she think he was crazy?

Another thought bothered Ben as well. Ever since the night when Shepherd arrived while Ben was in bed with Melissa, it seemed he showed an unhealthy interest in occupying Ben's senses when he was with Melissa. Was it just writer's ego, stoked by Melissa's effusive fandom? Or was it something else – had Shepherd's exposure to their intimacy set a darker process in motion? Was his interest in Melissa's involvement the result of artistic vanity, or were they being stalked by a disembodied dirty old man?

`This is a good idea. You know it is.`
`You need to speak to her.`

As he paced, another thought occurred to Ben. He got the sense Melissa was increasingly suspicious of him. A couple of times she heard him talking to Shepherd, and she reacted as though she thought he was calling a woman. Maybe bringing her in on the deal would help with that.

No, no, that's crazy, crazy. She'll think you're nuts. She'd never believe it. Is this insanity contagious?

But wait a minute. This whole thing is real. You know that. What if he's right? What if she could help us get this thing done and over with quicker?

But then again, getting her involved in preparing the manuscript would also open her up to coming into contact with Robin. Bearing in mind you haven't exactly made a final decision where we're going, relationship-wise, that surely can't be good. It can potentially be very, very messy.

This is crazy.

But if you could get done sooner ...

Besides, admit it. You want someone to know. Sometimes you're just about bursting with this secret, and you can't tell anyone. And if you did have to tell someone, Melissa is perfect. She would believe you, or at least she's more likely to than any reasonably cynical person. She is such a huge fan she will *want* to believe it. People will believe anything they want to believe. She reads all that fantasy stuff, so she just might believe it.

Then again, if you do break up, and things get ugly, what could she do with the information?

Listen to yourself. This is madness. Stop it now.

Well?

I'll think about it.

Chapter 22

"You're lying! I don't believe you!" she shrieked.

"I wish I was," said Doug. "But the pictures in this envelope aren't."

-- David Shepherd, *Neck of the Woods*

Between the holidays, Ben and Shepherd did not get much work done. Ben and Melissa spent a good bit of time together, and Ben resisted Shepherd's increasing frustration with their slow progress. Shepherd appeared almost daily and berated him at length. Ben debated with himself at length about whether the plan to get Melissa involved was a good idea, wavering back and forth several times a day. Fortunately his workload was light over Christmas week, for he felt distracted and unable to concentrate.

Toward the end of the week, he kept coming back to one thought – how hard it was to keep such a huge secret to himself, and how much he wanted someone else to know. But the prospect of telling Melissa was terrifying. He always played the calm and strong one in their relationship. She unloaded everything on him, sometimes to a point he could hardly stand. But he hardly ever confided any insecurities or fears to her. Of course Ben didn't have many insecurities or fears, but when he did, he tried not to let them show.

He finally decided to try explaining his bizarre predicament to her, but put the conversation off through New Year's Day. On the Sunday after New Year's, they made plans for a dinner and video evening in his apartment. Ben resolved to start the conversation and see where it went.

After they finished their Chinese takeout, Ben sat in the window seat, staring out at the lights of the entertainment district to the north. Melissa walked up thumbing through a handful of Ben's DVDs.

"I can't decide what to watch," she said. "I'm in the mood for something light and comic, but your videos are mostly action."

"Lis," he said, "there's something I need to talk to you about."

"Ooh!" said Melissa, in a chirp implying this didn't happen very often. She sat opposite him on the window seat, leaning forward and beaming. "Does this have something to do with the apartment?" Ben knew from her tone what she was thinking.

"Sort of," said Ben, carefully modulating his tone to sound neither too upbeat nor too glum. She cocked her head and waited.

"This is really hard for me to say," Ben began. Immediately, her whole countenance changed. Her fingers rose to her lips, and she leaned back. Ben sensed she was trembling a bit.

"Oh, God," she said, her voice wavering. "This is it, isn't it? Wait, don't make any decision yet. Give me another chance. Tell me what's wrong. I'll change, I promise, I know I can. I'll be less needy. I won't make demands on you. Just … just ..." She lifted a hand to her cheek and he saw a tear form in the corner of her eye.

"Wait," he said. "Do you think I'm breaking up with you?"

"Uh, no, no, … I don't know ... are you?"

"No, no, not at all," he said. He reached out and took both her hands. "No, far from it. This is hard because ... I have something to tell you you're going to find hard to believe. I don't know if you'll even believe me."

"OHH!" she exclaimed, squeezing his hands so hard he almost pulled them away. "Of course I'll believe you! I love you! You can trust me!"

"Well ... " Seize the moment. Go right there. "It's kind of about Shepherd."

"Shepherd?" she said. "David Shepherd?"

"Yeah. You know how sometimes you say you can feel his presence here?"

"Oh, yes! I stand here and look out the window and I think, 'This is where it happened! He stood right here where I am now and worked up all those wonderful stories! It's so exciting! But I thought you thought that was all nonsense."

206 | *Ghost Writer*

"Well, not entirely. I've had some ... some experiences of that kind myself here."

"Oh, you mean you feel him here too? That's wonderful!"

"Uh, not exactly. I wouldn't say I feel him here. I, uh, this is the strange part ... I hear him."

"You ... huh?"

"I hear him. I hear his voice."

"His voice. He ... what, you hear him talking?"

"Yeah, he talks. To me."

"Talks to you? You ... hear this?"

"Yeah."

"Has anyone else heard him?"

"Nope. It's not even as though his voice is in the room. It's like it's right here, inside my head. I could clamp my hands over my ears, and I'd still hear him plain as day."

Melissa stared at him uncomprehendingly for a moment. Then she said, "You're not trying to backdoor break up here, are you? I mean, you're not trying to weird me out so I'll leave you? 'Cause it's working. The weirding out part, I mean, not the leaving part."

"No, no," Ben protested, squeezing her hands so hard she flinched. "I don't want you to leave. This is weird for me, too. That's why it was hard, I was afraid I'd drive you away. But I have to tell you, because I need you more than ever right now! I need you to help me through this!"

It was as if Ben, facing fourth and long, threw a perfect pass for an 80-yard touchdown to win the game. The apprehension and confusion melted from Melissa's face, and she pulled their hands to her chest. "Oh, Ben, if you need me, I'm here for you! Just tell me everything, and we'll find a way through this! You can trust me!"

She dropped his hands, folded hers, and rested her chin on them, staring at him intensely. "Okay, tell me everything. What, exactly, do you hear?"

"A voice, here in my head. A male voice, baritone. Excellent vocabulary, kind of professorial tone. Asking me questions, making observations, giving me directions. He can see what I'm looking at, and hear what I can hear. He can't hear me thinking – I have to tell him."

"Tell him? Out loud?"

"At first it was out loud. Now, it's kind of internal. I just sort of develop an intention to say something and launch it. He hears that, or at least responds to it."

"Hmm. What makes you think it's him?"

"He knows stuff. Like stuff the publisher said, or stuff you said that I didn't know. I don't know, he told me he was Shepherd. He seems to know what Shepherd would know. Everything I've looked into checks out."

"How long has this been happening?"

"About a month. It started just after I moved into the apartment, and it's picked up since then."

208 | *Ghost Writer*

Her eyes widened. "And you're only telling me now?"

"I was afraid ... I didn't want you to think I was going crazy."

"Have you ever heard voices before? I mean, voices of people who weren't physically there."

"No. Never. That's why it's so disturbing."

Melissa looked hard at him, as if assessing his sanity. "Don't take this the wrong way," she said. "Have you thought about the possibility it's your own consciousness, reprocessing information you know in a weird way? Maybe you have more conflicted feelings about living in a space where a man died than you realize. What if this is just your mind's way of dealing with that? Maybe it's an Oliver Sacks kind of thing."

"Um, no, I hadn't thought about it that –"

`Have her test me.`

"What?" he blurted.

Melissa recoiled. "I didn't say anything."

"No, no, it was ... I was talking to him. He's here. He just showed up."

A look of shock crossed Melissa's face. "You're ... you're hearing this voice, right now?"

"Just a moment ago. He said test him."

"What?"

Test me. Have her ask me questions
from the books. Anything. The harder, the
better.

"He says to test him. He says to ask him ... ask me something from the books."

Melissa looked stunned. "You want me to ask you about the books?"

"Yeah. You've read them. I haven't. I don't know anything about them. If you ask me a question from the books and I can answer it, you know it's coming from him. Not from the depths of my consciousness, because there's nothing about the books anywhere in my consciousness."

Melissa regarded him in silence for a moment. Warily, she began. "Okay. In *Neck of the Woods*, how was the poison administered, and how did Doug figure it out?"

Ben closed his eyes. Did you hear that? Should I repeat it? He listened for a moment, then said out loud, "It was painted in a thin layer on the eraser of Miggleman's pencil, which his assistant would have seen him chewing. Doug realized it while he was drinking a salty margarita."

Melissa recoiled, and her eyes opened wide. She stuttered, "Uh, uh, okay. All right, in *Rib of Adam*, why did Doug's secretary, Mrs. Filbert, quit at the end of the book?"

Ben listened for a moment. "Because she was secretly the mother of Randy Ryder, who went to prison because of the evidence Doug found."

"No," she exclaimed. "That's wrong. Randy Ryder and Heck Ryder were brothers. There was a scene where Doug interviewed their mother at their father's medical office and she gave him a phony address."

Ben listened for a moment and, "Remember when Doug asked Mrs. Filbert about her early days as an actress, and she started crying inexplicably?"

"Uh, yeah ..."

"That's because she gave birth to Randy during that time, and she had to give him up for adoption. She couldn't care for him, so Dr. Ryder and his wife adopted him."

Melissa's blinked in surprise. "Oh, that's right! I remember Mr. Filbert was a theater producer! That makes sense."

Her eyes narrowed, and she leaned forward intently. "Okay, a hard one. A really hard one. In *Hand of Kindness*, who mailed the bus locker key to Doug?"

Ben paused a moment, then said, "Doug mailed it to himself."

Melissa's mouth flew open. "What?"

Ben listened. "Uh, uh, Doug knew Corrigan's men would search him on the way out, and he'd be finished if they found the key on him. So he put an envelope in his coat pocket – remember he picked up his mail on the way over?"

"Yeah."

"Well, he put a blank envelope in with his mail. While Corrigan was distracted on the phone with Barry, he swiped the key from the desk. Then when he left Corrigan's office, he wrote his own address on the envelope, put the key in it, and dropped it in the mail slot in the hallway. That way he didn't have the key on him when Corrigan's men searched him, and he got it in the mail the next day."

Melissa's face twitched with wonder as she thought this over. "Of course! I totally missed that! I thought he had a contact inside Corrigan's gang, who was never mentioned otherwise. It seemed so deus ex machiney. But it works! Wow! That's so ..."

She stopped and stared at Ben with astonishment. "He's in there. He's really in there!"

She leaned back. "So he's talking to you? Just talking? What does he have to say?"

"Well, remember when the publisher was here, and I told you about the manuscript?"

Melissa's eyes grew wide. "The Doug Graves manuscript? The twelfth novel?"

"Yeah."

"So there is a manuscript? Where is it? Where?"

"No, there isn't. He burned it."

"*What?*"

"He burned it. He planned to restart, but he never had the chance."

212 | Ghost Writer

"Oh, no! So there is no ... wait, I'm confused. If there is no novel, what does he come for?"

"That's where I come in. He asked me to collaborate on producing a new manuscript."

"Producing?"

"He is, um, telling the story, and I am transcribing it. We're producing a new manuscript, and I am to take it to the publisher and say I found it hidden."

Melissa's mouth dropped open. "You're writing a manuscript?"

"He's writing it. I'm typing it."

Melissa leaped up and leaned with her hands on his knees. "You're writing the twelfth Doug Graves novel? Omigod, omigod! I told you, this is magical! It's so exciting! Is any of it done?"

"We've been working on it for about three weeks. We have about 45 pages done."

"So what is happening? Doug was in a coma at the end of the last book. How did he come out of it? What is the storyline about?"

"Well, Doug was out of the coma at the beginning, but he's broke. So this society girl is found murdered, and her boyfriend from the wrong side of town is the main suspect. He hires Barry to defend him, and Barry gets Doug to investigate the case. He says it's a big story leading to Doug's redemption."

"Oh, that's not right."

"What?"

"Doug doesn't need redemption. He's a good guy that bad things happen to. If anyone needs redemption, it's Barry. It was his fault Doug was in the coma."

Ben stood up and paced away. "I don't believe this!"

Melissa jumped up and followed him. "Don't believe what?"

"Here I am, pouring out my heart about the most disturbing thing that's ever happened to me, and you're giving me a literary critique! You care more about this story than you do about me!"

"I'm sorry," she said. "It's just that ... Omigod! Omigod! He can hear me, right?" She grasped his arm and stared at him intensely, as though trying to look past him and see something behind his eyes. "I'm sorry, I'm sorry! I didn't mean it! You're a great writer, and I would never never tell you how to write your stories! I'm sure whatever you have in mind will turn out just great. I'm so so so sorry –"

"Hey!" said Ben, pulling his arm away. "Talk to me, not to him! Sheesh!"

"Okay, okay. Do you think he heard me? Will he be mad?"

"See what I mean? Ten minutes ago you had no idea he still existed, and now you care more about what he thinks than what I'm going through!"

Melissa pulled him back to the south window seat and knelt in front of him. "I'm sorry, babe, I'm sorry. You're right, my first responsibility is to you. But why didn't you tell me sooner?"

"Like you would have believed me. You would have thought I was crazy. Even now, you weren't going to believe me until he told me to answer your questions."

"So, so, why did you tell me now?"

"Because we need your help."

An expression of pure wonder passed over Melissa's face. "You need ... *my* help?"

"Yeah. In fact, it was his idea for me to tell you, because we aren't making very good progress. We thought it might go more quickly with your help because you, uh, because you know the books and the characters. Rather than me trying to get the text down perfectly, we thought I could pass the information along to you and you could type up the final product. Because you're so much better at ... editing, and getting it right, and so on."

Melissa hopped up and down, clapping her hands together in excitement. "Oh, Ben, this is the best thing that has ever happened to us! I'm so excited! We're so lucky to be in on such a historic event!" She threw her arms around his neck and kissed him.

Delighted by how well this was going, Ben knew how he wanted to celebrate. "Yeah, it's great for us." He kissed her back and slid his hand onto her back under her sweater. But Melissa had other ideas. She pushed away from him and said, "How much did you say you have written?"

"Uh, about forty some pages."

"Well, let me see it! Let me see it!"

Ben disengaged and picked up his computer from the desk. He turned it on and opened the novel document. "Here it is."

"Omigod! Omigod!" Melissa seized the computer out of his hands, sat down on the north window seat, and began reading.

"Uh, I guess I'll, I guess I'll just watch something ... while you're reading," he said, but Melissa was already deeply absorbed in the first pages.

As he walked away she said, "Oh, by the way, is he there when we, you know ..."

"Oh, no, no," Ben lied. "I know when he's in. He'd never do that."

"Oh, good, 'cause I don't know exactly how I'd feel about that. It would be kind of ..." Her voice trailed off and she was lost in her reading again.

`That went well, I think. Very well!`
`I'm encouraged.`

Yeah, right. Well, you can get lost now. It's only forty pages.

`Certainly. Have fun, kids.`

Ben could think of a few adjectives to finish Melissa's last thought.

Chapter 23

> "It's a perfect plan," said Barry.
>
> "It'll never work," grumbled Doug.
>
> "Why not?"
>
> "Because they're not idiots."
>
> -- David Shepherd, *Leg of Lamb*

Ben and Melissa arranged to begin work the next evening. When Ben arrived home from work, Melissa was already waiting outside the apartment with her white MacBook under her arm. While eating the takeout he brought, they discussed how to proceed.

"I've installed this voice recognition app on my computer," Ben said. "I figure I will just repeat what Shepherd dictates to me. The VR will type it into a file. Once I get enough text down for you to work with, I'll save it. I'll configure your computer for file sharing on my network, so all you have to do is open the most recent file. There will be errors and misinterpreted words, but since you know his style, you can edit it and load it into the master file while I'm dictating the next section."

"Oh, this is exciting!" exclaimed Melissa. "I can hardly wait."

Melissa set her MacBook on Ben's desk near the window, and Ben logged it into his home network. She retrieved his master file and began editing it. Ben settled into the north window seat with his computer in his lap, waiting for Shepherd. Before long he heard the telltale hiss announcing Shepherd's arrival.

So our little team is assembled? Excellent! Let's get to work, shall we?

Ben donned the lavaliere microphone that came with his voice recognition software and repeated the plan out loud, so both Shepherd and Melissa could hear.

Splendid. Shall we begin? Show me where we were so I can pick up again.

Ben looked at the concluding page of the manuscript from their last session, and Shepherd began dictating the next lines. After each sentence he paused and Ben repeated what he said into the microphone, watching as the words scrolled smoothly across the screen of his computer. Melissa worked for a while on the master file, but before long she stopped and just listened as Ben recited the lines. After he read three pages onto the computer, Ben saved the text to a new file for Melissa to open and edit.

"Question," said Melissa after a while. "Remind me again what the plan is. When we get this finished, how are you getting it to the publisher?"

"I'll print it up and take it in and tell Robin I found it in the apartment."

"Yeah, but I was thinking," said Melissa. "Didn't he type all his manuscripts on a typewriter? I remember you mentioned he didn't even have a computer."

"Uh, yeah, he typed them on this old Selectric. It was on the desk when I first came here."

"So, if he wrote them on a typewriter, wouldn't they be suspicious if you brought in a computer printout?"

The thought hit Ben like a bus.

`Oh, my God. She's right.`

"But … but we know she wants in the worst way to believe it's here somewhere, so she'll be overjoyed to get it," said Ben.

`It will never work.`

What?

`Robin won't question it. As you noted, she will be too excited to have the manuscript at all. But her partner, Howard Bridges, is extremely cautious and analytical. He will be very concerned about authenticity. The young lady is right. A printed manuscript will never do. It has to be typed.`

Ben sat silently listening to Shepherd. "What's he saying? What's he saying?" Melissa asked.

"He says you're right. We have a problem. It can't be a printout. It has to be typed."

"I'm no expert on forensics and document examiners and stuff, but I do know it's pretty easy to tell a typed manuscript from a printed one."

```
The more I think about this, the worse
it gets. Not only will it have to be
typed, it will have to be typed on a
Selectric. Identifying the machine is
Documents Examination 101.
```

Ben repeated this to Melissa. She sat lost in thought for a moment, then smiled brightly. "I've got it. We go on eBay and find a Selectric just like his. You can find anything on eBay, I'm sure that would be a snap. We order it and type the final manuscript on it. Mission accomplished!"

```
Not so fast. Howard Bridges will
examine the manuscript under a micro-
scope. I think we have to assume that he
may even bring in a professional docu-
ments examiner. In fact I'm sure. He will
want to have a report stating that the
manuscript is genuine.
```

"But if it's typed on a Selectric, wouldn't that be close enough?" said Ben.

```
Not nearly. A skilled documents
examiner can identify not just the type
of machine a paper was typed on, but the
particular machine.
```

Ben had seen enough detective shows to realize that was true. He repeated this to Melissa, and her downcast face told him she knew it, too.

"Do they have your other manuscripts?" asked Melissa. "Other samples typed on the same Selectric?"

She asks excellent questions. I wish I had better answers. They have many of samples of my typing there – manuscripts, letters, all sorts. To make matters worse, papers typed on my Selectric would be very easy to identify. The capital D's are slightly dropped, and the spaces in lower case a's would often fill in. I sure they will try to verify that the manuscript was typed on my Selectric, and that test will certainly fail. I'm afraid it is quite hopeless.

Ben repeated this information to Melissa, and her expression passed from crestfallen to desolate. "What a crash," she said. "From the most exciting thing that has ever happened to us to complete despair in a matter of minutes. I don't see a way out unless we typed it on his own Selectric, but we don't know where it is."

True. It's gone. We have no idea what happened to it after they cleaned out my possessions. Probably sold it off for a few dollars in the estate.

Ben could think of nothing to contribute at the moment. Sometimes when a void of ideas as to what to say collides with a perceived need to say something, the mind has a perverse way of releasing words which, given even a moment of thought as to consequences, the speaker would never let fly. Over the coming days, Ben would many times regret what came out of his mouth next, but out it came.

"Oh, I know where it is."

"What?"

What?

"I know where it is. They have it at the Atwater and Bridges office. In a display case, with a plaque."

"Oh, that's fantastic!" exclaimed Melissa.

Magnificent! Hope springs again. We are back in business.

"When were you at Atwater and Bridges?" said Melissa.

"Oh, I stopped in to, uh, pick something up," Ben said.

"Well, that's great. We just have to figure out how to get hold of it."

"Hello?" said Ben. "Were you listening just now? It is in Atwater and Bridges' very public office, in a big glass case, right by the reception desk where everybody in the place can see it. They thought it valuable enough to get a damn plaque made for it. What do you think we're going to do, walk in and say, 'Excuse us, but can we borrow your heirloom typewriter for a couple of months? No, no particular reason.' It might as well be on the moon."

I can get you in.

"What?" exclaimed Ben.

"What did he say?"

"Nothing."

The office is secured at night only by a keypad lock. I know Robin thought I was a paranoid old man for not allowing my manuscripts into that office, but their security is atrocious. There are no cameras, no security guards. You can get in with a simple keypad. I know the code. I can get you in there.

"You're listening. He's saying something. What did he say?"

"Just crazy talk. I'm not going there. This conversation has veered into madness and the bridge back to sanity is washed out."

Look, this is a plan. Melissa mentioned that E-bait, or whatever, where you can get a Selectric? We get a twin to my typewriter, go in at night, and switch them out.

"Go in at night? Switch them out? My God, you're talking burglary here. A felony! If I get caught, my career is over and I spend the next several years of my life as a guest of the state of Missouri. I suppose I'd have the pleasure of your company in my prison cell, but I don't think I could claim I found your manuscript there."

"Switch them out at night?" said Melissa. In the heat of the discussion Ben forgot to channel his thoughts nonverbally. "How would we get in?"

Ben's rational mind screamed at him to take the Fifth at that point, but once again the words leaked from him like air out of a punctured balloon. He repeated what Shepherd said to Melissa.

She clapped her hands. "Oh, we can do this!" She turned to her MacBook and navigated quickly to the eBay homepage. "Let's see, search for 'Selectric.' Here's a whole page of them. What color? Red? Self-correcting or not? Here's one really cheap – oh, that's for parts only. I suppose if we're just switching it doesn't matter whether it's working or not. Better to get one that works. Ah, here's one. Is this right?" She showed Ben the screen.

`Yes, that's just like it. Perfect!`

Ben relayed the information, although he felt like he should bolt out of the apartment and escape these lunatics while he still could. Melissa clicked and pecked and clacked, then handed the MacBook to Ben. "Here, it's ready for you to put your credit card number in. It will be here in three to five days if we use the expedited shipping. This is going to work!"

Forlornly, Ben watched the wreckage of the bridge back to sanity wash downstream, as the decapitated bridge piers loomed like hulking prison guards over the broken remnants of Ben's career path.

Chapter 24

> The writer bears responsibility for the work. No one else can shoulder that burden. But trusted eyes can be a writer's most valuable resource, helping him refine his vision, polish his gems, and when necessary, turn him back when he strays from the path.
>
> -- David Shepherd, *The Writer's Journey*

The following Thursday, Ben was working at 6:00, as usual, when the alarm tone on his phone went off. Ben couldn't remember what he would have scheduled, so he looked at the alarm. The popup message reminded him the Well Read writers' group was meeting in an hour.

Ben looked at the pile of deposition transcripts, interrogatories, and requests for admissions scattered over his desk. He could put in another three hours plowing through this mess and still have to face it first thing in the morning. He really should put in a couple more hours, but ...

Ben thought back to how he felt after the last meeting, when his dialogue writing met with the group's approval. And his log of billable hours for the week already stood at 37; with all day Friday and a half day or two over the weekend, he could take the evening off and still make his target of 48. He had time to grab some dinner and still make the meeting.

An hour later Ben walked into Well Read just as the little circle was assembling by the front window. Glancing around the group in their casual dress, he wondered how out of place he looked in his crisp designer suit. Eric wore a sport coat, blue shirt and khaki dress slacks; at least someone else came straight from a serious job.

The group greeted him warmly enough. As an opening exercise, each of the group members spoke briefly about what writing they were working on. Since he wasn't working on anything, or at least anything of his own, all Ben could think of was how to fake his way through his turn.

When the others looked at him, Ben said, "Well, I haven't gotten much done. I've been busy at work, and what time I have available I've been helping out another writer with a project of his. It's been hard to work on anything of my own."

"That's great of you to help another writer," said Josh. "What kind of work have you been doing for him?"

"Oh, going over his manuscript, proofreading, editing, a little research – you know, second pair of eyes kind of thing."

"Has that been helping you with your own writing?"

"Oh, definitely. He is much more accomplished than I am, maybe than I ever will be. I've learned a lot from watching him work. In fact, I probably wouldn't have come here if working with him hadn't stimulated my interest."

"Has he been published?"

"Oh, yeah. I think he's published a thing or two."

Josh rubbed his chin. "You, know, I've been thinking of some new ways to expand our approach here. What if we were to bring in an experienced writer from time to time to share with us some of their secrets? Do you think your writer friend might be willing to join us?"

Ben recoiled. "Uh, I don't think that would work out. He's not ... local."

The group proceeded to readings of their recent work. Eric read a passage from his novel about the bridge engineer, and again he dragged the reader down a rocky path of technical detail Ben struggled to follow. Judging from the body language of the others, Ben surmised that some of them found the effort even harder to endure. Leila in particular squirmed in her seat, and the expression on her face alternated between pain and annoyance. Leila sat fidgeting while Josh and Ben offered a few comments, then she exploded.

"I'm sorry, but I could barely sit through that. You lost me at the beginning and I could never catch on again. Seriously, who do you think is going to want to read this? Who do you think is going to care? Why do you even do this?"

Josh intervened to try to smooth over the first open conflict in the new group. "I understand your feelings, Leila, but let's try to be supportive. Let's turn that question around a bit: what are you trying to do for your audience? What do you hope to accomplish with this work?"

Eric's eyes pointed toward the floor, as if the hostility in Leila's tone caught him by surprise.

"Why do I do this? Well ... look. I'd just rather spend my time doing this than whatever else I might do with it. I'm an engineer, okay? People find out what my job is, and they think because they know what I do, they know all about me, how I think, who I am. But I want to be more. I am more. I've seen things, learned things, I understand things. I know probably no one will ever publish my novel. Maybe no one will even read it. But I want to know that when I go, there will be something to show for all that was going on in my mind. It doesn't matter if no one reads it. It matters that I did it. It matters to me that I created it, that these things found their way from my mind to this paper. I know it's not good enough yet, but I want to be better. I guess that's why I do it. That's why I'm here."

They all sat in silence for a few seconds. Then Josh said, "Fair enough. That's why we're all here, I think. Anyone else?"

Dolores barely missed a beat, pulling a tablet with green and violet ink all over it. "I do. This is a poem inspired by a dream I had last week."

When the session was done, Ben waited until the group began to disperse, then approached Eric, as he was slipping his manuscript into his satchel. His expression was morose.

"That was a little rough," Ben said in a low voice. "I guess this group isn't exactly your target audience. But for the record, I'm finding your story interesting."

Eric smiled and chuckled. "Thanks, I appreciate that a lot. I'm glad there's someone here with some interest in what I'm trying to do."

"It's pretty technical so I can imagine why the others would be impatient. But I would keep reading until you finish laying the groundwork.

"This is actually the third novel I've started. Didn't finish the other two, but I think once I get past the groundwork, as you call it, this one is going to have legs. It could really be something."

"I also appreciated what you said. I can sense a lot of passion there. I have the same feeling sometimes. People hear I'm a lawyer, and they think they know all about me. They think they know how I think, how I react, what kind of person I am. Maybe writing is a way to show them there's more to me. Or to prove it to myself. I don't know. I'm just starting to explore."

Eric pulled on his coat and slung the satchel over his shoulder. "Just keep moving," he said. "Just explore. I am looking forward to hearing when you do get something of your own written. I promise I won't ask you why."

They left the store and walked toward their cars. As Ben stopped at his, Eric said, "See you next time?" It was a question as much as a valedictory.

"Sure," said Ben. At least in that moment, he meant it.

On returning to his building, Ben stopped in the lobby to check his mailbox. Jim came out of his utility room office and called to him.

"Hey, Ben. Package came for you. I signed for it. It's pretty heavy." He gestured toward a cube package about two feet on a side. Ben looked at the return label and saw it was from the vendor from whom they ordered the typewriter.

Jim lent Ben a hand cart to move the package into the elevator. In his apartment, he opened the lid of the box and brushed aside the Styrofoam peanuts to reveal the textured red metal surface of the Selectric.

Ben called Melissa to let her know.

"Oh!" she exclaimed. "The eagle has landed!"

"No, the typewriter came."

"So now we move to the next step in Operation Titania."

"Operation what?"

"Titania. From *Midsummer Night's Dream.* Because ... well, never mind. We're ready to make the switch."

They discussed how to go about the task. Ben expressed the need to make at least one trip to reconnoiter the building and familiarize himself with the route they would be taking. They decided to shoot for making the switch sometime in the middle of the next week.

On Friday evening, Ben carefully checked out the building after hours. Shepherd gave him the entry code that got him in through the front door. He saw no security cameras, guards or watchmen. So far, everything Shepherd said about the lax security checked out. Ben took the stairs to the sixth floor and peered in the glass door of the office. As he remembered, a central corridor led to the reception desk, with the individual offices opening into the corridor. A little after seven, the office appeared deserted. A pair of spotlights over the reception desk lighted the central corridor, but all the offices looked dark, and Ben could not see any people or movement. The light from the spotlights reached far enough for him to see the display case with the typewriter to the left, just outside the door of the left rear office, the one from which Robin emerged on his prior visit. A security keypad was mounted to the left of the door. Ben was tempted to punch in the access code Shepherd gave him, just to see whether it worked, but he decided it was too risky. The path to the typewriter case was maybe forty feet, straight in.

Ben reported back to Melissa, and they decided that since the office was likely to be deserted, the following Friday would be a good night to execute the switch. In and out. This was still madness, but methodical madness.

Chapter 25

> Doug froze. The sound of the footsteps drew near, and stopped right outside the door Doug huddled behind. He held his breath. If they found him here, he might not be doing much more breathing.
>
> -- David Shepherd, *Finger of Fate*

The following Friday, Melissa arrived at the apartment about eight. She was dressed in a black leather jacket, black jeans, and boots, with a black leather cap pulled over her eyebrows, and leather gloves. "They were on sale at Marshall's," she said. "How do I look?"

Ben scanned her outfit. "Like the IT tech for a biker gang. What do you think we are here, ninjas?"

"I just wanted to get in the mood for our caper."

"You mean our criminal enterprise."

"We're not stealing," said Melissa. "We're switching. They'll never know the difference."

"I doubt that the courts have decided the issue, but I'm pretty sure it's still theft if you take something and leave something just like it in its place."

"Nothing to it. In and out in five minutes. It will be our great adventure. Are you wearing that?"

Ben wore jeans, a work shirt, a Royals cap, and a utilitarian blue jacket. "Some of us plan our nocturnal breakins with more than style in mind," he said.

He handed her a business card he composed just for the occasion. It showed a business called "T&S Office Supply Co.," with a fictitious address on 31st Street and the slogan "Office equipment and technology – sales, service, repair." He also typed out a convincing invoice for repairs on an IBM Selectric ordered by Atwater and Bridges Publishers with a handwritten notation in bold marker, "Needed ASAP! Pick up immediately!"

"Oh, that's clever," Melissa said. "If someone questions you, you're returning or taking the typewriter for repairs. But what about me?"

"You gave me a ride over on your bike."

Melissa drove them over to Robin's building in her blue Mini Cooper and parked at a meter near the building. They took the elevator to Atwater & Bridges' floor, Ben hauling the replacement typewriter on a hand cart. Ben looked around nervously but saw no security cameras. With a stylus pen, he punched in the six numbers Shepherd gave him for the entry code to the firm's suite.

"How does he know the numbers?" Melissa asked.

"They're Robin's birthdate. Her father set the combination when he was president."

Melissa thought for a moment. "Hmm. She's older than us. She's over thirty."

"So?"

"Just sayin'."

The entry area was illuminated by a single spotlight over the reception desk. The typewriter was in the glass display case on the left wall, as Ben remembered. Ben wheeled the duplicate into the office and parked it behind the display case. He tried to lift the glass cover, but he couldn't.

"Damn! It's locked. Why would somebody lock up an old typewriter?"

"Maybe they thought some crazy people might break in and try to steal it," Melissa suggested.

Robin keeps her office keys on a chain on the left side of the center drawer of her desk. Her office is the door on the left, next to the reception desk.

Ben wasn't excited about the prospect of rooting around in Robin's office, but they had come this far, so he might as well get the job done. "I have to go into the office for the keys," he said to Melissa. "Make sure no one is coming."

"Right. I'm the lookout!" Melissa saluted and ambled toward the front door.

Robin's office was a long, narrow room, with a wall of windows on the left side. The glow of the streetlamps and city lights gave Ben just enough light to navigate through the room without turning on his flashlight. Against the far wall he saw the desk behind a coffee table and several chairs. To the right of the desk was a door, evidently into a small conference room. Ben was tempted to run his flashlight around the room, examine it for images or objects to give him some insight into the lovely presence that occupied this room each day, whose choices transformed the room into an expression of what she was and what she wanted to be. But it was dark, and Ben wanted to get out of that office as quickly as possible. He rounded the corner of the desk and pulled open the center drawer, willing himself to focus on the keys and not stop to look at anything that might get him thinking of the office's occupant.

Ben spotted the keys right where Shepherd said they would be. As he reached for them, Melissa burst into the room and dashed toward the desk. By the light of the streetlights outside, he could see stark terror on her face.

"Somebody's coming!"

Ben rushed to the door and looked around the edge. He had a clear line of sight to the lighted front corridor. He could see Robin in her winter coat, reaching up to punch her access code into the keypad. An older man stood beside her, rubbing his hands on her coat. Because of the spotlight in the reception area, Ben and Melissa could not escape the office without being seen. They were trapped.

`Into the conference room!`

Ben remembered seeing the conference room to the right of Robin's desk. Taking Melissa's hand, he pulled her into the room. Looking around, he saw it was no more than ten feet square, with a small table surrounded by four chairs, bookshelves lining the walls, and a reading chair and lamp in the corner by the window. Between the inward-opening door and the bookshelf on that wall was a nook only a couple of feet wide. Ben backed against the wall and pulled Melissa tight against him, behind the door.

`Don't close the door. She always leaves it open. If it is shut she'll notice. Just stay behind the door. Don't move. Don't - make - a - sound.`

Ben made the "zip lips" signal to Melissa. Her face in the dim glow of the streetlights told him she didn't need the advice.

The light in Robin's office came on. They heard two voices, Robin's and the man's. Both sounded giddy and volatile.

"In here, in here," Robin's voice said.

"You're lucky I didn't take you right out in the reception are. The security guards would have a show."

"Oh, there aren't any guards." Ben noted this with relief, although it was the least of his concerns at the moment.

"How about the conference room? There's a table in there," the man said. A tsunami of panic washed over Ben, and he felt Melissa gasp audibly.

"No, it's too small. I wouldn't trust it with both our weight on it. Here, here, use my desk."

They heard sounds of a chair scraping and papers being pushed aside, followed by a series of grunts and murmurings. The desk where the amorous couple were negotiating their merger was on the other side of the thin partition wall against which Ben's back was pressed, less than five feet away from them. Ben couldn't avoid contemplating the events occurring nearby, events he had rehearsed in his own mind. The imagery, combined with the pressure of Melissa's backside against his front, kindled an involuntary physical reaction.

`Oh, you can't let that happen. You have to stop it!`

Ben looked down at Melissa's face, contorted into a mask of disgust. Clearly the situation was not having the same effect on her libido it was having on his.

`You have to get your mind off it. You have to think of something else.`

A high-pitched squeal from the other side of the wall rendered that impossible.

`Baseball. Think about baseball. The 1985 Royals. Concentrate with me now. Catcher, Jim Sundberg. First base, Steve Balboni. Second base, Frank White.`

Ben tried to screen out the crescendo of gasping and groaning on the other side of the wall. To make things harder, someone was bracing against the wall, which was now thumping rhythmically.

... George Brett. Left field, Lonnie Smith. Center field, Willie Wilson.

A crescendo in the racket arrived at a cadence, and by the time Shepherd reached Mike LaCoss in the bullpen, a falling off in both pitch and volume signaled that the parties had arrived at their respective destinations. Ben relaxed, careful to avoid an audible sigh, as the vocalizations dropped to a husky postcoital murmur.

The man's voice spoke first, "Oh, babe, you're the best."

Robin's voice sounded a breathy note of satisfaction the like of which Ben had heard only in fantasy. "Of course I am." Robin suddenly began laughing.

"What's so funny?" the man asked.

"I was just thinking that tomorrow I'll tell my partner I was still bent over my desk at eleven p.m. Of course I won't elaborate."

"Hah, hah. Tell him I was probing you with a new project." Scraping sounds of the chair moving.

"What, are you going already? Why such a hurry?"

Ben heard the sound of a zipper and a belt buckling. "Aw, babe, it's nearly eleven already. She's going to be wondering where I am. I gotta get back."

"Oh, screw her. No, on second thought, don't."

"I'm sorry, babe, but I told you, things are a little sensitive right now. She's fragile. I'll make it better, I promise."

"So, when will I see you again?"

"I'll see you this weekend. No, wait, we're meeting up with her parents at the lake. It'll have to be sometime next week."

Ben heard Robin sigh for dramatic effect. "Seduced and abandoned, again. Can you at least console me by sending me that epilogue you promised?"

"Ah, I'm still working on that. It's coming slowly."

"Unlike the author," Robin said. "Well, try to find time. I need to get to press by February."

"For you, babe, anything." Smacking sounds indicated the parting ritual. A man's footsteps echoed through the office and into the reception area, and a moment later the front door slammed. They could hear some papers shuffling and objects being moved on the desk. Then a lighter set of footsteps echoed through the office, and the office light went out. Ben and Melissa remained still until they heard the front door close and the lock click. After another minute or two of silence, they peeked around the conference room door, then tiptoed through the office to look into the reception area. It was dark except for the single light, just as when they arrived. They saw no sign of Robin.

Ben retraced his steps to the desk and opened the drawer to fish out the key ring, trying not to visualize the desk's most recent employment. He found the key to the glass case, unlocked it, and made the switch. Back on track with the plan, they made sure everything was exactly as they found it, wheeled the Selectric to the elevator, and took it to the ground floor to load into the Mini Cooper.

Melissa drove back to Ben's building in icy silence. Ben thought perhaps he should break the tension by talking about the experience, but he did not know how to read her expression or what to say that wouldn't set her off. She pulled into the basement parking garage, drove up to the elevator, and popped the hatch lid, leaving the engine running. Ben got out and unloaded the typewriter. He thought she was going to park and come up with him, but she rolled down the window and leaned out.

"You owe me!" she snapped. "You *so* owe me!" She rolled up the window and pulled away, tires screeching as she drove toward the exit.

Ben shouted after her, "What happened to *our* great adventure?"

`Don't worry, she'll get over it.`

Oh, shut up.

Chapter 26

"Come on, you gotta help me," Barry pleaded.

"Nope," said Doug. "I'm done with sleuthing."

"Oh yeah? You've been a sleuth all your life. What else are you gonna do?"

"Something. Anything. Anything that doesn't make other people's business my business."

-- David Shepherd, *Belly of the Beast*

Over the next week, Ben and Melissa worked several evenings with Shepherd. The pace of the work picked up somewhat, but the addition of Melissa to the team did not improve their rate of production as much as they hoped. Melissa caught up with them quickly in her editing work, and turned her attention to the typing on the Selectric.

Ben insisted that Melissa wear gloves when handling either the typewriter or the paper; he felt paranoid about getting their fingerprints on anything. It occurred to him they might even check the manuscript for Shepherd's fingerprints, which would be missing. They couldn't do anything about that, though.

The approach of having Ben repeat what Shepherd dictated did not work out well. The pauses seemed to derail the train of Shepherd's thought, so they returned to having Ben type out what he wrote, without worrying about accuracy or corrections; those were left for Melissa to fix. Even then, Shepherd seemed less enthusiastic, less animated, more tentative in his dictation.

On the Thursday after the typewriter caper, Ben arrived home about nine, too late to call Melissa to come over. Shepherd didn't arrive for a long time, until Ben thought he might have a night off. Shortly before eleven, Shepherd checked in. They started in with their usual routine: Ben read back the last section they completed, and sat ready to receive the next passage from Shepherd. But the words didn't come.

Well? Where do you want to go from here? Time's wasting. I have to go to work in about eight hours. I can't wait all evening.

Shepherd dictated a few lines, without his usual urgency and flair. Then he fell silent for a moment.

`I'm sorry. Maybe this was a bad idea.`

What? This chapter seemed to be going well until we got stalled. What's a bad idea, the railroad swindle subplot? We can change it, or leave it out if you don't think it's working.

`No, all of this. The book. It seems like I'm just doing telling the same story I have several times before.`

But your readers want it. You have to give them closure.

It's not right, me demanding so much of you, pushing you to take chances with your very promising lives, putting you in a dangerous position the way I did.

Oh, the typewriter incident? Okay, that was a scare, but it's done. We took the chance, now let's make it pay off. Come on, where do you want to go from here?

Maybe it was that debacle at the Atwater and Bridges office. I've been thinking, you young people have your own lives. Maybe I have no business hanging on like this. Maybe I should accept I've had a fine life, and let you go on with yours.

A bolt of panic surged through Ben. Shepherd never talked like this before.

It's no problem, really. Don't worry about it. We're both into this project, we both want to finish it. Let's just get working, okay?

Shepherd paused again.

I was warned this was a bad idea, but I insisted. Sometimes that is how they teach us here, by giving us our way and letting us find out for ourselves.

Hey, come on. We have something good going here. We don't mind, really. In fact you were right – this has been good for us. It's brought us closer together. I've been stretched in a whole new direction, and I'm starting to enjoy it. We can't stop now.*

He heard no response. Ben felt a need to keep talking, to get him through this. *You know what it sounds like to me? You sound depressed. I don't know anything about what it's like over there, but maybe people in your ... state get depression too. So talk to me – what is the problem? What has changed?*

    I am feeling as though this whole
effort is just my ego, my not letting go.
It's just that ... I don't understand it.
I don't understand why I was taken away,
just when my most important work remained
to be done.

Well, that's one mystery I can't help you with. I mean, we're human. And death is part of life, as they say. But you've been given an extraordinary second chance. You need to make the most of it.

    I should have been the one finishing
this. It would only have taken me a few
weeks to retype the novel with the
changes I had in mind. But to be snatched
away just at that moment – it's just
cruel, unnatural. I don't understand it.

Don't understand what? Why you had the heart attack?

That's one thing I don't understand. I was healthy. I went in for regular physicals. I walked a lot. I never experienced any heart problems. Yes, I was overweight, I had diabetes. But still, I was healthy.

Weight, diabetes? Those are risk factors. I don't know what you know about the big picture, but I wouldn't read any cosmic murder plot into that.

Yes, I had risk factors. But my health was excellent. My diabetes was completely controlled. I was on this new miracle drug, and I felt virtually cured.

A cold shock of foreboding struck Ben. *Miracle drug? What miracle drug?*

A terrific new medication, just introduced, called Eonocin. Great stuff.

Now it was Ben's turn to sit quiet for a moment. Ben knew the name Eonocin.

DuAllen Pharmaceutical, a medium-sized firm based in Minnesota, manufactured the diabetes drug, Eonocin. Ben's law firm, Block Stahl, did a lot of business in pharmaceutical product liability defense. DuAllen was a client of the firm in liability cases relating to a number of its products. Ben worked on a couple of DuAllen cases himself – Pazefrin, a sedative, and Hemaplex, an anticoagulant. Although he was not part of the team handling the case, he knew from meetings and communications that the firm was also representing DuAllen in a liability case relating to Eonocin. Ben didn't know the details of the Eonocin lawsuit, but suddenly he was chilled by the realization that Shepherd began taking the drug shortly before his untimely demise.

You're suddenly reticent. What are you thinking about?

Ben's instinct was to remain quiet. The principle of client confidentiality had been drummed into him since his first year at law school, and talking about a client's business, especially with any potential of risk to the client, was against his nature. He needed to proceed carefully.

You were on Eonocin? How long did you take it?

I participated in a clinical trial a few years ago. Then when it came on the market last spring, I started again. It worked quite well for me. My blood sugar readings had been spiking into the high hundreds, but after a month or two on Eonocin they dropped into the 80's and stayed there. My doctor was very pleased, and I felt better than I had in years.

Ben searched his memory for anything he remembered about the Eonocin case. There must have been some safety issue with the drug, or there wouldn't be a liability case for which DuAllen would have hired Block Stahl. Ben wished he could remember what it was.

`Why are you so curious about the drug?`
`Do you know something?`

Confidential, confidential. Ben shouldn't say anything. *I can't say.*

`Can't say? Can't say? You do know`
`something, don't you? What is it?`

Honestly, I don't know anything. I just know ...

`Know what? Tell me. I have a right to`
`know.`

Okay, how could you violate confidentiality by telling a secret to a ghost? A ghost with no access to the world except through your own mind? That's no more a violation of confidentiality than writing a memo to yourself, is it? Ben was pretty sure no ethics opinions addressed the subject. And the case itself was on the public record.

Okay, all I know is that my firm, my law firm, represents the manufacturer of Eonocin in a number of matters. And there is an Eonocin case. I'm not on that case and I don't know anything about it, but usually if we are defending a case it means there's some safety issue. That's all I know. Really.

`This is the first I've heard of any`
`safety problem. My doctor said something`
`about side effects and the instruction`
`sheet had the usual small-print blather,`
`but I didn't read all that. Can you find`
`out for me?`

Um, I'll check when I get to work tomorrow. That's all I can tell you. I'll look into it.

Well, good. I need to know. I really need to know about this.

So, can we get some work done? I can afford another half hour or so.

No, I'm much too distracted. I should leave now. Will you have an answer for me tomorrow?

That guarantees he's coming tomorrow. Maybe he'll settle down and we can get back to work again. Melissa will be over tomorrow night expecting new material to type on the Selectric. *I'll find out what I can. Talk to you tomorrow?*

Tomorrow then. The hiss faded away and he was gone.

Ben closed his laptop and dropped into the south end of the window seat. What did this evening's strange conversation mean? If it turned out there was an Eonocin connection to Shepherd's death, what difference would that make? Was Shepherd quitting? Ben didn't even express to Shepherd the thought that disturbed him most: if he quits, if there is no novel, how do I break it to Melissa?

Chapter 27

> She blew a smoke ring that turned into a cloud about the time it hit Doug's face. "So, you think I should give you another chance?"
>
> "Nope," said Doug. "I'm not here for romance. I'm here on business. I got something to ask you about."
>
> She smirked. "As if it was ever anything but business with you."
>
> -- David Shepherd, *Mouth of the River*

Ben's schedule for Friday was full, but he felt an obligation to honor his commitment to Shepherd to check out the Eonocin issue.

Under his firm's intranet setup, each major client had their own section of the firm's shared storage. Each area was protected, so only authorized users could gain access. Ben could enter the DuAllen directory due to his involvement in the Pazefrin and Hemaplex cases, but he wasn't sure whether his password would get him into the Eonocin subdirectory. He logged in and quickly found the Eonocin case among the matters in which the firm represented DuAllen. He clicked into his directory, and the pleadings folder in the Eonocin subdirectory came up.

Ben opened the original petition to see what the case was about. The firm was representing DuAllen in a case filed in the 17th Circuit court,

Johnson County branch. The plaintiff was Vincent L. Black, of Warrensburg. Reading through the paragraphs of the complaint, Ben learned that Black, born in 1952, suffered from Type II diabetes, and began taking Eonocin in the winter of the previous year, a few months before Shepherd did. Like Shepherd, he had no history of coronary problems and was healthy other than his diabetes diagnosis. The complaint went on to say that about four months after beginning the regimen, Black suffered a devastating heart attack. Due to quick medical attention, he survived, but his health was seriously worse after the heart attack. The complaint alleged, without much detail, that the switch to Eonocin caused the heart attack, and that DuAllen failed to document or disclose the risk of heart attacks in its statement of side effects of the medication.

Ben clicked through the pleadings file to see what attorneys from the firm were handling the defense. One name jumped out at him. The attorney signing most of the discovery filings was Jennifer Saxton.

Ben knew Jennifer well. They joined the firm in the same class of new associates four years ago. Like Ben, Jennifer was just out of law school, in her first legal job. Ben and Jennifer spend a lot of time together that first year, learning the ropes of the discovery process that would consume much of their time as associates.

Jennifer was a petite brunette, smart, attractive, and ambitious. Ben's relationship with her mixed

camaraderie with friendly but vigorous competi-
tion. Jennifer often joined the group of young
lawyers who would head for the bars after work to
release the day's tensions in alcohol, loud music,
and friendship. Although they were part of a social
circle of peers, Ben felt some chemistry between
him and Jennifer. They both worked far too much
to cultivate any kind of social relationships during
that first year, and Ben observed a firm policy of
avoiding romantic attachments with coworkers in
close quarters. After the first year their assign-
ments changed and they moved to different floors
and different projects. Ben thought once they established some professional distance, maybe they
might explore what developed between them.
Before Ben could take any steps to make that
happen, however, he met Melissa, and he did not
see much of Jennifer over the past two years.

To make matters worse, the firm granted
Jennifer partnership in the last year's round of
offers. Ben felt stung that she received an offer
when he did not, but he tried to suppress his envy.

Still, they had a relationship of sorts, and Ben
thought Jennifer might be his best information
source on the Eonocin case. At noon he took a trip
to the fourteenth floor where Jennifer was now
based. Her assistant told him she was out to lunch,
but he might find her in the firm's cafeteria on the
second floor, where she often grabbed a quick meal
on busy days.

Ben took the elevator down to the second floor
and entered the cafeteria. Scanning the tables, he

saw Jennifer hunched over a table in the back, leafing through a file as she munched on something.

Ben bought a sandwich and a drink, and carried his tray toward the back of the room. He walked past her table and turned back, feigning sudden recognition.

"Hey, Jen," he said. "It's been a while. How have you been?"

Jennifer looked up from her tuna sandwich. "Hi, Ben." How embarrassing would it be if she struggled for his name? "Yeah, time flies, doesn't it?"

She looked great, her hair and makeup styled with much greater care than it was before, her suit and jewelry obviously expensive. Ben gestured toward the seat opposite her. "You mind?" She waved her hand at the seat, and he sat down.

"So," she said. "How is it going for you? You up for shareholder this time around?"

"I hope so," Ben said. "I'm working hard on it."

"Best of luck," she replied. "You still seeing that girl – what's her name? You married yet?"

"Melissa," he answered. For some reason he felt crestfallen she knew he was attached, or that she would assume he and Melissa were married. "No, we're still in about the same place. You know how it is, it's hard to make any commitments when the partnership thing is up in the air. You?"

"Nothing going on, really. It doesn't get that much better even if you get partner. I'm not going to play the card about men and successful women, but being a female shareholder doesn't seem to do much for one's stock in the dating market. Still doing discovery?"

"Mostly. I do more motions and hearings than before, but I'm still spending most of my time on discovery. Hey, since I ran into you, I needed to ask you something. You're still on DuAllen projects, aren't you?"

"Yeah, one. I'm heading up the discovery team on the Eonocin case. "

"That's one I was wondering about. I'm doing a couple of DuAllen projects, and I am hoping to compare the way they handled that to some of the things I'm dealing with. That's the diabetes drug, right? What's the case about?"

Jennifer hesitated, balking at Ben's attempt to divert the conversation into shop talk. "Oh, it's a liability case. Diabetic, overweight, drinker, smoker, and of course his heart attack is our client's fault. You know the drill."

"Do you know anything about the background? Is there any evidence on the link to coronary issues?" He paused, but Jennifer didn't respond. "I'm wondering because we have some concerns in our cases about the extent of disclosure. Just wondering how thorough DuAllen has been about identifying side effects in other cases. To compare to ours."

Jennifer's countenance hardened into a poker face, the kind a lawyer wears while weighing what to say in a sensitive situation. "Oh, nothing major I recall. I don't recall seeing anything particularly problematical in the discovery materials. I guess Linda Peterson would know more about that. She is lead counsel on the case. I wouldn't want to say without checking with her. You've worked on DuAllen, you know how nuts they are about confidentiality. I mean, I know you're in the firm and all, but I'd want to talk to her. "

Linda Peterson was a top litigation partner. Ben certainly didn't want her hearing about his inquiries. He needed to bail out, to minimize the impact of his inquiry. "Ah, it's no big deal. I just wondered, since we happened to be talking. Every case is different, you know."

"Yeah, they are." Jennifer crumpled the remains of her sandwich onto the tray and slung her purse over her shoulder. "Well, I gotta go. Nice talking to you again. Best of luck with – you know. With everything." She turned to go.

"Yeah, thanks. Nice to see you," Ben called after her. After she left, he sat and mulled whether he learned anything from her response. She dismissed the concerns pretty casually, but her reaction showed more defensiveness and tension than he would usually expect between peers in the same firm. His reading of the case file and his conversation with Jennifer did little to soothe his concerns about the Eonocin connection. He could not afford more time on the inquiry that day, but at least he had something to report to Shepherd. Would that keep him coming back? Ben was surprised to realize he hoped it would.

Ben got home to the apartment about seven, and texted Melissa to come. As they finished their Chinese, he told her he didn't have any new material for her.

"So what is happening?" she asked between forkfuls of fried rice. "You haven't had anything new to type in over a week."

"Shepherd seems to have run out of inspiration again. After all the trouble to get that damn typewriter, he goes drifting out on us."

"Oh, no. We can't let him quit now. What's the problem? Is he having trouble working out the plot?"

"It seems he is thinking more about his own life and death. We had this strange discussion about why he died. How many people can claim they've had a conversation with a dead person, complaining about why they died?"

"I don't know. Based on your experience, maybe more than we ever realized."

Ben chuckled at the thought. "So anyway he spends more time puzzling over this heart attack than he does dictating his story."

"What's to explain? He was in his 70's. Heart attacks happen."

"I guess when it's your own life you ask these questions. Here's the odd thing. He was taking this new diabetes medicine, Eonocin. Supposed to be a miracle drug. The thing is, my firm is involved in this liability case on Eonocin. For some reason I got curious and checked, and you know what? The claim in the liability case is that the Eonocin causes heart attacks."

"What, do you think there might have been a connection? Between this new medicine and his heart attack?"

"I don't know, but Shepherd is badgering me to check into it. It puts me in kind of an uncomfortable position, because all the information I have access to is confidential. I'm not even supposed to be talking to you about it."

Melissa paused. "What if there is something to this? What if this drug, this drug your firm is defending, really does cause heart attacks?"

"I've done a good deal of work on pharmaceutical cases. There's a long Food and Drug Administration process to determine risks like that. I trust the process."

"What, big Pharma and government bureaucrats? 'Trust' wouldn't be in my top ten word associations for those two."

"The process is a big deal. It's very long and meticulous. They can't even move to human testing until they file an application for approval with the FDA. It's called the IND process, and they have to do that before they can even do small-scale tests in humans."

"IND?"

"Investigatory New Drug. Then after the initial tests, they file the NDA, before it will be approved for commercial distribution."

"NDA? You're acronymizing me again."

"Sorry, New Drug Application. This application is huge, 100,000 pages or more. It summarizes all the studies and trials they've done, all the configurations and applications of the drug. It's very carefully scrutinized by the FDA. It usually takes at least a year and a half, and that's if all goes well.

"Then they do more studies and trials. By the time it's approved for the public, a new drug will have been exhaustively tested. I'm sure a major issue like causing heart attacks would be picked up and considered. I trust the process."

"But don't some drugs go through the whole rigmarole and still cause problems? I recall there was one taken off the market a couple of years ago. It was big news story, as I remember."

"You're probably thinking of Vioxx. That was withdrawn by the company after approval, based on a study they did after it was approved. To this day some people still think Vioxx was safe."

"So if this process is so great, why didn't they know about the problems with Vioxx? If they have 100,000 pages of data, shouldn't they know whether the drug is safe or not? Obviously the process isn't perfect."

"No, there's never certainty. It isn't black and white as to whether a drug is safe. The whole thing is statistical, a matter of probabilities and risk benefit analysis. A percentage of people may experience a health complication, especially since these drugs are given to people with risk factors to begin with. It only becomes a safety issue if the incidence reaches a certain level of statistical signi-ficance. In one study the incidence of a problem may be perfectly normal, and then in another one it may come in high. You only know there's a prob-lem when a condition reaches a certain level over multiple trials. Even then you have to balance the benefit of the drug against the risk."

Melissa parked her chin on her palm. "Okay, I understand the testing and the probabilities and the risk-benefitting. But I can understand why it's so important to David. Like you said, when it's your own life, you would want to know. You'd just have to know."

Ben squeezed a soy sauce packet between his fingers. "Tell me about it. Ever since the subject came up, it seems to be all Shepherd wants to talk about. I didn't sign up for this. The deal was, get the novel done and get him on his way. Now he wants me to poke into all these things. I'm not sure it's good for my career."

258 | Ghost Writer

"For your career? Why not? They assign you to work on those things, how can they object to you wanting to find out about them?"

"Because it isn't my case. It isn't my business. It's distracting me from the things I need to be doing, and getting me into areas where I don't belong. Lord knows I have enough of my own work to do. I asked a lawyer who was a pretty good friend about it, and she ... I got this clam-up reaction that kind of surprised me. Like it's a sensitive subject."

Melissa sat silent for a moment, stirring her won ton soup. "Okay, don't take this the wrong way. But suppose it turns out this is a problem? Suppose the information you find means this drug isn't safe, that it does cause heart attacks, like David's. How would you deal with the fact that a product made by a company your firm is defending might be killing people? How do you handle that?"

"Handle it? I have to. It's not like these people are murderers or something. They develop these drugs to try to help people."

"And make a ton of money."

Ben bristled. "Well, yes, that too. But they aren't ogres. Their job to make drugs to cure people's illnesses. We aren't some kind of mercenaries for evil. We're just trying to get good people through complicated situations."

"I'm not criticizing or accusing you or anything, I just wonder how you come to terms with the possibility that what the firm does for the company isn't what's best for the people who use the drug. How you deal with that as a person."

"I get what you're asking. Criminal defense attorneys get that all the time. 'How can you get someone who is guilty off? How can you defend people who do those horrible things?' People are entitled to have their point of view represented. That's our job as advocates, to give people their best chance."

"But what if the truth isn't in their favor? Don't you have an obligation to the truth, too?"

Ben didn't really want to debate legal ethics, but he thought it important she understand what he did. "It's more complicated than that. One of the things I learned early is there's no one simple truth. Every story has two sides, at least. You ever see the movie *Rashomon*?"

"No."

"Classic Kurosawa film. Four witnesses to a murder each has a different story about what happened. They're all partly true, but affected by their own agenda. 'Truth' is selective. It's our job to make sure our clients get the best presentation of their own version of the truth we can make. It's someone else's job to decide which version of truth will prevail."

"So, you're counting on the process again?"

"Not entirely. We do have obligations. We can't assist them in any fraud. We can insist the other side meet its burden of proof, but we can't manufacture or misrepresent or destroy evidence."

"But you still want to know the truth."

"Every lawyer knows there are several different truths – the one you know, the one you suspect, and the one you can prove. The last one is the only one that counts, at least for professional purposes."

Melissa sat in silence for a moment. "That was an important qualifier – your professional purposes as opposed to – what? You still feel the need to look into it, even though it isn't part of your job. It seems to me something else is driving you personally. That's what I'm curious about. You're not just doing this to get David off your case, are you? This bothers you, doesn't it?"

Ben didn't want to answer. How did she pick up on that? This story was drawing him in, and it wasn't about David. It wasn't about work. It wasn't normal for him. What was happening to him, and how did she know?

Chapter 28

"Is that the file?" Doug said.

The clerk heaved a large carton of papers onto the table. "The first box. I'll bring the other two down in the morning. I'm going home. Turn out the lights when you're done. The door will lock behind you." He left the room and Doug heard the office door slam.

Doug stared mournfully at the thick cluster of dusty papers. They think sleuthing is an exciting business, but often this is where you find what you need. Buried somewhere in a moldy old file.

-- David Shepherd, *Neck of the Woods*

After Melissa left, Ben anticipated he might hear from Shepherd. The hiss came in about 10:30. Ben opened up his computer and waited for Shepherd to begin dictation, but all Shepherd wanted to talk about was the drug. Ben filled him in on what he found out.

So I'm not completely off the wall about this, am I? You think there may be something to it, don't you?

Maybe, I don't know. But what's the difference, really? What's happened can't be undone. We need to turn our attention back to the task at hand.

What difference does it make? In my case, it made a life and death difference! Can you just look away?

It isn't my job to right every wrong in the world. I said I would check it out, and I did. Can we please get back to work?

Well, aren't you going to follow up? You can't just tell me, yes, there may be something here, maybe this drug did kill you, now let's just get back to work. Aren't you going to investigate?

Investigate? Now, look. You dragooned me into typing out this novel for you. We are halfway through and I've invested a lot of time here. I want to get this done. I didn't sign up to use my professional status to poke into things that are none of my business. Do you want to do this novel, or don't you? You've hardly given me anything in the last week.

Okay, okay. Let's make a deal. I will come ready to give you more of the novel every time, and you will check a little more for me. My time here is defined by the novel, so if I don't work on it I won't be able to come any more. But you'll look up what you can for me in the time we have left, okay?

Ben worried at the prospect of poking around any further. But at this point he wanted to see the novel done. If this is what it would take to keep

Shepherd engaged, maybe that was what he had to do.

All right, I'll check a little more. But I need some details. Exactly when was this trial you participated in? Exactly. Month and year.

Let's see. I was in the trial for about three months. It started in March. My quarterly doctor visit was in February. That's when we discussed it, and he got me into the trial a few weeks later in March.

March – March of what year?

It would have been about two - no, three years ago. What date is it there? Time works rather differently here.

It's January 25. You died in November, about two and a half months ago.

Then it would be three years. I was in the trial for a few months, then it stopped. Then the drug got approved a year later and my doctor put me on it. That would be in March of last year.

What, the trial started in March or it came out in March?

Both. I started on the drug the second time this last March, less than a year ago. There was a year in between. So the trial would be March three years ago.

And how long were you in it? When did it stop?

The following June. I'm sure of that. Stuart and I were planning a fishing expedition in Manitoba, and I found out the trial was cancelled when I called to get a supply to take with me. Stuart died the November before this last one, and he was too sick to travel for most of that year. So it definitely would have been two years before last March.

Okay, so we have the time frame firmly in mind, March to June three years ago. The next important detail – who sponsored the study? Was it DuAllen?

I was told it was a company-sponsored trial, but we didn't get the drugs from the company. It was some local medical office, over on the Kansas side. I can't think of the name. It was a strange name, with two X's in it.

Ben thought for a moment. *Axxiom. Was it Axxiom?*

Axxiom! That's it!

Ben knew the name. Axxiom Research, a laboratory located in a medical park in the Kansas City suburb of Leawood, Kansas, often served as a contract research organization conducting studies for pharmaceutical firms. Their work often showed up in Ben's pharmaceutical cases. Ben found it completely plausible that DuAllen would contract with Axxiom for NDA trials, and that Axxiom would recruit study participants through Kansas City area physicians.

Okay, now we're on to something. Since I know the dates and the CRO ...

CRO?

Contract Research Organization. Companies often contract their research work out to laboratories like Axxiom to manage their clinical trials. With the dates and the CRO, I can find the study up online at clinicaltrials.gov. I can look it up right now.

Ben punched the keys of his computer. *Ah, here it is. Axxiom Research, Effect of cinefitide – that's the generic name – on geriatric diabetes patients. Site is Kansas City, begun January ... hmm, no results reported.*

No results? Isn't that a red flag?

No, not really. I hoped we'd get more information from two outfits like Axxiom and DuAllen, but they aren't required to report their results, and many of them don't. Here it just says no information received after June. That confirms what you said – it ended in June.

What can you find out about it? Does that tell you anything?

I have access to the full New Drug Application on the disk at work. It's probably enormous, so I didn't look for it when I was checking around today. I'll take a look at it tomorrow and see what it says about the Axxiom trial. So, now can we get to work?

Shepherd obliged by dictating a few pages of the novel, but without his usual enthusiasm. The new material didn't have the energy and polish Ben sensed in his previous work. They were barely halfway through the book, and already Shepherd seemed to be losing interest. Ben wondered whether their joint venture would even go on once Shepherd had the answers to his questions.

Ben had a busy day at work the next day, so he didn't find time to delve into the Eonocin directory until after six. He texted Melissa that he would be working late, hardly unusual, and ordered a sub delivered from Jimmy John's. He opened up Clearwell, the firm's case management database, to search for the Eonocin NDA, and found it quickly – all 124,618 pages of it.

He searched the NDA document for any reference to Axxiom. He found references to an animal study Axxiom did early in the investigative stage, but none to the geriatric trial Shepherd participated in. That's odd, Ben thought. Even if the study was canceled for some reason, he would expect some explanation in such an extensive report.

Ben ran another search for the term on the other documents in the folder. He read through a couple hundred emails from the period from late April until June. Many of them discussed the trial as though they fully expected it to be completed and included in the NDA. On April 24, Sherry Bowman, the research physician who served as the project director, sent out an email dated discussing the timeframe for incorporating the Axxiom study into the application. Then Ben found a series of emails from Bowman to project staff, dated June 7, tersely informing them the Axxiom study had been canceled. She offered no explanation.

Ben focused on Bowman's emails around the period, and found one from Aram Vardanian, the medical director of DuAllen, informing her that the study was canceled. Bowman wrote a couple of emails in response asking for an explanation, but Vardanian's responses were evasive. Finally he wrote that the decision to cancel was made by Jeffrey Lennox, the CEO of DuAllen, and no further explanation was to be offered.

Ben turned his attention to Vardanian's directory, but he could not find anything that shed light on the decision to cancel the study. Like all the other emails Ben read, everything in Vardanian's emails indicated that up to June 6, he fully expected the study to continue,. Then the simple directive to Bowman on June 6. In his word processing files, Ben also found a terse letter to Charles Smith, research director of Axxiom, also dated June 6, confirming his telephone call of the same day to notify Axxiom that the contract for the study was canceled. The letter included some routine instructions for winding down the trial, and concluded by reminding Smith that DuAllen insisted on strict observance of the confidentiality of the project. Ben found no documents dated after June 6 referring to the Axxiom trial.

Ben leaned back and looked at the clock. It was already 9:45. After looking at hundreds of documents, he still had no better idea what happened with the Axxiom study than when he started.

Ben heard the sound of Shepherd arriving.

`Where are you? You're not at home, are you?`

No, I'm still at work. I've been here three hours, trying to track down this trial of yours.

`So what have you found out? Was there a reason it was stopped?`

I haven't been able to get any answers, even after three hours and hundreds of documents I've looked at. I don't know whether I can find the answers you're looking for.

`Isn't there something else you can check?`

Look, I don't know what you want from me. All of this is confidential information. I couldn't do anything with it even if I found something. And what difference does it make? What would it change at this point? It wouldn't bring you back.

I know. But what about the others?
What about the ones who are still here?

Ben pushed away from his desk.

I'm sorry. I signed up to help you finish your novel. That's what you're here for. I'm no crusader. I have a job and a career, and I'm not putting them at risk to satisfy your curiosity. Now I'm going home. You can come with me and work on the novel for a while if you want, but I'm done with Eonocin for the night.

Ben packed up to leave. He had another idea to try, but it would have to wait until Monday. And he needed to think about how far he was willing to go with this.

Chapter 29

> For this kind of dirt, Doug had only one place to go – to Louie the Rat. Louie's real name was Rattigan, but his only gainful occupation had cost him the last two syllables. Doug found him in his usual dive on Prospect. He took the barstool next to Louie. "Hey, Lou, I need some information."
>
> Louie gave him a bleary stare. "Oh yeah? Well, buy the *Star*. I ain't in the information biz no more."
>
> Doug laid his wallet on the bar. "Mr. Jackson here says otherwise."
>
> Louie eyed the wallet disdainfully. "Jackson? I don't work for Jackson no more. Ben Franklin, maybe."
>
> -- David Shepherd, *Chest of Drawers*

Ben went in to the office on Sunday, much to Melissa's displeasure, and worked his way through several hundred more documents. He found countless references to the Axxiom study, but the vast majority of them bore dates before the June 6 cancellation. After that, a pall seemed to fall over the entire division. The Axxiom study just disappeared from their communications. But nothing he could find shed any light on why the trial was canceled. Nothing pointed to any problems prior to the cancellation.

About 5:30, after several hours of poring through countless emails and reports, Ben pushed away from his computer with a sigh of frustration. He felt as though he was searching for a grain of sand on a beach – a grain that might have washed out to sea. The search capability built into Clear-well was powerful, but it wasn't leading him to the nugget of information he was looking for.

Ben had an idea how to cut through the task of searching through the thousands of documents in the Eonocin directory. The Information Technology department had search tools capable of cutting through the clutter on the directory in minutes to find things it would take him hours to search. Ben happened to have a contact in IT, and that contact happened to owe Ben a favor.

Rick Thomas, an analyst in the IT department, joined the firm about the same time Ben did. He and Ben were members of the group that fre-quented the Power and Light district bars during Ben's first years with the firm. Ben stopped run-ning with that crowd about the time his relation-ship with Melissa solidified, but he stayed in contact with Rick, and still kept up their friendship from those days.

Besides, he had helped Rick out. A year or so ago, Rick got into some legal trouble with a former girlfriend, and turned to Ben for help. Ben not only got him out of the situation on very favorable terms, he did so off the books, so nobody else in the firm ever found out about it. So Rick owed him, big time.

On Monday, Ben took a break to head down to the lower level of the building, where the IT department offices were. Rick greeted him warmly. "What's up, bro? You doing right by that girl yet?"

"Same old same old," Ben replied. "Look, man. I need a little favor. Could you do a little search for me?"

"What? Hey, you could teach me Clearwell. What could I possibly do for you?"

"Well, I need something Clearwell isn't finding me. I need something a little more powerful."

"What, you want a machine search?"

"Yeah."

A look of concern crossed Rick's countenance. "Gee, man, I don't know. They control those things pretty carefully. Who is authorizing this?"

"That's my problem. This one is kind of off the books. I was hoping you could find me something without going through channels."

The concern on Rick's face changed to alarm. "An unauthorized machine search? Geez, man. Do you know what you're doing here?"

"Of course I do it. Look, I need to know – can you do it? For me? As a favor – a big favor."

Rick fretted for a moment. Clearly he was weighing his debt to Ben against the risk of what Ben was asking. "All right, man, for you, I can probably sneak one in. How much do you need to search?"

"Maybe three months. Four or five users."

"Three months? No frigging way. That would take an hour and show up like a great big zit on the logs. I can maybe sneak in two weeks, two or three users. That will run in under fifteen minutes and maybe no one will notice."

"Okay, deal. Do that and we're square." For a moment Ben wondered if that reminder was over-playing his hand.

Rick picked up a scratch pad and a pen. "All right, give me the details. What directory?"

"Black v. DuAllen. The Eonocin case."

"What time period? Two weeks."

"Three?"

"All right, three. You're killing me, man."

Ben looked at the calendar on his smart phone. "May 25 through June 8." He added the year.

"What users? Three, absolute max."

Ben thought for a moment. "Aram Vardanian, medical director. Sherry Bowman, project direc-tor."

"One more. Before I change my mind."

Ben took a breath and let it fly. "Jeffrey Lennox."

Rick looked up from the pad, his mouth open. "Uh, dude, even this dumb i-tech knows that Jeffrey Lennox is the CEO of DuAllen. You want me to do an unauthorized machine search on the CEO of a zillion dollar client?"

"Yep. Yes, I do."

"Damn, you're hunting for bear. You did say you know what you're doing, right? Okay, I need search terms. Three. No more."

"Okay. Must include Axxiom. A-X-X-I-O-M, two X's. Alternate terms – you can do wild cards, right?"

"Yeah. Exclamation point for forms of a word."

"'Cancel-exclamation. Termin-exclaim. I want to catch all variations on 'cancel' or 'terminate.'"

"You're sure I can't do anything else for you? Like slash my wrists so you can drink my blood?"

"Drama queen."

Rick shook his head. "When you need it?"

"When can you let me know?"

"I'll try to slip it in after hours today. Or tomorrow. I'm going to need a drink afterward. Meet you at Gordon Biersch?"

"Oh, I'd like to, but I promised Melissa dinner tonight. I kind of owe her."

"Okay, while I'm at it I'll pick you up some new balls. Looks like yours are in custody."

Ben ignored the needle. Rick was doing him a huge favor. "Thanks, Rick. It's important. I wouldn't ask otherwise."

"Yeah, well, I'm not sure I want to know why. Talk to you tomorrow then."

Ben bid Rick farewell and caught the elevator back to his floor. If this didn't work, he was finished. He had done all he could. His access to the information was extraordinary, and he was out near the border of abusing that access. This was more than Shepherd could reasonably expect. Tomorrow the questions would be answered, one way or another, and they could get back to the novel, and he on with his life.

When Ben got back to his floor, Lesley told him Mark was looking for him, and wanted to see him in Mark's office.

Ben swung by Mark's office. "You wanted to see me?"

"Yeah, come in," said Mark. "And, uh, get the door behind you."

Ben didn't particularly like the sound of that. He pushed the door shut and took one of the leather chairs opposite Mark's desk. Mark brushed aside the papers covering the walnut desk. "So, uh, how's it going?" he asked.

"Pretty good. Everything's under control."

"You keeping busy?"

"Here? There's always plenty to keep busy with. You know I got that big email production on the Midwest Dynamics case. We talked about the possibility of getting some temps. You were going to look into that."

"Oh, yeah. Well, you know, budgets. I'll ask about it again." He left the thought hanging in the air, as though he really didn't mean to talk about Ben's cases.

"So, anyway," Mark continued. "I got this call. It seems you were asking some questions of one of the other attorneys about a case. One you're not involved in. One of the DuAllen cases?"

Ben was startled that word of his conversation with Jennifer would make it back to Mark.

"The Eonocin case? Oh, that was just a lunch-time conversation. She was a classmate of mine I haven't talked to in a while, and I knew we were both working on DuAllen cases, so I was just making conversation."

"Oh, yeah, I'm sure that's all it was. Well, anyway, I guess it's kind of sensitive or something, so it was mentioned to me. I thought we were keeping you pretty busy, so I just thought I'd ask. In case you needed more work or something."

"Oh, no, nothing like that. I was just looking for something to talk about. I didn't think it would ruffle any feathers."

"It's not a big deal, just something that was mentioned to me, so I've mentioned it to you. That's all. But while we're on the subject, maybe we should talk a bit about the process."

Ben didn't need clarification on what process Mark was talking about. The fact that he would bring up the partnership issue during the same conversation did not bode well.

"So you're in the home stretch here," said Mark. "Just five more months until the partnership committee meets. I don't have to tell you this needs to be the strongest five months of your time here. But lately it seems you've lost some drive, as though you're distracted by something."

Ben struggled not to let his discomfiture show. "Distracted? My hours are right up there. My results ... "

"Oh, I'm not faulting your hours, or your results. It's just ... it's just something intangible in what I've seen. Sometimes it seems your mind is somewhere else, as though you'd rather be doing something else. I've never gotten that impression before. I just want to keep the lines open. If there's something wrong, you can talk to me about it. How is it with ... with the girl?"

"Oh, fine," said Ben. "Things on hold. Same as ever."

"You got a new place, right? Everything okay there?"

"Yeah, it's great. Sometimes I wish I could see it more in daylight, but it's great. That's not a complaint."

"Folks okay? No family issue?"

"No, everyone's fine."

"Not drinking more, or anything?"

"No, no. Nothing like that."

Mark leaned back in his chair. "I don't mean to pry, but I've seen it happen sometime. An associate works like a dog for years, gets right on the brink, then suddenly they lose the drive. As though somehow getting close to the finish line makes it more real, and suddenly they don't want it enough. Or maybe it's unconscious. Like they stop just short of the goal."

"Like Colin Smith."

"Who?"

"Oh, one of my movie allusions. *Loneliness of the Long Distance Runner.* Never mind, I'm sorry. Back to your point."

"Anyway, the point is, you have to decide who you want to be. Do you want to be the kind of lawyer this firm wants? Are you ready to give 110%, maintain your discipline and consistency over the long run, always be a rock for the clients of this firm? Because that's what you need to show the committee, and to show the committee you need to show me. I always thought I saw that in you. I still think it's there. Are you going to show me you have it?"

What else could Ben say? "Sure I do. Sure I will."

"Okay, great. Five months, Ben. Focus like a laser. Make me proud of you. Help me sell you to the committee."

"Sure. I'll do my best."

"Okay, thanks. I'm glad we had this talk." Mark picked up a file on his desk, signaling the conversation was over.

Ben made his way back to his office and shut the door behind him. He slumped against the wall. This was a wakeup call, he thought. This Eonocin thing isn't a casual favor. It is starting to look career threatening. I've come all this way. I've worked so long and so hard. I'm right on the threshold. Why me? Why now?

He sat down at his desk and logged on to his computer. The thing to do now is dive into the work. If he didn't get those temps, he better look into that email review. In the back of his mind he wondered whether he should call Rick and cancel the search. But he got involved in something else, and the thought got lost in his mind.

Chapter 30

Doug picked up two beers at the bar, sat at the table and slid one over to Perkins. "So what brings you to our humble city from the great metropolis of Chicago?"

The older man lifted the brew to his lips. After a big swallow, he said, "Looking for a runaway husband. Girlfriend has family in Kansas, wife thinks they may be hiding out here."

"Coulda saved you a trip. I could run that down for you."

"I know, but the dame wants me on the job. She's loaded, so she gets what she pays for. But it's good to see you again."

Doug didn't answer, but he felt the same way. It was good to see his old friend again.

-- David Shepherd, *Finger of Fate*

Ben worked until 8:00 that night, too late for dinner with Melissa. He stopped at Panera for a pick two, and got back to the apartment about 8:30. After he ate, he turned on the computer and waited for Shepherd, but nothing happened. He felt sad about it. Despite the shock of the day's events, he found himself looking forward to receiving more of the novel. He was caught up in the story, and wanted to know where it was going. The whole process had been such an exceptional incident in his ordinary life that he was disappointed to feel it slipping away.

He considered giving it up and watching some television or going to bed. Then he thought of something else. He searched through his emails until he found one with an attachment. He opened up the spreadsheet, picked up his phone, and dialed the number he found. After a moment of ringing, he heard the phone on the other end being picked up, and a nasal voice answered, "Hello?"

"Hello, Eric?" Ben said. "This is Ben Trovato – remember, from the writer's group?"

"Hey, man!" the other voice spoke, brightening with recognition. "How ya been?" We've missed you. It's great to hear from you."

"I thought I'd call. Remember how you were telling us about the Heart of America, and how no one ever thought of the work you did on it?"

"Yeah."

"Well, I just wanted to tell you I drove over it the other day and thought, hey, this is Eric's bridge. So you can stop saying 'no one,' because now there's at least one."

Eric laughed heartily on the other end. "Oh, that's rich! My moment of immortality! Thanks, I really appreciate your telling me that."

"No problem. So how's your novel coming?"

"Funny you should ask. I just had a break-through. A huge one. Remember how Josh was always getting on me about needing more conflict, how it wasn't enough that the bridge might fall down?"

"Yeah, I remember him saying that."

"Well, I was looking through some old folders I keep and I found this one I started a couple of years ago, when I got interested in cults. All this stuff on cults. So all of a sudden this idea pops into my head – how can I work a cult into my story?"

"So did you?"

"I did! And it turned out great! As soon as I started thinking about it, all this stuff comes pouring out. So get this – while Victor is trying to convince the bureaucracy the bridge is unsafe, he finds out this cult has the same idea and is planning to sabotage the bridge just when this big parade is passing over it."

"Do cults do that, or terrorists?"

"This one's a little of both. Kind of a cross between Charles Manson and bin Laden. So anyway, it turns out the head of the cult is a former classmate of Victor's. They were rivals in school, but this guy lost his license after a bridge he designed collapsed, and now he's bent on revenge! So that's how he knows the bridge is bad – he knows it for the same reasons Victor does!"

"Oh, that's good. Man against man conflict superimposed on man against nature."

"Ha ha. What, you've been to two meetings, and already you've absorbed Josh's shtick?"

"So, do engineers join cults?"

"No, we're too analytical. We wouldn't join one, but we might start one. The control thing." Ben suppressed the charismatic engineer joke that came to mind.

"So anyway," Eric continued, "Victor finds out about this, and now there's a race against time – he's got to persuade the bureaucracy to close the bridge before the cult can bring it down."

"Sounds like Josh really helped you with that. It's shaping up as a juicier already."

"Oh, there's more. Victor finds out because there is this young woman in the cult, an engineering student who fell in love with the leader. The cult leader knows that if anyone catches on to his plan it would be Victor, so he sends her to romance Victor and find out what he knows. But when she gets to know Victor, she becomes conflicted. Finally she confides in Victor, and he starts working to get information out of her, and something develops between them. So there's this romantic triangle, too."

"Oh, a romantic plot. Have you ever written a sex scene?"

"I've tried, but the results were pretty awful. It could be the scariest scene in the book."

Ben chuckled. "The best thing about writing sex scenes is the research is so much fun."

Eric laughed. "I'll have to try that one on my wife. 'But honey, it's for the book!'" Ben realized it never occurred to him that Eric may have a wife. Somehow he visualized Eric in his parents' basement. Stereotypes.

"So, are we going to see you again?" Eric asked. "I didn't know if you'd be coming back."

"Well, I got distracted with some stuff. I didn't make it last time, but I still think about it."

"You should come. You don't need to bring anything, just come and listen. Really, we'd love to see you."

"I don't know. I'm interested, but I haven't done the work like most of you have. I haven't been reading, I haven't written anything but papers and legal stuff since high school. You've been spending much of your time working on your writing for what, twenty years?"

"Closer to thirty. But hey, man, you're young. You've got years to find your voice yet. You just need to keep with it. You have talent, you know? The dialogue you wrote in that exercise Josh gave us was really good. My dialogue sounds like characters giving speeches. Yours sounds like people talking. That's a gift, man. You can develop it, if you want to."

"When I listen to you guys, I feel like a dilettante. You're totally committed. I never find the time to write."

"You just have to make the time. A writer writes, that's all. You know what we call someone who wants to write but can't find the time?"

"I don't know, what?"

"I don't know either, but we don't call him a writer. You just have to decide whether you want to do it and make the commitment. You have to sit down and do it. It doesn't matter if it's good. You just have to get the fingers going. Do you want to be a writer or not? You need to decide who you want to be."

"Heh. Funny you should say that. My boss just told me the same thing today."

"What?"

"That thing about deciding who I want to be, in another context. Only it sounded more ominous coming from him."

"Well, I've got this thing I call the rule of threes. If one person says something to me, I'm like, okay, thanks for the advice. If two people say it, maybe it's something I should be thinking about. If three people tell me, then the proverbial two by four to the head is next."

"So if someone else says it to me, then maybe I should, uh ..."

"Do it. Or put on a helmet."

"Okay, okay. Well, I gotta go. I think maybe I should come to the group again. I like what it makes me think about, even if I'm still not doing anything."

"Yeah, just show. Use the gift, man. Keep it alive."

"So, yeah, I think I'll try it again. I'll see you there."

"I'll look for you. Thanks for calling, man. It's great to hear from you. Bye."

"Yeah, great, Good night."

Ben pressed the button to hang up the phone. He sat back and thought about what he and Eric discussed. Shepherd said the meaning is what makes the story. He should listen for the stories. When he thought about it, that was what the group taught him – not to express himself, but to listen. The rest will come, he thought. You have to listen.

He shut down the computer. As he did, he noticed one of the Doug Graves novels Melissa left for him. He picked it up, carried it over to the chair by the window, and turned on the reading light. Time to listen for a while.

Chapter 31

Doug stared at the faded sheet of yellow legal paper. He read it again, then another time. That was one time too many. He knew what that scrawled notation meant. Some things are too dangerous to know.

-- David Shepherd, Neck of the Woods

About eleven the next day, Rick called Ben on his cell phone. "I got something for you."

"I'll be right down," Ben said.

Ben hurried down to the lower level and found Rick's cubicle. Rick set his personal notebook computer up on his desk and plugged in a flash drive.

"I ran the search and looked through the results. About a hundred documents meeting your criteria. They're on here."

"Thanks, bud. I appreciate it," said Ben.

"Most of them are just emails that don't seem like much to me. Mostly just followup on the cancellation. But there's one I thought you should see."

Rick pulled up a document. "This is a Vardanian document. The weird thing is it wasn't in his directory – it was a deleted document."

"Deleted?"

"Yeah. People who aren't very computer literate often think when they delete a document it's gone. But it isn't. The system just changes the first character in the file name, so it doesn't show up in the directory. But it's still there. That's where I found this one. Here, read for yourself."

He slid the laptop across to Ben, and Ben read the document on the screen:

FROM: A. M. Vardanian, MD

TO: Eonocin file

DATE: June 6

RE: Meeting with JLL on Axxiom

I met today with JLL to go over the implications of the information Charles Smith of Axxiom conveyed to me in this AM's phone call. I informed him CS says trial is showing cardiac incidents above statistical significance and he will be reporting this to institutional review board. I advised that previous tests were too close to SS line for comfort and a trial over the line would be a problem in Phase 3 application. Study likely to be halted by IRB. We would need a strategy to deal with this in NDA application and may need to delay application for additional trials.

JLL was unsurprisingly quite upset with news. He insists that NDA application will go forward on schedule. I raised question how we will deal with Axxiom results, and he said Axxiom trial will not be part of NDA application. He said if CS is going to IRB, we should cancel immediately to preempt this. I expressed ethical reservations of cancellation in face of unfavorable result, but he was unpersuaded. He specifically directed me to cancel Axxiom contract stat and inform CS we will insist on confidentiality. He made this directive very clear in face of my reservations.

I am writing this memo to

The memo ended there. Ben reread it, then read it a third time. "Holy crap," he said.

"That was my reaction," said Rick. "But I defer to your qualified professional judgment."

"This is ... my God. This was a deleted document?"

Rick pulled out the flash drive and handed it to Ben. "Yeah. My guess is he started writing it then had second thoughts. It's bad, right?"

"You bet it's bad. If this is true, the CEO killed an adverse study on the eve of filing their approval application. And it's right on the issue our litigation is about."

"But you can't do anything with it, can you? There's all kinds of confidentiality and stuff."

"I don't know. This is serious stuff. There are rules about what you have to do when you find out your client has committed a fraud."

A pained expression came over Rick's face. "You don't mean ... you don't plan to show this to anyone, do you? That wasn't the deal."

"I thought I just wanted to find out what happened to the project for my own information, but this is a whole new ballgame. I have to figure out what I'm supposed to do."

"Look, man," said Rick, a catch in his voice. "You can't show this to anyone. It can be traced back to me. We could both get fired. I trusted you, man. You said you knew what you were doing. I didn't think to ask whether it involved us getting flushed down the toilet!"

"Don't worry. I'll find a way. I'll make sure nothing gets back to you. This is just a lead. It just points me in a direction. It'll be all right, I promise."

"Okay. Just ... just don't save that on any firm computer, okay? Don't show it to anyone. I tell you, we're both in over our heads here. Don't make me sorry I helped you."

Ben promised he wouldn't, and put the flash drive in his pocket. The rest of the day he could feel it burning a hole in his thigh.

Ben sat in the south end of the window seat, his notebook on the window ledge, staring out at the city lights to the north. Of all the nights for Shepherd to take his time arriving. Ben closed his eyes and concentrated, calling out with the inner voice he used to speak to Shepherd, trying to summon him from whatever alternate dimension he resided in.

Finally he heard the background noise signaling Shepherd's arrival.

`Did you find anything out? Is there any news?`

Ben took his time, and told Shepherd everything he learned step by step. He opened up the file with the memo on his notebook, so Shepherd could read it with him.

`I knew it! The bastards! They knew that drug was bad, and they pushed it onto the market anyway! They don't care who dies, as long as they make their bucks!`

Ben let Shepherd rant for a while. He supposed under the circumstances, he would be pretty upset as well.

`So what next? What are you going to do about this?`

There's not much I can do. All I have is this memo, protected about five layers deep in confidentiality. I can't use the memo, or my friend and I could both get toasted. I would need to find some corroborating evidence that isn't confidential. I don't know how I could do that, I don't even know where to look. They've buried this thing pretty thoroughly. People with a lot more leverage than I didn't find it.

Didn't find it because they didn't know about it. Isn't there something you can do? Someone you could leak it to who would be able to dig it out?

Now what you're asking is for me to violate the letter and the spirit of confidentiality. I could be disbarred if I did that.

A million lawyers in the United States, and I get the one that gives a damn about ethics. Isn't there some kind of exception if your clients are killing people? Because I assure you, people are dying right now from this drug. It's too late for me, but what about them?

Ben hesitated. He did his reading on the issue, pulling up a copy of the Rules of Professional Conduct to review what they said about confidentiality. He remembered something about an exception allowing a lawyer to reveal a confidence when necessary to prevent a client from doing harm. Even after reading the rule, Ben had his doubts. In his situation, where he had learned about the harm through means not entirely above board himself, he stood on shaky ground.

I'm not sure what I can do. Aside from putting my whole career at risk, this is a complicated question. I don't know what to do. I thought I might talk to someone who knows this stuff better than I do, but I don't know who I can trust.

Can't you get an ethics opinion or something? Doesn't the bar association do that?

The Legal Ethics Counsel does, but they're tied in to the disciplinary system itself. I am not about to go to an office under the Supreme Court and say, hey, a dead guy asked me to check something out, so I pulled a favor and got some information I'm not entitled to, saying our million-dollar client committed a fraud that may be killing people. I don't have a professional death wish.

Now it was Shepherd's turn to be silent for a moment.

Okay, you say you want to talk to someone you can trust. May I make a suggestion? Years ago I had some legal work done by a gentleman in your firm. Name was Roger Donns. Do you know him? I believe he's semiretired now.

Ben remembered the name. *Yes, he is – or was – a senior partner. I've seen his name on various things. I remember he used to do a lot of the firm's CLE in ethics.*

CLE? You're using acronyms again.

Sorry, continuing legal education. I remember he did the ethics section of our orientation when I started at the firm. Other than that I've never met him.

Well, he is definitely someone you can trust, if ever I could say that about anyone of your profession. As I recall he was active on the ethics committee or something. Anyway, if you need advice, perhaps you could speak to him.

The idea struck Ben as a good one. If Donns still had an active license, he could consult with him as his own counsel, and anything Ben told him would be confidential. Ben thought this was a good point to cut off the discussion of the Eonocin situation.

That's a good idea. I may just do that. Maybe he can help with the next step, if there is a next step. I'll give him a call tomorrow. Now, can we get something done on this novel? I could use the distraction.

Shepherd agreed to resume work on the novel. He began dictating more text, but again he lacked his usual passion and intensity.

Come on, **Ben encouraged him.** *You've done this all your life. You know where you're going with this. Just let it flow, anything. We can fix it up later. We just need to get moving again.*

This is different. It's just ... I don't know how to explain it. I know, this is my only chance, if I don't get this done now, the window will close, but ...

But what?

Did you ever have the feeling that everything you have worked on, everything you wanted to accomplish, all depends on what you say right in the moment, yet your mind is blank, just frozen? That's how it feels.

Just throw something out. Just to get moving.

The problem is, it's not right. This story is going down the same track as the one I burned, and I'm unhappy with it for the same reasons. Doug Graves deserves a better story than this, but I just don't know what that story is. If I don't finish it now, when I have the chance, I never will.

But you have to finish it. You can't leave it where it was, with Doug in a coma. Everybody who knows the stories says so. They are all looking for some closure. You have to give it to them, even if it isn't your masterpiece.

Maybe the Doug Graves cycle will forever remain unclosed. Something is wrong, but I don't know how to fix it.

Ben felt a deep frustration. Rather than moving forward, Shepherd was slipping further and further away from completing the novel. He tried to talk him through some of the plot issues Shepherd struggled with, and found himself pleasantly surprised with how much substance he was able to contribute and how well Shepherd took his advice.

But the hour grew late without significant progress, and by the time Shepherd bid him good night and faded out, they added only a few more paragraphs to the manuscript. They were stalled at 51,000 words, and Shepherd wanted to discard more than add. Ben went to bed knowing tomorrow he would plunge into the Eonocin mess again. Maybe Donns could help him close that down. Maybe he would never hear from Shepherd again. Whether on the novel or on the drug, it seemed the more he did for Shepherd, the further away the end appeared to be.

Chapter 32

"I can't tell you. It's better you don't know," said Doug.

"Come on," said Barry. "Hey listen, make me your lawyer. Then anything you tell me is privileged. I can't tell anyone, and nobody can make me. Here, just sign this retainer agreement and you can tell me everything."

Doug eyed the lengthy form Barry shoved across the table. "This says I owe you five hundred bucks."

"That? Just legal mumbo jumbo. Don't worry about it."

-- David Shepherd, *Hand of Kindness*

When Ben arrived at work in the morning, he checked the entry for Roger Donns in the firm directory. His recollection was correct; Donns was still listed, but his title was "Of Counsel," a designnation often given to attorneys who retire from active participation in the firm, but keep their licenses current so they could still practice law. Donns did not have an office or a telephone extension in the building. His entry listed a residential address in Lee's Summit.

He called the number on the listing, and an amiable older man's voice answered. Ben identified himself and explained that he had an ethical problem. "I know you were quite active in the field of ethics when you worked with the firm."

"Yes," Donns replied. "I served on the ethics committee for many years. Chaired it for a couple of terms. Somebody had to do it."

"That's why I wanted to speak to you. I need some advice on an ethical issue. I'd prefer not to discuss it here at the firm. Would you be available to speak to me on an attorney-client basis? To give me your advice as my counsel, not as a representative of the firm?"

"Hmm, so you can have the benefit of confidentiality? Certainly, I can do that. I'm glad to help a young lawyer who takes his ethical responsibilities seriously. When would you like to get together?"

Ben arranged to meet with him early in the afternoon. About his normal lunch time, he drove onto I-70, and reached Donns' home in an upscale neighborhood southwest of Lee's Summit half an hour later.

Donns met him at the door. He looked like the senior attorney from Central Casting, with distinguished silver hair lining a wrinkled, but tanned and cheerful face. He wore a pullover sweater and jeans, a perquisite of the retired after years in the office wearing expensive suits, white shirts, and ties. Like Ben's.

Donns ushered him into his study, a quiet room lined with bookcases and furnished in luxurious walnut. Ben noted the only computer in the room rested on a credenza on a far wall, inaccessible from the desk and clearly not a central focus of the room. He gestured to a thickly padded chair, and Ben sat down and faced him across the expanse of the burled walnut desktop.

"Do you still practice much?" asked Ben.

"I do some estates work for friends. I volunteer for some charities. Some of my old clients call from time to time," said Donns. "One of the benefits of retirement is that I can work only on matters that appeal to me. Digging into the ethics field again is certainly an invigorating challenge. Tell me what's bothering you."

Ben gave him an outline of his foray into the Eonocin matter. He fudged the facts a bit, saying he became involved at the behest of a friend who lost a loved one to a heart attack shortly after going on the drug. It wasn't completely a lie, he figured; Shepherd was undoubtedly his own "loved one." Without naming Rick, he said he came across a memo while looking at files he wasn't really authorized to see. Based on the memo, he had reason to believe the client may have committed a fraud on the Food and Drug Administration, securing authorization for a drug that might be unsafe, and that the distribution of the drug under approval gained by fraud may pose a risk of serious harm or death to unsuspecting consumers. He added that he doubted anyone else at the firm knew about the fraud yet.

Donns sat in thought for a moment. "Have you looked at the rule yet? Rule 1.6 of the Rules of Professional Conduct, as I recall. It addresses the situation of client fraud resulting in harm to others."

"I looked at the rule and read the comments," said Ben. "It seems to be a borderline case. I'm still not sure where I stand with it even after reading them several times."

"Let's look, shall we?" said Donns. He turned and pulled a volume off the shelf, within easy reach right behind him. It was a bound version of the American Bar Association Rules of Professional Conduct. Ben just looked up the rule online.

"Here it is," said Donns. "Rule 1.6(b)." He read out loud: "A lawyer may reveal information relating to the representation of a client to the extent the lawyer reasonably believes necessary ..." He ran his finger down the page and read further:

> (1) to prevent reasonably certain
> death or substantial bodily harm.

He set down the book. "For that exception, you have to be reasonably certain the conduct will result in death or bodily harm. Based on what you know, do you think it is reasonably certain that consumers will suffer death or substantial bodily harm?"

"I'm convinced on the personal level. But can I prove it as a lawyer? Probably not. That's why it seems like a borderline case to me."

Donns read over the rule again. "We should check whether the Missouri rule tracks the model rule." He reached behind the desk and pulled out the current year's update volume of the Missouri Rules.

"Hmm, the Missouri rule – Rule 4-1.6(b) – is slightly different. 'To prevent death or substantial bodily harm that is reasonably certain to occur.' The language is stronger than the ABA rule, which says to me the Missouri Supreme Court intends to enforce the prohibition on revealing confidences even more strictly than the ABA standard. In my view that should caution you against taking any chances about revealing anything you learned because of your position with the firm."

Ben shifted uncomfortably in his chair. "That's what I suspected. I wondered just how imminent the threat has to be before I could reveal it."

"Comment 6 helps with that," Donns said. "It gives the example of a lawyer who finds out a client is discharging toxic materials into the town's water supply. The lawyer could reveal that, if 'if there is a present and substantial risk' that people would contract a fatal or debilitating disease from the water."

Ben grimaced. "It still seems borderline. I know the company considered the threat of heart attacks serious enough that they killed the study. There may be a direct link between people taking the drug and dying of heart attacks. Is it certain? I think you would need a lot of data to answer that

302 | Ghost Writer

question. I strongly suspect the drug is causing deaths, but I can't say I'm certain. I just don't know enough. Nobody does, because the company sabotaged the process by which the question would have been answered."

"Comment 12 specifically discusses the steps you should take in such a situation," said Donns. He read the comment out loud:

> Where practicable, the lawyer should first seek to persuade the client to take suitable action to obviate the need for disclosure. In any case, a disclosure adverse to the client's interest should be no greater than the lawyer reasonably believes necessary to accomplish the purpose.

He closed the book and looked across the desk at Ben. "I realize you are in a very difficult position. But the rule we have gone over places a strong emphasis on the certainty of the harm caused by the client's conduct, and it seems you are less than certain of the consequences here. It might be wise to bring the information you have come across to the attention of the counsel handling the case, and allow them to make the decision as to how to approach it. You may want to look at Rule 5.2 as well. As a subordinate lawyer, you do not violate the Rules of Professional Conduct if you act in accordance with your supervisory lawyer's reasonable resolution of a question of professional duty. If you inform those above you on the chain of authority what you know, and defer to their resolution of the issue, you are in the clear. Under the circumstances, I think you are fully justified in maintaining your silence here."

Ben considered that advice for a moment. "The problem is … what I am really struggling with is … I hate to say it, but I don't really trust those above me in the chain on this. My question is not whether it is okay for me to remain silent, but whether there is any way I can do something about this, if they don't. I understand the importance of confidentiality. But I can't just sit back and shut up, knowing people may be dying, because they don't know something I do. I understand my role as a lawyer. But I'm also a human being, and I don't want people to die because of my silence."

Donns sat back and gazed intently at Ben. "You really are unusual, you know? I saw hundreds of ambitious young lawyers on the way up in my years at Block. Almost all of them, if you tell them it is in their professional interest to keep quiet, they would clam up like the dead. Not too many would express such a concern. I do respect that."

Donns folded his hands and rested his chin on them for a long moment. "You know, I worked with DuAllen, back in the day when they were just a small startup company. They were known as Duane and Allen then. I enjoyed dealing with them, because they took their responsibilities seriously, just as I did. Marvin Duane, who was the

CEO for so many years, was one of the most principled and ethical people I knew, in any profession. He's gone now. He and Dr. Grace Edwards were the heart and soul of the company. They were the company back then, thirty years ago. Do you know Grace?"

"The former medical director? I don't know her, but anybody who has worked on DuAllen cases has seen her name all over the file. She retired, didn't she?"

"She didn't retire. After Mr. Duane died and the new guy came in as CEO, she stepped down, to let him make his own choice as Medical Director, and she went back into the lab. That would have been about four years ago."

"About when I joined the firm."

"Grace and I are still in touch. The last I heard from her, she was still working in the lab. That was her first love, working on the chemicals, developing new drugs. She must be in her seventies by now. She's an amazing person. It was never easy for her, an African-American woman in a white men's business. But Mr. Duane believed in her, and she succeeded. She's a very good research physician, and also one of the wisest and most insightful people you would ever meet."

Donns sat silent for a moment. "I just had a thought," he said. "You might be able to use Grace as a resource to address your situation."

"My situation? How is that?"

"Your problem is that you need more information. What is the story behind the cancellation of this trial? How significant a risk does this drug pose? Dr. Edwards might be able to give you some perspective on that. Since she is still employed by DuAllen, she is still within the circle of confidentiality owed to the firm."

"Are you suggesting I talk to the former medical director about whether the company's drug is killing people? She was probably in charge of the early stages of the development of the drug. That seems like a tremendous risk to me."

"It seems like an option if you insist on discussing this with someone. With most people, I would agree. But Grace is as straight a shooter as you will ever find, and a person of her word. If you tell her something in confidence, your trust will be safe with her. I think Grace might be the best person to answer the questions you have. No course is free of risk, but speaking to her is one path you are allowed to take under the rule. It's your call. That's the best advice I have for you."

Ben and Donns talked some more about people in DuAllen and Block Stahl. After about an hour Ben got up to leave and they shook hands. Ben thanked Donns for his time and offered to pay him for it, but Donns declined.

"I really respect your concern for doing the right thing, and doing it the right way," the older lawyer said. "It gives me hope for the future to see young lawyers who think seriously about their responsibilities."

Driving back to Kansas City, Ben weighed the course Donns suggested. Speaking to the former medical director, without the knowledge of the lawyers working on the case, seemed suicidal. But something about Donns' calm assurance appealed to Ben. He went to Donns looking for options, and now he had one more. Yet somehow the knowledge he could do something was more frightening than the feeling he could do nothing.

Chapter 33

> "Hey, I know people," said Barry. "I got a buddy in Cleveland who can get anything done. Anything you want."
>
> "If he can do anything," said Doug, "how come he can't get out of Cleveland?"
>
> -- David Shepherd, *Palm of God*

The next day, Ben went over his January time-sheets in preparation for sending out billings. He added them up three times, not believing what he found. His January hours totaled nearly twenty percent below his usual pace. Even allowing for the holidays, that was not the kind of pace he needed when his name came before the partnership committee. During January, Ben felt as though he was working as hard as ever. The business with Shepherd, the novel and the Eonocin inquiry, must have been distracting him much more than he realized, just at the time when he needed to be at peak efficiency.

About 10:00, he received an email through the e-filing system on one of his cases. Stunned, Ben read an order denying an application for relief. He didn't anticipate any problem with the motion. Ben pulled up the application. Reading over it, he realized his work on the application was hasty and shallow, not up to the standard of his usual work.

A deep sense of shame and apprehension swept over Ben as the twin humiliations sank in.

For his whole career, Ben always took pride that diligence and reliability were his strongest assets. No one worked harder; no one maintained his standard of excellence. His January lapses not only let down those who depended on him, they threatened the image of hard work and competence at the foundation of his professional life. Ben plunged into his work, toiling furiously for the next several hours, as if he could make up for a bad month in a single day.

About four, Rick Thomas called. At first Ben feared Rick's call would yank him back into the Shepherd inquiry, distracting him from his new-found focus. But Rick just asked if Ben would meet him for drinks at a bar in the Power and Light District after work. That sounded like a great idea to Ben. It reminded him of the old days when he and Rick and their circle of friends would collect at one of the bars for good times after their long days at work. After the events of this day, Ben could really use a drink.

Rick was already well into his first beer when Ben arrived. He nodded absently as Ben slid into the seat next to him.

"So what's up?" asked Ben after he ordered a drink.

"I was wondering if you would be available Saturday to help me out, packing up my stuff for a move."

"Sure. A move? You getting a new place?"

"No," said Rick. "I'm out of here. A college buddy of mine is IT director of a firm in Cleveland. He's been on me to come work in his department for a while now, so I decided this is the time to take him up on it. So today was my last day, and I'm on the road Saturday."

The news knocked Ben back in his seat. "You're leaving? You quit?"

"Yeah. I figured, Cleveland in February. Practically paradise."

"Damn," said Ben. He took a sip of his beer and studied the bottles behind the bar. "Is this about the search?"

"What do you think?" said Rick. He left the question hanging in the air.

"Gee, man, I'm sorry. I mean, I hope the Cleveland thing works out for you, but, damn. I'm sorry. I didn't mean to cause you a problem."

Rick stared at the bubbles in his beer for a moment. Then he said, "Look, I'll be fine. I trust you know what you're doing, but I sure as hell don't. You're messing with people who aren't to be messed with. I just don't want to be here when the shit hits the HVAC."

"I know what I'm doing. I'm just doing a little research. I don't even plan to do anything with it."

"A little research? I looked up your trail. Man, you've been living in that Eonocin cabinet."

Ben took another swallow. "That bad?"

"I deleted as much of it as I could, but I couldn't get it all. I hope you know what you're doing. You better hope no one looks."

"Jeeze," said Ben.

"Look, I'll deny this on a stack of Bibles if anyone asks, but I erased a lot of stuff. That file I showed you, gone. All traces of the search, gone. Access records for both of us, nuked. I may have violated every standard of my profession and a couple of criminal laws, but that crap is vapor now."

Ben looked down at his beer. "Rick, I ... I don't know what to say. I'm sorry. And thanks."

"Well, I owed you. See you Saturday. About eight."

"Sure," said Ben. Rick dropped a bill on the bar and left. Ben raised his glass to his lips and held it, inhaling the dusky scent of the rich dark brew. Rick said "owed." Past tense.

Distracted, Ben picked at his dinner. While Melissa packed their leftovers away, Ben inserted the flash drive into his computer and examined the memo for the fourth time. He printed a copy, folded it, and stuck it into his wallet. Then he sank into the south window seat and stared at the Bartle Hall towers.

Melissa dropped into the seat opposite him. "So, what's wrong?"

"Nothing's wrong."

She leaned forward, elbows on knees, eyebrows arched. "Yoo hoo. It's me, Lis. I know you, and I know something's wrong. What is it?"

Ben flinched, and looked off toward the western skyline. "I've just got a lot on my mind. Work and all."

"You always have work and all on your mind. This is different. What's up?"

He didn't answer, but she persisted. "Is it the Shepherd thing? Did you find out something about that drug?"

He couldn't hide much from her inquisitive stare. "I did find some stuff. I can't tell you. It's confidential."

Her eyebrows arched again in an expression of disbelief. "No, really," he said. "I don't want you to know. We're not married, so there's no privilege. Someone could force you to testify. I don't want to expose you to that."

Her eyes widened. "Testify? Ben, there isn't a power in this world who could make me say anything to hurt you. Please, let me help you. Tell me."

He sighed. "I found something buried in some documents I wasn't even supposed to be looking at. It's huge, and it goes straight to the top. I may be the only person who knows – well, me, and one person who helped me. And now you. It's a bomb-shell. It's dangerous to know."

"Dangerous?"

"You've got to realize how much is at stake. What I found is evidence of deliberate fraud. They might have hidden information that will lead to people dying. The company has made nearly a billion dollars on this drug, and there's billions more in the future. There could be lawsuits, fines, criminal prosecutions. Who knows what they'd do to protect themselves?"

"My God," she said. "You're making this sound like a spy thriller."

"The thing is ..." Ben covered his face with his hands. Even talking about it stirred up his doubts and fears. "I've never dealt with something like this before. I've handled cases where plenty of money was at stake, more money than I'll ever see in my life. But this could mean people's lives – people other people love, people with something to give to the world. I've never been in a position where someone could live or die, depending on what I do."

"Oh, Ben."

"I don't know what to do. I never asked for this. I don't know why this is happening to me."

Melissa sat silent for a moment. "Okay, I know you don't always agree with me about this, but hear me out," she said. "I believe things happen for a reason. We've been assuming this whole thing is all about David and his novel. But since this drug business came up, I've been thinking. What if this is what it's about? What if this is the real story? And this is your story, not David's. It happened to you because it had to happen to you. Maybe you're the only person with the intelligence and the knowledge and the information to put it all together. Maybe of all the people who know, you're the only one who's not in on it, the only one with the conscience to do something about it."

Her comments only stirred Ben's agitation. "But I don't know what to do about it. I can't even reveal how I got the information. I'm not supposed to have it. Bringing it out could ruin me and someone who trusted me and helped me. One false step and I could lose everything I have, everything I've worked for and hoped for. My job, my career, my license. And it's not just my future any more. It's yours, too. I need to think about what I owe you."

"What you owe me? Listen." She knelt before him and placed her hands on his knees. "You need to figure out who you are, who you're here to be, and then do whatever is true to that person. That's what you owe me – nothing more, and nothing less. I think I know what the man I love will do, but you're the only one who can make that decision. Just do that, and I will be right there beside you, and we'll face it together, wherever that road takes us."

She rested her head on Ben's knees, and he leaned forward and buried his face in her hair. He still had no idea where his next steps would lead, but the path ahead seemed a little less lonely.

Chapter 34

"His Honor will see you now," said the secretary. She escorted Doug into the Mayor's office.

His Honor looked up from the pile of papers on his desk. "Graves, huh? I know everyone that matters in this town. I never heard of you."

"Just a guy working for a living," said Doug.

"Well, I got something I need you to do."

"I'll have to ask my boss."

"What do you mean, ask your boss?" snarled the Mayor.

"I work for my boss. Just like you work for your boss."

-- David Shepherd, *Belly of the Beast*

When he got in to work the next day, Ben put off the task of looking up Dr. Edwards' number for several hours. He was encouraged by Donns' testimonial, but the act of calling a highly placed person in DuAllen terrified him, even if she was no longer in a position of power.

About eleven, he logged on to the DuAllen website and located a staff directory. He found Dr. Edwards' number, listed as a research physician in one of the labs. He jotted the number on a sticky note and pasted it to his monitor. He stared at it a couple of times in the next few hours, before summoning the courage to call. He picked up his personal cell phone and punched in the number. His call went into her voice mail.

He identified himself, and then paused before leaving his carefully framed message. He left his cell phone number and hung up.

An hour or so later his phone rang. Glancing at the display, he saw a number with a 612 area code – Minneapolis, the site of DuAllen headquarters. He pressed the icon to answer the call.

A husky, amiable contralto answered his greeting. "Hello, this is Dr. Grace Edwards returning your call."

A surge of anxiety ran through Ben. He had rehearsed what he wanted to say, but the knowledge that he was talking to a highly placed former executive in the company rang alarm bells in his mind.

"Hello, Dr. Edwards. Thanks for calling me back. I am dealing with an issue regarding the process in an FDA approval application. It's quite a sensitive matter. A person I trust suggested you are someone I could look to for advice."

"Well, that's very flattering. Do you mind telling me who you spoke to?"

Ben remembered that Donns said he and Dr. Edwards were still on very good terms, so he figured it could help to drop the name. "Roger Donns. He told me about all you did for the

316 | *Ghost Writer*

company back when he was active in the firm and spoke in the most glowing terms of your expertise and discretion. I'm in need of both." It couldn't hurt to lay on the flattery pretty thickly.

"I appreciate that very much. Roger is such an extraordinary man. How can I help you?"

Ben considered his words carefully. "I have come across some information that causes me concern, about the handling of a clinical trial that may have adversely affected an NDA."

"I'll be glad to help if I can. Is this one of our company's products?"

Choppy waters here. Must be careful, Ben thought. "Yes. These events occurred recently, after your tenure as Medical Director."

"Which product?"

"Eonocin." Ben waited for a reaction.

"Hmm. I oversaw the early development of the cinefitide project, but not at the NDA stage."

Ben took a deep breath and gave her a carefully edited lead up to the question. "Did you know about the cancellation of the Axxiom clinical trial?"

"We were informed that a number of Axxiom projects were cancelled all at once."

"They cancelled all of their projects? At the same time?"

"Yes, about three years ago, a year after I stepped down. I was sorry to hear about that, as

Axxiom did a lot of excellent work for us over the years."

"Do you know why that was done?"

"I wasn't told. I assumed it was for financial reasons. Axxiom did first-class work, but they were expensive."

"One of those was the clinical trial on cinefitide for geriatric patients. Did you know anything about that?"

"That trial was planned while I was still Medical Director, but I wasn't much involved with it. My successor, Dr. Aram Vardanian, oversaw that project and would certainly be a better source of information. He is very competent and diligent."

This was getting very tricky. "The reason I am asking is that I have come across some information, very confidential information, that the cancellation of the trial might not have been for financial reasons."

"What sort of information?"

"Preliminary results may have pointed to some complications – complications that may have made approval of the NDA more difficult. My question is whether, from a practice standpoint, the cancellation of a trial with possibly adverse results would be reason for concern."

The tone of Dr. Edwards' voice grew urgent. "It would certainly be cause for concern if that was true. You always want to know as much as possible about an adverse finding, no matter what the status of the application. It's difficult for me to believe, knowing the people involved as I do, that the study would have been cancelled for that reason. It would be highly improper."

"That's what I wanted to check out with you. It seemed to me from a legal perspective that we would want to know the results, but I needed to hear your medical perspective before I look into this any further."

"What reason do you have to believe the cancellation was because of the results?"

"There is a memo."

"What does the memo say?"

"I hate to hold back information, since I got you involved with this, but this is really very sensitive and I can't share it with you at this time. I'm sorry, but I'm feeling my way very carefully here. I hope you understand."

"Well, now you have me wondering. Listen. I can make some inquiries. I might be able to find out. I'm sure you'll find there's a reasonable explanation."

A stab of anxiety jolted Ben. He wanted to know anything he could about the cancellation, but it seemed dangerous for Dr. Edwards to be poking around. "I didn't expect you to do that. I just wanted your perspective."

Dr. Edwards' voice sounded firm and decisive. "What you've said raises a serious question about the integrity of this firm. I need to know, myself."

Ben did not get the impression he would talk her out of asking her questions. "Dr. Edwards, the person who recommended I call you particularly emphasized your discretion. Please, I'm asking you, be very careful in what you say about this. I'm not making any accusations against anyone. I'm just trying to find out whether there is a problem I should bring to the attention of the appropriate people. I don't want to make any waves if it's unwarranted."

"Don't worry. I won't reveal anything about you or your memo. I know who to ask and what to ask. I will find out what happened, and hopefully put your mind at ease. I will call you back when I know anything."

Ben thanked Dr. Edwards and hung up. He was filled with trepidation at the idea of her asking around at DuAllen about the study, but at the same time the slight improvement of his chances of answering his questions about the trial intrigued him. What happened at DuAllen was out of his control, but at least he had done what he could.

Ben arrived at the office in a good mood on Friday, his anxiety over the call with Dr. Edwards eased. As he passed Lesley's cubicle, she looked up with an expression of concern.

"Valerie from the 23d floor called. Mr. Abel wants to see you. Right away."

The 23d floor was the top floor of the building, housing the executive offices of Block, Stahl. "Mr. Abel" needed no explanation. That was William Abel, the firm's principal managing partner.

Ben had met Mr. Abel twice – once during the group orientation for his associate class when he joined the firm, and another time at the firm's annual Christmas party, when Mr. Abel passed as he arrived for his ceremonial sweep through the party. Both times Mr. Abel greeted him with a handshake, but his gaze swept over Ben's eyes as if he wasn't there, moving on to the next person he was obliged to acknowledge. Ben doubted Mr. Abel would even recognize him in the elevator, or that he knew Ben's name other than as one item on a long list. Being summoned to the 23d floor to meet with Mr. Abel was either the best news a young associate could hope for, or the worst. Ben had no illusion it was the former.

Ben dropped his briefcase in his office and headed for the elevator. He wondered if he should stop in the restroom before stepping onto the elevator, but the urgency with which Lesley pronounced "right away" deterred him. Ben swiped his security card on the control panel and pressed 23. He felt a surge of surprise when the elevator began to move. Normally his security card would not give him access to the 23d floor. Someone had changed the programming just for the occasion.

When the elevator doors glided open at 23, Ben drew a quick breath. He had only been on the 23d floor once before, shepherded with a flock of new associates to a conference room for their brief meeting with Mr. Abel during their orientation. His eyes swept over the burnished walnut paneling, his feet pressed softly into the heavily padded carpet, his ears immediately picked up on the conspicuous silence of the acoustically muted background, and the rich scent of fine wood and lacquer tickled his nose. He turned to his right and saw an immaculately groomed receptionist sitting behind an intricately inlaid desk, far larger than any on Ben's floor. He walked up to the desk and said, "Ben Trovato for –"

"Mr. Abel is expecting you," she said. She gestured to a hallway running to her right. "Please wait in the foyer."

Ben trooped down the hallway, lushly carpeted and decorated with original art. He arrived at a foyer where another woman in an expensive suit sat behind an even larger, more ornate desk. Valerie, Mr. Abel's personal assistant, looked up, and without waiting for his name, said in a crisp voice, "Mr. Abel will see you now." She gestured to a pair of heavy, carved doors to her left.

Ben grasped the handle of one of the doors, which despite its great weight, swung silently and smoothly open. He stepped into a huge chamber, with a conference table, several padded chairs, extravagant artwork, and shelves and shelves of law books. A panoramic sweep of windows looked out over the Missouri River and deep into the Northland.

Mr. Abel sat at the far end of the room, behind a vast mesa of mahogany polished to a mirror-like finish. Ben padded softly up to the desk, and stood waiting for instructions. Mr. Abel did not look up from the desk, but leafed through a single legal file. He was a wiry man in his sixties, thinning gray hair sculpted and shaped like a warrior's helmet, muscles of his thin face tightly drawn into an austere scowl, reading glasses perched low on his aquiline nose. With a slight wave of his bony hand he gestured toward one of the riveted leather chairs by his desk, which Ben obediently took. Mr. Abel still did not look up or speak for some time.

Finally he said, in a stentorian voice, "Trovato." Ben jerked uncontrollably at the staccato pronunciation of his name. It sounded like an accusation.

"You are a fourth year," Mr. Abel said.

Ben felt no confidence that any kind of inflection or composed response would serve his interest. He merely said, "Yes."

"Product liability defense, discovery unit. Mark Masters is your supervisor."

"Yes," Ben piped, afraid his voice sounded shakier.

Abel closed the file and folded his hands into a steeple. His blue-gray eyes swung up to Ben's face for the first time.

"It is my understanding that you have done work on certain projects on behalf of our very good client, DuAllen Pharmaceuticals. Is that correct?"

"Yes." Ben tried to keep his voice as neutral as possible, with the slightest tilt toward warmth.

The steeple broke up and the hands lay flat on the desk. A dark current of annoyance welled up in the voice for the first time. "It is also my understanding that you are not assigned the Eonocin project. Is that so?"

Ben tried to force out another affirmative, but it would not come. He sat silent, panic rising fast through his chest.

"I take it my understanding is correct. I am informed that after you questioned a member of the Eonocin team about details of the project with no relevance to your assigned work, your supervisor spoke to you about the importance of concentrating your attention on your own work." He did not even pretend to ask a question, and Ben made no effort to answer.

The anger in his voice rose a notch. "So we were surprised when our IT department detected a remarkable surge of activity from your network address accessing the documents generally reserved for the Eonocin team. After normal working hours, and after the conversation with your supervisor."

A dark, dank tide of despair struck Ben. Everything was known. He had no secrets. He was caught, exposed, busted. Thoughts of jumping up and running from the building, never to return, crossed his mind. He sat stock still, all his muscles immobile and unresponsive, though his heart was pounding uncontrollably.

Abel planted his palms on his desk and leaned forward, lowering his head as his voice dropped into a snarl.

"Then imagine my astonishment when I received a call, late last night, from Jeffrey Lennox. You do know who Mr. Lennox is, don't you?" Ben sat frozen. "*Don't you?*" barked Abel.

"Yes," Ben said barely above a whisper. "He is the CEO of DuAllen."

"That's right. The CEO of DuAllen, a very, very valued client. Do you know how much this firm's billings to DuAllen were in the last year?"

"No, sir," Ben said. He was locked in the game now. He had to play by his opponent's rules.

"Well into eight figures. Certainly, the value of that client's good will to this firm exceeds your value by many orders of magnitude. Do you know what Mr. Lennox had to say?"

"No, sir."

"He was irate. No, he was enraged. Livid. It seems that a certain young associate in this firm has been spreading rumors in his company questioning his very integrity. He was so furious that he spoke of seeking other counsel to represent DuAllen in their various matters. He demanded an explanation."

Ben plummeted down, down into a dark ocean of guilt, betrayal, and loss. All his dreams, all he had worked for vanished from sight in the gloom of those turbid waters.

The chairman pushed back from his desk and crossed his arms. "As a result of your actions, we are in damage control mode. Early this morning Jesse Horner, one of our senior partners, and Linda Peterson, the litigator in charge of the Eonocin project, took a charter flight up to Minneapolis to meet with Mr. Lennox in person and try to save the day. But the only person who can offer an explanation is the one who created the crisis. That, Mr. Trovato, would be you."

"I can explain –" Ben began.

The chairman rolled forward and slammed his hands on the desktop. His voice rose to a near shout, laced with rage and venom. "I don't want your explanation! I am not the person to whom you owe it. Here is what will happen. You are taking a charter flight to Minneapolis, right now. Our chief of security, Mr. Bruckner, will escort you."

He gestured toward the side of the room. In a chair by the window sat a brawny man, his arms folded over his chest, a scowl imprinted on his leathery face. Ben did not even notice him before.

"Mr. Bruckner is going to take you directly to Minneapolis, where you will stand before Mr. Lennox yourself and explain your actions. Mr. Horner will represent the firm at that meeting.

Understand that he has the authority to fire you on the spot. If it were up to me, Mr. Bruckner would be escorting you into the street at this very moment, while we do whatever is necessary to protect the firm with regard to your license and your employability. But Mr. Horner thought it best that you be brought before Mr. Lennox yourself. So that is where you are going. Now." He opened the legal file on his desk and looked down at it. He was finished.

The burly man by the window stood up and walked over to Ben. "Let's go," he said in a gruff voice. He turned and walked toward the door. Ben scrambled to his feet and followed.

Mr. Bruckner strode down the hall to the foyer, Ben tagging behind him. As they stepped into the elevator lobby, Ben said, "If we're flying to Minne-apolis, I better make a stop at the restroom first."

"No," said Bruckner. The elevator arrived and he stepped on. Ben had no choice but to follow. Ben stopped the elevator at his floor to retrieve his coat from the cloakroom. Bruckner stepped between him and the hallway to the workspace, making it clear he was not permitted to go to his office.

They rode the elevator down to street level, where a car was waiting to pick them up. Bruckner opened the back door and gestured for Ben to climb in. It felt more like an act of custody than courtesy. Bruckner spoke not a word during the twenty minute drive to Kansas City International Airport. The car drove directly onto the tarmac of a private section of the airport, where a small light jet was waiting for them.

Bruckner opened the door and waited for Ben to climb in. Ben took the bench seat facing forward and thought Bruckner would sit opposite him, but he took the seat next to the pilot. After about fifteen minutes of checkins, the plane rolled down the runway and took off.

Ben had nothing to do but look out the window and check his email occasionally. He sent Lesley an email telling her he was on an assignment and didn't know when he would be back. He wondered, would he ever be back?

He stared out at the airplane window at the banks of clouds below. He tried to rehearse what he might say, but he felt he was walking to the altar as the ritual sacrifice. What could he possibly say that would placate Lennox? That he knew what he had done? That his flagship product might be killing people? He thought about what he might do, where he might go if he was fired, as he almost certainly would be. That depressed him too much, so he struggled to keep his mind off that train of thought. Two hours in flight crept by at an agonizing pace. With all this time, Ben should have his opening perfected, his arguments plotted, his facts and conclusions all mustered in ideal order. But nothing took shape in his mind. He was a lamb heading down the chute toward the blades, and he couldn't do a thing to stop it.

Chapter 35

"And who are you to dictate terms to me?"
snarled the police chief.

"Just some dumb guy who knows who
paid you," said Doug.

-- David Shepherd, *Belly of the Beast*

The plane landed at Minneapolis-St. Paul
International two hours later. A car was waiting for
them on the tarmac. Fifteen minutes later, they
pulled into a modern office building Ben
recognized from photographs as the headquarters
of DuAllen Pharmaceutical.

For the second time in the day, Ben stepped
out of an elevator on the executive floor of a large
business to face the wrath of its head. This time,
unlike the solemn mahogany grandeur of the Block
Stahl executive suite, the office was designed in a
chic, expensive contemporary theme, flooded with
light from panoramic windows and a soaring sky-
light.

The security officer led Ben and Bruckner to a
foyer, where a woman sat behind a glass desk
bearing the nameplate "Carol." She gestured to a
teak door, elaborately carved in a Pacific style.
Bruckner remained in the foyer as the security
officer opened and held the door for Ben to enter.

Ben stepped into a long conference room, with
a panoramic window looking out over a wood

adjoining the office park. At the far end of the table sat the participants. Ben recognized the silver-haired man at the farthest seat on the left side of the table as Jesse Horner, a senior Block Stahl partner. Next to him sat a woman in her forties, whom Ben surmised to be Linda Peterson, the litigator in charge of the Eonocin case. Opposite them sat a fortyish man with dark hair and eyes, and vaguely Middle Eastern features. Ben guessed he was Aram Vardanian, the company's medical director. Presiding at the head of the table was a stocky man with thinning brown hair and horn rim glasses, whom Ben recognized as Jeffrey Lennox, chief executive officer of DuAllen. In the photos Lennox wore an expansive smile, but his face now was knotted in anger. All the other participants were dressed in perfectly tailored suits, but Lennox wore a white shirt with a tie loose around his neck. He glanced up at Ben, and his eyes blazed. No one invited Ben to sit, so he stood at the end of the table, like a defendant in the dock.

"So," Lennox said, his voice crackling with anger and sarcasm. "This, I presume, is my accuser?"

Jesse Horner spoke in an even tone. "Ben Trovato, correct?"

"Yes," said Ben, his voice coming out tense and fragile.

"Well," said Lennox. "Thank you for taking the time to join us." He did not sound the least bit thankful. "I have asked you all here because I am told that someone from your law firm has made calls to people in our organization spreading slanderous rumors about my integrity. Obviously, I am interested in hearing exactly what I am accused of. I am told the calls in question have been traced back to you, Mr. ... Trovato? I'd like to know exactly what I have done to offend you."

Ben's stomach seemed to be attempting an escape from his body, but his mind continued to function. Wait a minute ... calls? I only made one call. Traced to me? Did Dr. Edwards go straight to Lennox? Did she betray me? He struggled to find words to say.

"I came across ... I am not accusing anyone of anything ... I was just investigating, no, uh, trying to get information –"

"You were trying to get information?" Lennox exclaimed in a mocking tone. "My, my. It seems we have given your firm so much information that you have been charging us outrageous amounts of money just to go through it all. Pray tell, what information could we possibly have missed?"

"I had information ... I was informed ... I learned there was a study. A clinical trial that was canceled. I was trying to find out ... find out why. That's all. I was just asking a question about protocol, I meant no ... no aspersions –"

"A trial? Why it was canceled? Now, Mr. Trovato, and *please* correct me if I am wrong, you called a member of our staff to ask questions about Eonocin. From what these people tell me, it turns out you were not even involved with our Eonocin case. In fact, from what I understand, you were *meddling* in something that was *none of your business!"*

"I made an inquiry," Ben said, hating the equivocal, apologetic words spilling out of him. "I had a concern. I was just trying to find out whether it was a concern I should raise with the appropriate ..."

"You had a *concern,"* Lennox interrupted. "You had a concern which was, I repeat, *none of your fucking business.* Pardon my French." He glared down the table at Ben.

Play the Doctor Edwards card. You have to.

What? No way. She betrayed me. She went straight to Lennox. That's why I'm here.

You don't know that. Did you hear what he said? They traced the call to your number. If Edwards told him you called, why would they trace the number? You have to play the card. You have nothing else.

Ben had no better ideas. He summoned all his courage and looked Lennox in the eye. "I had information that you ordered the cancellation of a clinical trial that was going to show bad numbers on cardiac incidents. On the eve of an FDA submission." He heard a sharp intake of breath from Linda Peterson, and Dr. Vardanian stiffened. "I called Dr. Edwards because a trustworthy source advised me she was the best person to tell me whether that was a problem I should pursue."

Lennox seemed momentarily stalled. He double-clutched for a moment, then said, "You called Dr. Edwards. You called a former top executive on my team, who is *not* a part of the process. You admit that?"

"Yes." answered Ben. His anxiety fell away. At this moment, the only weapon he had was the truth. You son of a bitch. I know and you know what you did. You're attacking me because you are afraid of what I know. If you're going to destroy my career, it won't be without a fight. "I was concerned ... I *am* concerned that information about a potential health risk has not been disclosed."

"Listen, you twerp," snarled Lennox. "I hire your law firm; I pay you a great deal of money to look out for my interests. To do what I say. I do not hire you to have junior attorneys calling up my top people about your *concerns*," he pronounced the word with exaggerated contempt, "and making problems for me. This is none ..." -- he pounded the table between each word – "... of your ... damn ... business! And if your firm doesn't stand up for me and ream your ass out for meddling in my business, I'll find one that will!"

He glared at Ben. Ben needed to say something. He gathered up every iota of resolve he could summon. "If I'm wrong, show me. I want to hear it from Dr. Edwards. Bring Dr. Edwards in. If she tells me I'm wrong, if she tells me what you did is perfectly all right, I'll accept that. I won't bother you again. But I want to hear it from her."

Lennox sprang to his feet, his face contorted with rage. "Dr. Edwards works for me, not for you!" He leaned forward on both hands, his face flushed, veins of his neck bulging. *"Who the hell do you think you are?"*

Ben realized that everything he had done, everything he ever hoped for, all hung in the balance, depending on what he said in that moment. But his mind was blank. He couldn't think of another thing to say.

`You know. Tell him. Tell him who you are.`

Ben swallowed and spoke deliberately. "I am a lawyer who does discovery ten hours a day, six days a week. I know the law. I know our obligations. And I know that if that study exists, the law requires us to disclose it."

Lennox rocked backward, as if hit by a blow. He stared at Ben for a moment, his mouth working but nothing coming out. He swung his head to his right toward Horner. "Are you gonna ... are you gonna let him ... what are you gonna do?"

Ben braced himself. This is where the ax falls.

But Horner didn't speak. He sat immobile, his eyes cast down in thought for a long moment. Then he said in a calm voice, "I would guess everyone at this table values Dr. Edwards's point of view as much as I do. If she has something to say about this, I for one would like to hear it."

Lennox stared at him for a moment, his jaw quivering as if to speak. Then he reached out and slammed a hand on the intercom in front of him. "Carol!" he barked. "Page Dr. Edwards to the conference room."

He sat down and lapsed into silence. Ben felt awkward standing at the end of the table, so he took the seat next to Linda Peterson. I don't need any damned invitation, he thought. Not at this point.

They all waited in silence as thick as smoke for what seemed like an interminable time, probably about ten minutes. Finally the door opened, and an older black woman wearing a teal lab coat walked in, safety glasses perched in her silver hair. Her lined, friendly face swept over the assembled group.

"Well, Jeffrey," she said in a warm, booming contralto Ben recognized from his conversation with Dr. Edwards. "It's been a while since I've been invited to these lofty quarters. To what do I owe the privilege?"

She greeted the participants around the table. "Jesse! So great to see you again. It's been too long. Linda, hello, hello; we're so proud of what you've been doing for us. Aram." She looked at Ben, evidently the only person in the room with whom she was not on a first name basis. "Hello."

"Grace," acknowledged Lennox. He gestured toward the seats to his left. She circled the table and took a seat next to Dr. Vardanian.

"Dr. Edwards," said Lennox stiffly. "As you know, these people are from Block Stahl, who represent us in a number of our cases. Apparently this young man has some questions he would like to ask you about the Eonocin project."

"Well, as you know, I was only involved in the early stages with Eonocin, but I'll try to help in any way I can."

She turned to face Ben. Ben concentrated on formulating his questions.

"Dr. Edwards, my name is Ben Trovato. We spoke yesterday on the phone."

"Oh oh," she said. "I guess I know what this is about."

"Yes," said Ben. "I asked you a question about a memo I came across. Regarding a clinical trial in the latter stages of the process."

"Excuse me," she said. "Do you have a copy of that memo?"

Ben remembered the printout he stuffed in his wallet. "As a matter of fact, I do." He reached for his wallet and pulled out the folded rectangle of paper. Everyone in the room seemed riveted as Ben unfolded it. Dr. Vardanian gasped audibly.

"May I see it?" asked Dr. Edwards.

Linda Peterson spoke for the first time. "I think we'd all like to see that. Can we have copies made?"

Lennox rang for Carol. Ben didn't want to let the paper out of his sight, so he followed her to the copier. She made five copies and handed them to Ben. He returned to the conference room and passed them out. "I'll give you a moment to read this," he said, although all five were already deeply engrossed in the memo, poker faces all around.

Ben waited as long as he could stand, about a minute. The memo was short, but everyone seemed to be rereading it without looking up. Finally he said, "Okay, Dr. Edwards, my question is – "

Dr. Edwards turned to Lennox. "Is this true?" she said sharply.

A startled expression crossed Lennox's face. "What?"

"Is this true? Did you order Aram to kill a study showing a cardiac signal?"

"I ... I ..."

She swung her gaze to Dr. Vardanian. "Did he?"

Dr. Vardanian said nothing, but his eyes were 15-balls.

"The methodology ..." stuttered Lennox. "We thought the methodology might be off. They might have undercorrected for the age risk. It could be an anomaly."

Dr. Edwards shot him a penetrating glance, then addressed Vardanian again. "How much of a signal? How bad?"

Vardanian mumbled some numbers in relation to statistical significance.

Dr. Edwards parked her forehead on her palm. "Oh, Jesus!" After a moment she looked up and spoke again to Lennox. "Okay. Sometimes the methodology is bad. Sometimes you get an anomaly in a study. But you don't bury it. You find out whether it was an anomaly or something real. You report it, you figure out what was wrong, you fix it, and you run it again. "

"Run it again?" exclaimed Lennox. "Jesus, Grace! We were ready to go into Phase III! Running it again would have set us back a year, maybe two!"

"If that's what it takes to be sure it's safe, that's what you do."

"It would be a big fucking red flag! It took eighteen months to get the NDA through as it is. The vast majority of our patients love it."

"Unless it kills them."

"We don't know that it's killing anyone."

"That's just the point. You don't know."

"But this is a great drug. It practically cures Type II. Christ, Grace, we've got two billion tied up in this drug!"

"Is that what it comes down to? It's okay to cut a corner if the stakes are high enough?"

Lennox looked as if his face were about to burst. "Have you forgotten who you are speaking to?"

"Have you forgotten who gave you your tour of the building your first day here? Jeffrey, we built this company on the principle that the health and safety of patients always comes first. When did that change?"

Lennox dropped back into his seat, and sat silent for a moment. "You know, Grace," he said in a low growl, "if they succeed, if patients stop taking this drug, people will die. More people will die of the disease than would have from the side effect."

"Maybe they will," Dr. Edwards replied. "But you have to tell them. It's their decision, Jeffrey. Not ours." They glared at each other across the table in silence.

Linda Peterson turned to Ben. "Do you know any more? Is there anything besides this memo?"

Ben described briefly what he learned about the Axxiom study.

She turned to Jesse Horner and they conferred in whispers. Then she looked back at Ben. "Okay, you can go now. We'll take care of it."

Ben pushed to his feet. He wanted to turn and flee from the room, get away while he still had a job, a career. But something made him stop. He had come this far. He couldn't leave until he knew.

"Excuse me," he said. "I mean no disrespect, but what do you mean when you say you'll take care of it?"

"Don't worry, Ben," said Jesse Horner. "We know about the trial now. We'll find out what happened, and if it's responsive, we'll disclose it. We'll do what's right."

Ben could not think of anything else to say. "Okay, thank you," he said, and he walked away toward the door.

As he left the conference room, Linda Peterson sprang up and followed him into the foyer. Mr. Bruckner, sitting outside, stood up to join them. Peterson pulled out her smart phone, punched the screen, and lifted it to her ear. "Hello, Bill? Linda. I just stepped out of the meeting. This thing Trovato found? It's real."

She paused. "We don't know how bad yet, but it looks serious. Jesse and I are going to stay here and find out what happened. I'll get a team on it right away. I'm sending Trovato back to main office."

She listened for a moment. "What? No, no. He's fine. In fact, it's a damn good thing he found this before they did. I'll call you when we know more. Okay. Bye."

She folded up the phone and addressed Mr. Bruckner. "Take Mr. Trovato back to main." She turned to Ben. "I'm going to email Jennifer Saxton to take her team over to Axxiom and get that study. Brief her on everything you know when you get back." She turned and disappeared back into the conference room.

Bruckner said to Ben, "Let's go." He turned and walked toward the elevator.

As Ben passed Carol at her desk, he said, "Thank you." She smiled warmly and nodded. Ben guessed she didn't hear that phrase often working for Jeffrey Lennox.

As they entered the elevator lobby, Ben said to Bruckner, "Can I use the restroom now?"

"Sure."

How about that, thought Ben. There are four words in his vocabulary.

They drove in silence to the airport and back to the plane. Again, Bruckner directed Ben into the passenger compartment and took the seat by the pilot. As the pilot prepared for takeoff, Ben glanced nervously at the only door, located behind the pilot's seat. A terrible thought seized him. What if Bruckner had orders to "take care of" the problem by tossing him out of the plane? No, that couldn't be. But no one else knows about the trial.

He eyed the back of Bruckner's head nervously. Ben was pretty trim and fit, but Bruckner was built like a linebacker. Ben imagined himself hurtling through the air, plunging toward a fate of being crushed an inch thick in an Iowa cornfield. How would his parents feel? What about Melissa?

An idea took hold of Ben. If there was the slightest chance Bruckner was planning to throw him from the plane, maybe the knowledge that someone else knew where Ben was might discourage him. Ben pulled out his cell phone and punched the icon for Melissa's number. She was at work, so her voice mail came on. Ben spoke in a voice a little louder than necessary, to make sure Bruckner heard him.

"Hi, it's me. The firm flew me to Minneapolis for a meeting. But we're done and I'm in the plane coming back. I should be home around dinner time. Talk to you then. Love you." Ben paused, and said in a low voice, "I love you."

He disconnected the call and thought about calling Lesley for good measure. Or Rick. Did he have Rick's number? Rick would understand.

Ben shook his head. This is crazy. No one's throwing you out of the plane. The plane was too small. The pilot would know too. Nobody just falls out of planes. Conspiracy theories are the first sign of insanity.

As the plane began its taxi down the runway, Ben leaned back and remembered what Jesse Horner said. He didn't say, "We'll fix it" or "we'll take care of it." He said, "We'll do what's right." People thinking of murder don't talk like that. Sometimes you just have to believe that people mean what they say.

Chapter 36

> That's it. The trail was cold. She was as good as gone. Doug stumbled into the alley and slumped against the wall.
>
> -- David Shepherd, *Hand of Kindness*

Ben's fears proved unfounded. The flight back was uneventful and boring. They landed at Kansas City International about 3:00, and stepped into the car waiting on the tarmac. On the way back, Ben insisted on stopping at a fast food restaurant, since he hadn't eaten all day. Bruckner scowled, but he ordered a burger as well.

They arrived back at the office about 3:30. After Bruckner released him from custody in the garage, Ben went straight to Jennifer's office on the fourteenth floor. Jennifer acknowledged she had received an enigmatic email from Linda Peterson instructing her to go over to Axxiom on Monday and collect everything they had on some clinical trial she never heard of before. She listened open-mouthed as he laid out what he knew about the Axxiom study, minus a few strategic details, and the confrontation with Lennox. Ben finished his presentation and hurried out before she could recover her composure enough to start asking questions he didn't really want to answer.

When Ben returned to his own floor, he arrived at Lesley's cubicle to see her and Mark standing by her desk. They both looked at him, questions in their eyes. Ben paused for a moment and tried to decide what to say. Then he smiled and said, "You know what? I'm going home." He turned around and left the office without picking up his briefcase for the first time in four years. He felt light as a feather.

When he got back to his apartment, Ben dropped into the cushions of the north end window seat. He glanced at his cell phone. The time was ten after four. Melissa would still be at work until 4:30, so he set the phone down on the cushion beside him; it would be better to wait until then to call her. As he leaned back into the welcoming comfort of the cushions, a wave of exhaustion swept over him. All the adrenaline from the confrontation in the meeting dissipated, leaving him exhausted and limp. Since he couldn't call Melissa for another twenty minutes, maybe he could just relax and recover from the stress of the day. He closed his eyes and a very peaceful feeling came over him, very relaxed, very ...

Ben awoke with a start. The apartment and the skyline outside were dark, and the streetlights glowed. Ben reached for his phone, but didn't find it. He sat up and saw it had fallen onto the floor. He picked it up and pressed the screen – the clock said it was 7:25. Had he really fallen asleep for three hours? He checked the call log. It showed three calls from Melissa, two from Lesley, and one from Mark. Why didn't he hear it ring? He realized he never turned the ringer back on after silencing it for the meeting in Minneapolis. The vibration of the phone must have shaken it off the seat, and he never even woke up as it clattered onto the floor.

He pressed the speed dial icon to call Melissa. She answered immediately. "Ben! Are you all right? I called three times after I got your message, and you didn't answer. I was getting worried! I even checked the news to see if there was a plane crash!"

"No, I'm fine. It's so stupid. I just fell asleep. I'm sorry."

"You were in Minneapolis? What was that all about."

"Oh, Lis, it was the most incredible day. I think we've turned the corner on the Eonocin thing. I think it's all going to come out now."

"Oh, Ben! How did it happen? Tell me everything!"

"I want to, and I will, but I just can't now. I'll tell you everything tomorrow. But, what's up with you? What are you doing?"

"Me?" She laughed. "Oh, nothing much. I was just reading. I'm rereading *Hand of Kindness*. I think it's my favorite of the Doug Graves novels."

"Read it to me."

"What?"

"Just read it out loud. I just want to hear you read it. "

She let go a small nervous laugh, but it was one of surprise, not embarrassment. "Do you want me to start from the beginning?"

"No, no, just, wherever you are. Just start reading where you were out loud. I just want to listen."

"Okay. No, wait, I know what to read. Let me find this. Here it is. This is one of my favorite scenes. In this scene, Doug has traced this woman to New Orleans, but he's lost the trail. Now he's alone, and tired, and broke, and doesn't know where to go next. That's where this picks up." The tone of her voice changed as she began to read. Ben sank back into the cushions and closed his eyes, surrendering to the rhythm of her voice as she melted into the story:

> Doug closed his eyes and leaned back against the ancient saloon's brick wall. His hands fell flat against the bricks. He felt their rough, gritty texture, worn away by decades of exposure to weather, to the wear and tear, to all the attacks the city made on them. He couldn't move, couldn't summon any response from his muscles, couldn't think of anything to ask of them. It seemed his whole body was melding into the brick, becoming just another layer of the dirt and grime the street deposited there. He imagined himself still there years later, just another pattern time

carved onto the hard surface of the wall.

The sensations of the city melted together into a hum in the back of his mind as he let go. Suddenly, jostling its way to the front of the dulling sensations that bumbled in the foreground of his brain, a familiar scent insinuated itself into his mind. It was the sharp, sweet smell of jasmine. He realized it must be wafting down to him from a crepe jasmine vine wrapping around the streetlight opposite the wall. He focused on the distinct tinge of the scent. As he did, other odors crept in around the edges of his awareness: the oily scent of smoke from the cars passing in the street, the lingering weight of the passed rainstorm, a musk from the pools of dirty rainwater still accumulated in the gutter and the pockets in the street. Somewhere someone was cooking, shrimp or maybe crawdad, liberally seasoned with peppers, onions, garlic, and spices. He heard the sizzle of a pan, not far away, or maybe he imagined it. Then other sounds – the clicking of streetcar wheels a block or so away, the whirr of tires on uneven pavement, footfalls of people passing by, men's and women's voices rising and falling, talking, shouting, laughing at unheard jokes. Then, just as the jasmine had drilled its way through the fog in his mind, a sound bored through all the others and took hold of his attention. It started tentatively at first, a soft, buzzing drone from a saxophone. At first it explored, a note here and there, a quick run up and down a chord, a few disconnected phrases, searching for a tune. Then it found what it was looking for, and it began to sing, a slow, melancholy air. Out of the sadness it wound, out of the loneliness and pain and defeat. It gathered strength and began to soar, running through the flats and the sevenths and ninths, and the hard edges and endless comfort of the blues. Its fingers circled around Doug and overpowered the inertia of his muscles, pried him away from the wall, and it wrapped around him like a blanket and pulled him, like a firm but gentle hand, away from the wall and into itself.

Doug found himself moving, following that sound, guided by it. There would be music, and succulent food and rich red wine, and people talking, laughing, singing, and that was where Doug needed to be. Bourbon Street wanted to dance, and Doug didn't mind if he did.

Melissa's voice played on, moving the story forward. Ben surrendered to the familiar lilt. It wrapped around him, carried him away, away from Minneapolis, away from Grand Boulevard, away to a New Orleans of memory, where the living was easy and the good times rolled.

Chapter 37

> When the writer is on fire with a story, he ceases to feel fatigue. The demands of normal life fade to insignificance. He has no purpose, no reason for being, no other need until the marriage of the story and the page is consummated.
>
> -- David Shepherd, The Writer's Journey

As Ben drove home at 6:00 on the Friday of Presidents Day weekend, thick currents of snow made visibility even worse in the fading gray dusk. Melissa left earlier to spend the long weekend with her family. She asked him to come with her for the weekend, but Ben declined. After he guided his car into the garage, he texted her, and she responded that she was safe at her parents' house, to his relief. He didn't like the prospect of her driving her little car in a snowstorm.

Ben contemplated what he might do with his weekend. Usually when Melissa was away, he would put in time at the office for much of the weekend. But for the first time he could remember since joining the firm, he was caught up on everything. He wasn't sure what to do by himself. He could camp out in front of the television, or maybe he could read. Only three stories remained in *The Winterset Formation*; maybe he could finish the book and start on one of the Doug Graves novels.

His real hope was that Shepherd would come to work on the novel, but he had heard nothing from the writer's ghost for more than a week and a half, not since the encouragement the voice gave him during the Minneapolis meeting.

After heating up a frozen dinner, Ben carried his computer to the window seat and sat down in the north end. He started up the computer and tried calling with the inner voice again. *Are you there? I need to talk to you. Can you hear me?*

Still nothing. Ben wondered how long he should continue paying attention, at what point he should give up and move on with his life.

Maybe Melissa was right when she theorized that bringing the Eonocin problem to light was the real business of Shepherd's lingering presence in the world of the living, and the novel just wasn't meant to be. The last time they worked on it, Shepherd seemed unhappy with it, complaining it was going down the same dead end street as the manuscript he burned. Early in their collaboration Ben would have been delighted to be rid of the Shepherd project, but now it left him downcast. He had come to care about the characters and about seeing their story to a conclusion. Now he would be left in limbo, just like all of Doug Graves' fans.

The night before, he attended another meeting of the writers' group. They did some writing exercises, and the members of the group praised the descriptive scene Ben wrote. Eric in particular flattered Ben and encouraged him to work on his writing. Josh gave them a series of writing prompts, suggestions to get started writing. Maybe he could work on some of the exercises and have something to show the group at the next meeting.

He pulled out Josh's list of writing prompts and studied it. The first read, "Write down the first ten story ideas that come into your head, in one sentence." Ben chuckled and typed on the computer, "A man moves into an apartment and hears the voice of a deceased former occupant." He leaned back and stared off into the thickening snowstorm, trying to think of another idea. He remembered the first story in *The Winterset Formation,* about the man riding through the desolate Kansas landscape. He typed, "A man's desperation grows after his small car slides off a little-traveled rural road in a heavy snowstorm." He turned his thoughts to a third idea.

Oh, good. Are you ready to work?

Startled at the sudden appearance of the voice, Ben almost dropped his computer. *Is that you? I haven't heard from you in over a week. I didn't know if you would be coming again.*

Well, here I am. And there's much to do. We need to get to work.

Sure, sure. But first let me tell you about the Eonocin thing. Here's what I think will happen ...

No time, no time. We have to get to work.

No time? But the last time we spoke, it was all you wanted to hear about.

That was when I didn't know what to do about the novel. Now I do. The novel is what matters. Let's review what happens in the first few chapters.

Ben opened up the chapter outline document and studied the first few chapters. *Okay, Chapter one, the body of Kansas City socialite Regina Colston is found in a creek in rural Kansas. She has been strangled. She is still wearing the gown she had on the last time she was seen, leaving a gala event in Kansas City. Chapter Two. Regina's boyfriend, a penniless artist from Westport, is charged with her murder. Turned down by every other lawyer in town, he hires Barry Grounds to defend him. Chapter Three. Barry tries to get Doug to investigate the case. Doug, deep in debt with hospital bills from his time in a coma, is angry with Barry and refuses, but relents because he needs the money ...*

Okay, stop right there. Keep One and Two. Delete everything starting with Three.

Delete everything? That's twenty-one chapters. Don't you want to go through them and see what you want to keep?

Nope. We're starting over. Are you ready? Chapter Three: ...

Quickly Ben copied the first two chapters and pasted them into a new document. No way he was going to delete 50,000 words he already typed. But Shepherd plunged onward.

```
Barry hated hospitals. Maybe they
reminded him of all the hours he spent
trolling them in search of clients. But
walking into this one, he felt a sharp
stab of guilt and regret ...
```

Before, Shepherd usually spun out his text in a slow, conversational manner, as though he was telling a story. Ben could usually keep up with him in typing. This time, however, Shepherd barked out his dictation in a steady stream of words, as though he knew exactly what he planned to say and was in a hurry to get it out. Ben pounded furiously on the keyboard trying to keep up, and often asked him to stop so he could catch up with words he missed. Needing an optimal typing position, he moved from the window to his desk. Shepherd paused when Ben needed a moment, but quickly unleashed a new torrent of words as soon as Ben indicated he was ready.

As he churned out the text he was given, Ben realized that whatever doubts Shepherd felt about the direction of the story were gone. The tale unfolding under his fingers was completely new and different. Shepherd had not given up on the story; over the last ten days of silence, he completely rethought it, and found an entirely new point of view and direction.

For hours they continued. Ben pounded at the keyboard until his fingers hurt. He figured Shepherd's burst of energy would take him through a chapter or two, and then he would get a break. But the writer drove relentlessly on. As the hours passed, Ben lost any sense of the passage of time. He was an instrument of Shepherd's creation, a vessel through which the new story passed. He found himself typing as a virtuoso plays the piano, oblivious to the mechanics of the process as the product spilled out on the screen in front of him.

All evening they continued, deep into the night. Ben requested a break only when he desperately needed one, to use the bathroom or run water over his aching fingers. As soon as he returned Shepherd resumed his rapid-fire dictation. They continued until the early hours of the morning. Every muscle in Ben's body ached, but still he kept his concentration and touched the keys with his stiff fingers. Finally at 3:00 am, after a full day at work and eight hours of typing, Ben lost the ability to listen and type at all. Begging a break from Shepherd, he staggered to his couch and fell down on it. He was asleep within a moment.

He awoke at the sound of his alarm going off in his bedroom. Since he never made it to the bedroom, he never reset the alarm. He pulled his cell phone from his pocket. The display told him it was 7:00. He had slept less than four hours.

`Are you ready? You've had your rest. Let's go.`

Ben prided himself on his ability to work at full tilt on very little sleep. He pushed off the couch, took a quick shower, fried himself an egg and brewed a pitcher of coffee. Clutching a steaming mug, he headed to his desk.

I'm good. Let's go.

Go they did. Shepherd immediately picked up where they left off, and Ben kept up with him, word by word. All day they worked. Ben developed a technique of lightly touching the keys that hurt his fingers less, with only small compromises in his speed and accuracy. Shepherd pushed on with confidence.

Ben fell into the rhythm of the story. He saw where it was going, how it worked, where it circled back and branched into subplots. By the afternoon they were a smooth and efficient machine, generating a blizzard of virtual pages on the screen of the computer. Occasionally Ben glanced at the word count in the lower left corner of his screen. 15,000, then 20,000 came and went. Ben kept the pots of coffee coming, and made himself a peanut butter sandwich in the early afternoon. As he gulped it down, he remembered he would have spent most Saturdays at the office at least until now, but it never even occurred to him to go in, nor did he care. He quickly returned to the computer and resumed work. Shepherd, of course, was waiting for him. 25,000 flew by not long after.

He continued pounding away as fast as Shepherd could dictate the text. Previously, Ben found he could type faster and more accurately by tuning out the meaning of the words and reproducing the words he was given. Now, he couldn't help but listen to the story as it developed. After all the months of typing and reading, Doug Graves and his adventures seemed like a part of Ben's life, and he listened with the curiosity of an old friend anxious to know what was happening with the cranky detective. He found himself shooting ahead of Shepherd when he paused, finishing sentences before the writer spoke them, and often getting them right.

They continued at a rapid pace until Ben noticed the light outside was beginning to fade. He glanced at the clock in the lower right corner of the computer screen and saw it was 5:13, nearly ten hours after he began typing in the morning. His fingers were aching and he needed a break, so he told Shepherd to hold his thoughts. Ben put on his coat and walked down the street to Crown Center to get some dinner. The brisk February air and the crunch of snow under his feet provided a welcome break from his typing marathon. After a quick dinner he headed back to the apartment and fired up the computer a little after six. The word count stood at 27,848.

Shepherd was ready when he returned, the next several chapters queued up and ready to dictate. They resumed the furious pace. Regenerated, Ben attacked his task with zeal. They worked as one mind, the words flowing from Shepherd's inner voice to Ben's hands. By now, though, they collaborated. Ben pointed out occasional errors, such as conveying information already covered in a previous chapter, place names that slipped Shepherd's memory, suggesting sentence completions and alternate phrasings, advice Shepherd accepted without resentment. Far into the night they worked. By the time fatigue overwhelmed Ben, the word count reached 40,280. Ben plodded into his bedroom and collapsed, fully dressed, onto the bed. Before falling asleep he glanced at his alarm clock. It read 2:21. He had been typing for nearly 19 hours.

His alarm clock went off again at 7:00 am. Ben dragged himself out of bed and into the shower. All day Sunday they reprised the pace of Saturday's efforts. When Ben declared a break about 5:00, the word count reached 55,750. He took a leisurely walk after dinner, and returned to the apartment about 7:00 for another marathon. He collapsed about 4:00 a.m., with the word count at 68,734. They were submerged deep in the development of the plot. Ben wanted in the worst way to know where it was going, but his brain and body wouldn't cooperate, and he found himself typing gibberish, so he gave up and again collapsed onto his bed.

The alarm clock roused him again three hours later. Monday, Presidents Day. Normally Ben thought of legal holidays as days he could wear casual dress to the office. This time, however, he never entertained a thought of going in. By 7:20, the computer was up and running, and Shepherd was ready for him. All day they worked, at the same deliberate but driven pace. By the time Ben needed a break about four, the setup to the climactic sequence lay ahead.

Ben returned after about an hour.

`We're really making progress here. Do you want to take the evening off? You've been working hard.`

No. I want to get done. I want to finish this.

`Finish? We have eight or nine chapters left. That's maybe 20,000 words. If we do 1500 words an hour, it will take more than ten hours.`

We'll do it. Let's go.

They dived into the work. The last light drained away and darkness crept up from the street. For hours he pounded away as the story bent toward its conclusion. The fatigue began to eat at Ben, and his fingers ached with each keystroke, but he attacked the task with the kind of determination that made him so successful in his work.

As they drew toward the end of the novel, Ben loaded up his printer and began printing out the manuscript. Over the last several hours, the pages churned out as Ben typed, and he stacked them in a growing pile on the desk.

Finally Ben sank into the north window seat as the first traces of dawn began to filter in through the window. Every muscle in his body ached, and a helmet of fog hung around his head from sleeplessness. But he pulsed with a sense of jubilation like none he ever felt before, for the sheaf of papers resting on the window cushion in front of him, the better part of a ream thick, was the completed manuscript of *Heart of a Creek,* the final work of the late David Shepherd.

He turned on his phone, idle on the charger for the past two days. The screen showed seven missed calls from Melissa. Of course. She probably called from Sedalia. She certainly called as soon as she got back. He half expected she would be banging on his door at any moment.

He pressed an icon to speed dial her number. She answered immediately, although her voice sounded sleepy. "Ben? I called and called but you didn't pick up. Are you all right? Are you mad at me? I could hardly sleep."

"I'm fine," said Ben. "Shepherd came back. We've been working all weekend."

"What?" She clearly just woke up and was struggling to understand. "You've been working? On ... on the novel?"

"It's done."

"Done?"

"*Heart of a Creek.* It's done."

The phone was silent for a moment. Then she said, "I'll be right over," and hung up.

He put down his phone and picked up the sheaf of papers. He ran his thumb through the stack of over 400 pages. He sat in the north window seat and gazed down Grand Boulevard, watching for her blue Mini Cooper.

A parade of emotions passed through him, but a mounting excitement was the most powerful. He thought about how thrilled she would feel to be the first person to read the last Shepherd novel. He rehearsed handing the manuscript to her and enjoying her exhilaration. Of all the emotions coursing through him, the strongest was delight that he could do that for her, that he could provide her that once-in-a-lifetime experience, that he could give her that joy. He could hardly wait.

For some reason he thought of the first time he sat in the window seat, when he heard the voice that turned out to be Shepherd, on the first day he was alone in the apartment. He remembered sitting there after Robin left, waiting for Melissa to come for the first time. He recalled what he thought about then, flush with the passion Robin inspired in him. He had evaluated whether to stay in his relationship with Melissa. He had wondered whether she was good enough for him. He could have broken her heart. She could have been gone from his life, by his own choice. But he didn't make that choice. She still loved him, and she was coming to share this moment with him. A wave of gratitude welled up through him, and crested in his eyes.

A few minutes later, the blue marble rolled down Grand Boulevard and disappeared under the façade of his building. He wiped his eyes and walked to the foyer to wait for her. Moments later he heard the elevator in the hallway, the soft thump of her shoes on the carpet, and her knock on the door.

He opened the door and she stepped in. She had not taken the time to do her makeup or fix her hair, and she looked as if she had just climbed out of bed and thrown a sweatshirt and jeans on. But she beamed and effervesced with energy. He took her into his arms and held her close for a long moment. She hugged back, but then pushed away, her face aglow. "Well?" she said. "Where is it? Let me see!"

Ben led her to the window seat. He picked up the manuscript and handed it to her without a word. She grasped it and stared at it with wonderment. "Omigod! Omigod! It's really happened! This is really it!" She plopped down into the north window seat with the manuscript on her lap. Instead of opening it, she closed her eyes and raised her face upward for a moment, taking a deep breath. Then she sighed, and turned to the first page. She was already lost in the manuscript when Ben turned toward the kitchen.

He made coffee, eggs and toast. He wolfed some down quickly and carried a mug and plate over to the window seat where Melissa remained deeply engrossed in reading. Without looking up, she let go an appreciative grunt and turned a page. Ben swallowed the last of his coffee and walked toward the bedroom.

A long, steaming shower regenerated him. He cleaned himself up, shaved, and dressed in one of his better suits, a stiff white shirt, and a conservative tie. When he returned to the living room, Melissa was already several pages deep in the manuscript. He turned her face up and kissed her lightly.

"You aren't going to work, are you?" she said. "How much sleep did you get?"

"A couple of hours, yesterday. Or maybe it was Sunday. I forget."

"You can't work all day on no sleep. You have plenty of vacation days. I'm taking one."

"Can't," said Ben. "I'm scheduled for a hearing. I'll get back as soon as I can. Make yourself at home."

He pressed his lips against the top of her head, but she had already returned to Doug Graves's world. He took his coat from the hall closet, and cast a look back at her as he reached for the doorknob. It was everything he hoped it would be.

When he arrived at the office, he plunged into his work with a sense of exhilaration. Lesley asked him if he was feeling all right, and he answered truthfully he'd never felt better.

His 10:00 hearing went by without a hitch. He argued the case with vigor. The judge and the opposing attorney glanced at him oddly. Perhaps they had never seen an attorney bring such passion and energy to an argument on whether the work product privilege extended to the report of a safety expert.

When he got back to the office, Ben considered leaving early, but decided he should use his momentum to get ahead on his work, so he could possibly take the morning off and sleep in on Wednesday. He worked at a furious pace until mid-afternoon, when the fatigue suddenly hit him like a sledgehammer. He sat staring at the discovery request on his screen, suddenly uncomprehending, barely able to keep his eyes open.

He shut down the computer and staggered out to Lesley's cubicle. "I don't feel so great," he said. "I think I might be ... I think I'm ..."

Lesley gave him a long, maternal stare. "Ben Trovato, you look terrible. You've seemed ragged all day, and now you're getting worse. You may be coming down with something. Go home, right now. Take care of yourself. You don't do yourself any favors by trying to tough it out."

"That's right, I think I ... I think I'll ... I think I'm going home."

Ben labored through the trek down to the ground floor and out to his car, and the mile-long drive back to his building seemed to take hours instead of the eight minutes that passed on the clock. He plodded through the parking garage and leaned against the wall of the elevator as it made its slow climb up to the 11th floor.

As Ben entered the foyer, he remembered Melissa was in the apartment. She was perched on the south seat of the window extension, staring out toward the downtown skyline, her legs folded up against her chest and wrapped in her arms. The manuscript lay on the window ledge next to her. Ben dropped his coat on the floor and sat down opposite her. "Did you finish it?" he said.

She nodded. Her expression was desolate, and Ben could see damp lines on her cheeks. He remembered the ending of the story, and realized he should have been prepared for her reaction.

"I'm sorry, Lis. Up until last night, I really thought Doug would make it through."

She wiped her cheeks with the back of her hand. "Oh, I know. I'm not disappointed. It's just a really sad story. But it had to end that way."

"Uh-huh. He said last night it would be cheating for Doug to come out of the coma for a happy ending."

"But it was really a great plot. Having Doug communicate telepathically with Barry out of his coma – that was just brilliant."

"Yeah, I wonder where he got that idea."

"But it was so right. You see, in all the stories, Barry's been this sleazy rogue. This way, he could put you inside both men's point of view in the same story. You understood who Barry really was for the first time."

"I'm glad the lawyer wasn't the scoundrel, for once."

"And in the end, when Barry rushes to Doug's bedside to tell him they solved the case, only to learn Doug has just passed away, his grief is so intense and so deep. In all the stories, you never got the idea Barry felt anything for anyone. His emotions in that moment are so real and powerful. Somehow you know he'll never be the same again. It's so heartbreaking, so perfect, so Shepherd."

"Umm," said Ben. "You know, you're the one who set him on track."

"Me? How?"

"Remember the night I told you about Shepherd being in my head? The first thing you said was, that's not right. You said it wasn't Doug who needed redemption, it was Barry. He said he was annoyed about that at first, but when he thought about it, he realized you were right. That was what was wrong with the draft he burned – he was writing the same story over again. Once he changed the focus, it all just fell together. He said to thank you for that."

"Wow. Wow," Melissa said.

Ben leaned back against the cushions. The fatigue overwhelmed him again. He couldn't move, couldn't keep his eyes open.

Melissa crossed the space between the seats and slid next to him on the north seat cushion. "But you know what?" she said, barely above a whisper.

"I could hear your voice in there too. Maybe no one else will, but I did. Ben? Ben?"

Ben's head dropped back against the pillow. Melissa lowered her head to his shoulder and nestled against him. His fingers curled around her shoulder just before sleep overtook him. They remained there as the sun sank down into Kansas, and the streetlights came on all up and down Grand Boulevard.

Chapter 38

"He needs a lawyer. I'll do it for a thousand bucks," said Barry.

"All he's got is a hundred," said Doug.

"Good enough. Bring him to me," said Barry.

-- David Shepherd, *Leg of Lamb*

The assistant named Natalie looked up as Ben walked up to the reception desk. "May I help you?" she said.

"Ben Trovato for Ms. Atwater. I called."

"She's expecting you. Please take a seat."

Ben didn't have a chance to take a seat. Robin came bounding out of her office door to the left of the reception desk. "Ben!" she exclaimed, reaching for his hand. "I was so surprised and delighted to hear from you."

Ben shook her hand, and the warm touch of her skin sent a momentary shock through him. He released it quickly. She looked much like she did the last time he saw her in December, her auburn hair cut a little shorter with more of a wave, a little deeper tan on her sculpted cheeks. She wore an elegant violet blouse under a well-tailored black pants suit, with an intricately carved necklace and matching ear bangles. Ben willed himself not to cast more than a quick glance anywhere other than her face. Damn, she looked good.

She stepped back toward her office and gestured toward the door. He followed her in and cast his eye around the room, noting in daylight details he missed in the low illumination of his previous visit. "Beautiful office," he commented. "You have excellent taste in decorations."

"Thank you," she said, circling behind the desk. "Have you been in my office before?"

"I think I would remember if I had," Ben said, taking one of the chairs opposite the desk. He hoisted his briefcase onto a coffee table topped in travertine. She eyed the briefcase, eyebrows arched.

"So," she said, "it was such a delight to hear from you. I thought after our dinner in December I would see you again. Are you enjoying the apartment?"

"Oh, of course. Great place. I've been doing some projects, which in a way is what brings me here."

"Oh, really?" she said. She gazed at him intently. Oh, those green eyes. "Do you have something to share with me?" A current of anticipation betrayed itself in her carefully chosen words.

"Perhaps," Ben said, laying a hand on his briefcase for emphasis. "But before we get into that, let's revisit our conversation that first day we met, at the apartment. I believe you mentioned that if I was able to find something of interest to you, there might be a finder's fee involved. I wonder whether you could elaborate on that a bit."

Robin sat bolt upright and her face brightened. "Oh, yes, of course. Well, as I mentioned, we believe there may be a manuscript of a nearly complete David Shepherd novel hidden somewhere in the apartment."

"I agree there is reason to believe that."

Robin's eyes widened momentarily and she took a sharp breath. Quickly she returned to her smooth, professional tone. "If that were to be so, we would definitely be happy to pay a finder's fee. I think for a nearly complete Shepherd novel, we would be prepared to offer you a fee of one thousand dollars."

"Well, hypothetically speaking, that would be very kind of you," Ben said. "Of course, a Shepherd novel ... as I have learned, Mr. Shepherd's work represents nearly a fifth of your company's entire catalogue, and I would guess they provide a considerably larger percentage of your sales, as they seem very popular. In fact, the last, posthumous novel, the conclusion of the immensely popular and commercially very successful Doug Graves series ... why, I would imagine that would be very valuable to your firm. Very, very valuable."

"Five thousand dollars."

"Hmm, I was thinking of something with a percentage sign next to it. Shared fortune, shared prosperity, you know."

An expression of alarm crossed her face. "A percentage? You didn't write this thing, you know."

"Assuming hypothetically that 'this thing' even exists."

She stared darkly at him for a second. "Okay, strictly hypothetically. What percentage were you hypothetically thinking of?"

"Five seems like a nice round number."

"FIVE PERCENT?" She rocked back in her seat, eyes wide. "The author only gets a royalty of ten to fifteen percent of retail sales. And may I remind you, this book is ours. We paid a very substantial advance for it."

"All right, three percent."

"Do you have any idea how narrow our margins are in this business? One-half of one percent."

"One percent on print copies. Two percent on ebooks. And the five thousand."

Robin leaned forward, both hands on her desk. Her entire body trembled like an engine running on idle. A gamut of unidentifiable expressions passed over her face. She stared at Ben, and then at the briefcase, and at Ben again. Finally she spoke. "Deal!"

"Oh, one more thing," said Ben. A look of shock passed over her face. "Assuming you published a posthumous novel, would you include a forward or afterword, acknowledgements and such?"

"Why, yes, under the circumstances I would think we would."

"If so, brief acknowledgement. Ben Trovato and Melissa Sturgeon."

"Acknowledgement? For what?"

"Nothing specific. Just a nod."

She reached for a notepad and scribbled on it. "Ben Trovato and Melissa ... Sturgeon? Like the fish?"

"Like the fish." She wrote it down.

Ben smiled. "It's such a pleasure to be of service to you." He turned to the coffee table and snapped open the latches of his briefcase. Robin's green eyes grew wide, and she gasped at the sight of the thick bundle of typewritten pages inside. But instead of the manuscript, Ben pulled out his tablet computer and started entering numbers into a document.

"I worked up a little agreement here," he said. "Do you have Bluetooth?"

Chapter 39

"It's true," said Barry. "I read it in the paper this morning."

"Just because you read it in the paper, doesn't mean it's true," said Doug.

"What, the paper lies?"

"No. They just never know the whole story."

-- David Shepherd, Mouth of the River

Missouri Lawyers Weekly, April 21

Verdicts and Settlements

- Case: Black v. DuAllen Pharmaceuticals, Inc.

- Court: Johnson County Circuit Court

- Counsel for Plaintiffs: Lawrence M. Dixon, Shane & Dixon, PC, St. Louis

- Counsel for Defendants: Jesse C. Horner and Linda S. Peterson, Block, Stahl, & Stonewahl, Kansas City

- Settlement: Undisclosed

A lawsuit alleging a user's heart attack resulted from the use of Eonocin, a top-selling diabetes drug manufactured by defendant DuAllen Pharmaceuticals of Minnesota, has been settled. The settlement is confidential.

Since its introduction three years ago, Eonocin has surged to become one of the most prescribed diabetes medications. However, according to the petition, numerous instances of heart attacks in users have been reported. The plaintiff, Vincent L. Black, had no history of heart problems when he began taking the medication, but suffered a heart attack after three months of use. He survived. Court documents allege that he experienced pain and suffering and incurred substantial medical expenses. The company denied liability.

Lawrence Dixon, counsel for Black, told a reporter the settlement vindicates his client's concern about the effects of the drug. He expressed confidence that the lawsuit had brought the issue to the company's attention and that it would serve the interests of Eonocin patients as a whole. He stated attorneys in other states with similar claims have contacted him about the matter.

Linda G. Peterson, litigation counsel for DuAllen, told a reporter that DuAllen places a high premium on patient safety and that Eonocin has been of great benefit to most of its users. She pointed out that the drug was approved by the Food and Drug Administration, and added that the company conducts ongoing research on the effects of its products and will fully cooperate with the FDA in monitoring the safety of those products.

U.S. Food and Drug Administration, News and Events, June 18

FDA Alerts Health Care Providers of Recall of Diabetes Drug Eonocin

The U.S. Food and Drug Administration is alerting health care providers and patients of a voluntary nationwide recall of all lots of Eonocin (cinefitide) by DuAllen Pharmaceuticals, Inc., of Minneapolis, Minnesota. Eonocin is used to treat Type II diabetes.

Until further notice, health care providers should stop prescribing Eonocin and return the product to DuAllen Pharmaceuticals.

According to the company, a clinical trial program showed an increased rate of heart attacks and other cardiac incidents in patients aged 60 years and older. DuAllen is conducting further research into these adverse results.

"Although we believe Eonocin is safe and effective, we have requested this pause to allow us to conduct additional studies to assure that this product is safe for all our patients," said Jeffrey Lennox, Chief Executive Officer, in a press release. "The DuAllen Corporation was founded on the principle that the health and safety of our patients always comes first, and we remain true to this commitment."

Customers may call the company's hotline or consult www.DuAllen.com, its website, for additional information.

The FDA asks health care professionals and consumers to report any adverse reactions to the FDA's MedWatch program.

Wall Street Journal, July 11

DuAllen Head Steps Down

Jeffrey Lennox, Chief Executive Officer of DuAllen Pharmaceuticals, Inc., Minneapolis, has resigned effective immediately, a company spokesperson stated.

The spokesperson stated that Lennox's decision to retire was motivated by a desire to spend more time with his family and pursue other interests. She denied that his departure had anything to do with the recent recall of Eonocin, the company's flagship diabetes drug, announced a month ago.

Lennox will receive a severance package in cash and stock options estimated at $20 million based on the contract he signed four years ago, when he took over the reins at DuAllen from the company's longtime CEO, Marvin Duane.

Grace Edwards, Medical Director Emerita, will serve as acting Chief Executive Officer while a search for a permanent successor is underway.

Chapter 40

> "Were you family?" asked the nurse.
>
> "No," said Barry. "Just a friend."
>
> "Well, I'm sorry for your loss." After a pause, she added, "I have to break down the room."
>
> "Right, right. Of course. I'll be on my way," said Barry. He turned to go, but paused at the door. He stepped back to the side of the bed and picked up the worn leather briefcase. The embossed initials were faint but visible: DG.
>
> Barry grasped the handles of the briefcase and turned into the hall. His footsteps echoed down the empty corridor.
>
> -- David Shepherd, *Heart of a Creek*

Ben was on the office phone with a client when his cell phone buzzed on his desk. He picked it up and read a text from Melissa:

@ the <3 of America. B there in 15.

I stopped for gas. Not txtg whl drvg. Don't yell @ me. ☺

<3u, M

Ben was on the call for several more minutes. When he hung up he heard Lesley's and Melissa's voices outside. He went into the main office. The two of them were admiring the sign installed on the front door of the office earlier that afternoon:

TROVATO LAW OFFICES, LLC
Benjamin J. Trovato, Attorney

Lesley Verlander, Legal Assistant

MST INVESTIGATIONS, LLC
Melissa S. Trovato

Licensed Private Investigator

"It looks great!" said Melissa. "It really feels official now."

"Who was that on the phone?" asked Lesley.

"A potential client," answered Ben. "A potential paying client."

"Potentially a client, or potentially paying?" said Lesley. "I'm learning to appreciate the difference."

"Did you find the place?" Ben said to Melissa. Ben's client owned a garage in Buchanan County that collapsed in a windstorm, damaging several classic cars. He retained Ben to sue the contractor, and Ben hired Melissa to drive up and take pictures of the damage.

"Yes, I found it," she said. "What a mess. They had a blue '67 Charger, beautiful car, except the roof is all smashed in. Broke my heart to see it, but the pictures are terrific."

"Great," said Ben. "How are we doing for time?"

"It's 4:15. It runs until five, so we have time to get over there if we go now."

"Go. Get out of here," said Lesley. "I promise you, nothing will happen in the next 45 minutes I can't handle."

Ben and Melissa took the stairs down three flights, as the elevator in their old building on 47th Street could be slow. They emerged to a crisp December afternoon. Country Club Plaza was already filling with people out to shop and dine and enjoy the brisk weather. The Christmas lights lining the Spanish style buildings of the Plaza glowed, and a festive atmosphere prevailed. Ben took Melissa's hand as they made their way through the crowds on 47th Street. They paused to let a light-lined, horse-drawn carriage in the shape of a pumpkin pass before crossing the street to the big box bookstore.

Outside the bookstore, they read the sign announcing the event:

NOW ON SALE

HEART OF A CREEK

BY DAVID SHEPHERD

The Triumphant Conclusion to
the Famed Doug Graves Series

Robin Atwater, publisher and creative trustee of the legacy of David Shepherd, will discuss the process by which this posthumous masterpiece was brought to publication, and sign copies.

3:00 PM to 5:00 PM

"Let's go!" said Melissa. "I can't wait to see it."

They entered the store. Right inside the door, a tall rack displayed dozens of copies of the hardbound edition of *Heart of a Creek,* priced at $29.99. Several patrons had already seized their copies.

Ben and Melissa each picked up a copy. Ben looked at the back cover. The photograph showed Shepherd posed at the Selectric, hands over the keys. He looked stern, as though annoyed at being distracted from his writing by the photographer. He also looked younger than Ben remembered him. Ben wondered when the photograph was taken. He could see the right edge of the window seat in the corner of the picture. The sash bound the curtains back.

They turned to the forward by Robin Atwater, discussing the literary legacy of David Shepherd, the enduring popularity of the Doug Graves series, and the extraordinary discovery of a virtually complete manuscript of the current novel after the author's death, hidden in his apartment. The forward did not mention by whom it was discovered.

The forward concluded with a set of acknowledgements. The last of these read:

> The publishers are grateful for the invaluable editorial assistance of Natalie Wilson; Gwen Majors; Ben Trovato; and Melissa Sturgeon.

Ben remembered that the assistants at Atwater and Bridges were named Natalie and Gwen.

Melissa chuckled. "Story of my life. I finally get my name in lights, and it's the wrong name."

She cast her glance to the back of the store, and Ben followed her gaze. Robin sat at a table behind a pile of books, engaged in conversation with three patrons, each clutching a copy of the book.

"Are you going to say hello?" Melissa asked.

"No," said Ben. "No need for that."

"Well, I am," said Melissa. She bustled off toward the back of the store.

Ben leafed through the copy he held. He remembered typing every word. He thought back to that torturous weekend in February, as the words echoed in his mind, flowed through his fingers, and out his printer. He recalled the laborious weeks of work reading the lines to Melissa as her gloved hands flew over the keyboard of the Selectric and carefully extracted each page of bond. He winced at the memory of the furtive second nocturnal visit to Atwater and Bridges, to switch back the typewriters. At least that one passed without incident. He glanced back at Robin, still talking to the earnest readers as Melissa waited behind them, flashing him a mischievous grin.

Let her enjoy her day in the sun. With
no more Shepherds in the pipeline, things
are going to get worse for her.

Ben almost dropped the book, startled to hear
a voice he thought was lost forever.

*You came back? I didn't think I'd ever hear from
you again.*

Oh, I couldn't miss this. Had to pull
some strings to get here, but it's completely worth it.

Is this it, then? Is this the last time?

Yes, I'm pretty certain it is.
Unquestionably, my work here is done.
Congratulations, by the way. I'd forgotten how lovely Sedalia can be in the
fall.

*You were there? I thought I heard you. Why didn't
you say something?*

It was a special day for you two. I
didn't want to be a distraction. But I
did want to be there in spirit. So to
speak.

I'm glad you made it back. Do we have much time?

The sound of Shepherd's voice was weak, and
the static masked it. Ben sensed their connection
was fragile and becoming weaker.

No. I just wanted to see this scene.
To see the story to an end.

And this is the end?

```
Yes.
```

Anxiety seized Ben. He had so much to say. He needed to think of it all.

There's one question I need to ask you. Were you – were you in love with her? With Melissa?

Shepherd did not answer immediately. Finally he spoke.

```
That   is   a   difficult   question   to
answer. The  easy  answer  is  that  the  way
you   think   of   love   has   little   meaning
here. But  in  another  view,  yes,  in  a  way
you cannot understand, although you will,
someday.
```

But you ... you wanted us together. You saw to that, didn't you?

```
Yes. You and she, you were – you are –
a  story.  I  had  to  make  sure  it  came  out
right. And it did.
```

Well, thank you. Thank you for that. And, and for everything.

```
My pleasure. My honor.
```

The voice was fading, falling below the level of the hiss. They were running out of time.

```
So  be  sure  to  look  me  up  when  you  get
here,  many  years  from  now.  They  all  know  me.
A lot of fans.
```

Ben laughed. *That's it? All we went through together, and you leave me with a lame joke like that?*

`Just one more thing ...`

Shepherd's voice fell below the level of the static. Ben felt an urgent need to hear that one more thing, whatever it was.

Say that again. I didn't hear.

He heard a pulsation in the static, the modulation of Shepherd's voice, but he couldn't make out the words. Ben closed his eyes and concentrated with all his might.

Please. Once more.

The static broke for a moment, and Ben heard the voice through the noise.

`Take care of her.`

I will. I will.

The static returned, and Ben could hear no more over it. Slowly the hiss faded away, and Ben heard nothing more in the chamber of his mind where their conversations took place. A deep sadness welled up through him. He felt dampness in his eyes, and wiped it away quickly.

Melissa came up the aisle, carrying the book.

"Just as I thought," she said. "She didn't remember me."

She opened the front cover to show him. Ben read the neat handwriting inscribed there:

To Melissa. Thanks for reading. Enjoy!

Robin Atwater

Melissa closed the book and clutched it to her chest. "You know what?" she said. "I think we invaluable editorial assistants deserve an extravagant celebratory dinner. Maybe the American. What do you think? Ben?"

But Ben's mind was elsewhere. He was thinking back on all that happened, and wondering whether there was a story in it.

Edwin Frownfelter lives in Lee's Summit, Missouri. He has practiced law for many years, currently in Kansas City, but never in a large law firm. *Ghost Writer* is his first completed novel.

26875475R00219

Made in the USA
San Bernardino, CA
05 December 2015